THE BETRAYAL YOU SERVE

USA TODAY & WALL STREET JOURNAL BESTSELLING AUTHOR

TRACY LORRAINE

Edited & Proofreading by Sisters Get Lit(erary) Author Services

1

———

KANE

"**S**he's fucking pregnant," Letty screams, her voice cracking with emotion as tears cascade down her cheeks. "She's fucking pregnant with your baby."

My world begins to spin, confusion fogging my brain as I stare back at her.

What the hell is she—

"Surprise, sweetie," Alana breathes as she wraps her hands around my upper arm, her presence startling me yet her voice turning my blood to lava.

Ripping my eyes from a shattering Letty, I stare down at her in disbelief.

My heartbeat pounds in my ears as I try to gain a grip on reality.

"I'm sorry, that wasn't how I intended on telling you. I wanted to surprise you with it on Wednesday night, but you know how things went," she says, lowering her voice and wiggling her brows.

My stomach churns at the reminder of the other

night, threatening to expel its contents right here in the parking lot.

Looking away from her vindictive eyes for a beat, I find that Letty is gone. My body screams at me to run, to chase her, to tell her this is all one big joke and to pull her into my arms. But I have no idea if any of that would be true, because I have no fucking clue what is going on right now.

I turn back to Alana, the accomplished smirk on her face causes something to explode inside me.

Red hot fury replaces everything else as I grab her by the throat and pin her back against the side of my car.

A terrified gasp rips from her lips before I crowd her, staring down into her now tear-filled eyes.

"You're lying," I say, although, I want to scream it in her face. I don't need her to see how fast I'm losing control right now.

"N-no, I'm n-not," she stutters, her entire body trembling against my rough hold.

I stare down into her eyes, needing to know the truth.

I already know she's a lying, vindictive cunt. I have zero reason to trust a single word that comes out of her mouth.

The fact that Letty was the one to spill her supposed secret has alarm bells screaming in my head.

Why would Letty know first? How does Letty even know Alana?

I only have one answer.

Alana.

"Get in the car," I growl, ripping the back door open and damn near throwing her inside.

She squeals before scrambling across the back seat to sit up.

"What are you—"

I slam the door on her so I don't have to hear her fucking irritating voice for a second longer.

Locking the car to ensure she doesn't escape, I start pacing.

The parking lot is empty now and as far as I know, no one witnessed what just happened. Hell knows the team couldn't have because I guarantee if they'd had seen or heard anything right now then I probably wouldn't be standing.

"Fuck. FUCK," I bellow into the silent lot.

My hands tremble as I pull my cell from my pocket and find Letty's number.

I hit call and lift it to my ear, but as I expected, it just rings.

I knew staying away from her the last few days was a mistake. But after Wednesday night, I just couldn't look her in the eye knowing that I'd betrayed her. Instead, I holed up with Reid in the hope we could come up with some kind of plan. One that could get me out of all this shit without having to kill anyone, namely his cunt of a father.

I continue pacing, knowing that I need to calm the fuck down if I'm going to get into that car and have to deal with her without strangling her.

After swiping up my duffel from when I dropped

it the first time Letty ran, I pull the driver's door open and drop down.

"Kane, I—"

"Don't talk to me. Do not say a fucking word to me right now unless you don't intend on getting out of this car alive."

I watch in the rearview mirror as she swallows nervously.

My eyes hold hers, begging her to defy me, to tell me that she's lying, to give me a reason to wrap my hands around her throat and squeeze the fucking life out of her for doing this to Letty.

My mind flicks back to reading that letter, of her telling me all about our baby.

Fuck.

My fingers tighten around the wheel in a painful grip as I try to imagine just how Letty felt right now.

Feeling myself starting to lose control once more, I rip my eyes from hers and start the car.

My wheels screech on the asphalt as I floor the accelerator.

The inside of the car is silent aside from my heaving breaths and her quiet whimpers in the back. Her sounds ensure that the darkness that's trying to seep through my veins hovers right on the edge, threatening to take over.

It's not until we're out of Maddison County that she speaks. Although I have no idea why she asks the question she does, it's fucking obvious.

"Are you taking me to the Creek?"

My teeth grind at the sound of her voice.

"I'm taking you to hell. And if it turns out you're playing me, it's going to be a one-way ticket."

"Not my husband," she begs, forcing me to picture one of Victor's men. A man who, apparently, only has Alana around for show because he never fucks her. I have a few theories as to why, but mostly, I don't give a fuck.

I can't help the laugh that falls from my lips.

"Your husband is too nice." We both know it's a lie. He's one of Victor's most loyal members, and he's anything but fucking nice. "You're going straight to the devil."

A whimper rips from her lips as I assume she pictures Victor.

If that's the case, then she's going to be sorely mistaken, because if my gut feeling is anywhere near right, then that's exactly what he's expecting me to do.

It's obvious the moment she realizes that we're not in fact heading for Victor because she sits up a little, staring out of the window with interest.

"There's no point memorizing the journey in case you need an escape. Something tells me that you'll never be leaving."

"W-where are we?" she breathes as I pull down a dirt road on the outskirts of the Creek.

We are literally in the middle of nowhere. It's the perfect place to deal with scum like her.

"It's a surprise," I say, keeping my voice menacingly low.

I pull to a stop outside of a huge set of gates. If

you didn't know that someone lived down here then you would never find them with the way they're cleverly hidden behind the trees and bushes. But when you know, you know.

After a couple of seconds, they begin to open for me, alerting the person inside to his visitors.

"Holy shit," Alana gasps as the house finally comes into view.

I understand her reaction. The building is hauntingly beautiful.

Harrow Creek manor house sits high up overlooking the shithole town beneath. Its Victorian-style has had a complete overhaul in recent years, only adding to its sinister look. Everything is dark and twisted. Much like the person who lives inside.

Killing the engine, I climb out, ripping her door open and wrapping my fingers around her upper arm to haul her out.

She stumbles as she tries to find her footing, but I don't wait for her, instead just drag her to the front door as it magically opens for us.

"I'd have dressed up if I knew we were going to have a party," Reid says, taking in the woman trailing behind me.

He's standing in only a pair of gray sweats, his hair disheveled like he's either just woken up or thrown a woman or two out.

"You look perfectly fine to me," Alana purrs.

"Shut the fuck up," I bark, all but throwing the traitorous whore at Reid.

"Hey, darlin'. Looks like we're going to have some fun with you."

From the way Alana's eyes darken as she stares up at him, it's obvious she has no fucking clue what he means.

Gripping the back of her neck harshly, he steers her into the hallway as I trail behind.

He goes straight to the door I was expecting him to and pulls it open.

"You hungry, darlin'?"

"Y-yes."

"Great," he breathes, his voice full of evil intent.

He pushes her through the door before he looks back at me and nods, an understanding passing between us.

"Beers are in the fridge. I'll only be a few minutes." He continues forward before the heavy door falls back into place with a chilling bang.

Smiling to myself, I make my way to his kitchen and pull out two bottles before dropping onto one of the couches at the other side of the room.

As promised, he's two minutes tops.

"What'd she do?" he asks, knocking the top off his beer and downing half in one go. He falls onto the opposite couch as if it's normal to lock a woman in your basement before even asking why.

I sit forward, resting my elbows on my knees and drop my head into my hands.

"She showed up after the game."

"Sorry about your loss, man. Coach fucked up not letting you start."

I nod at him, appreciating his comment and support.

"Yeah, well. Letty was waiting for me but before she got to me, that bitch barreled through her. She's claiming she's fucking pregnant with my kid."

"What the fuck?" he balks. "Alana?"

"And Letty already knew."

His eyes widen. "They know each other?"

"Not from the way Letty was shooting death stares at her, no."

"Shit, so... Alana's playing games? Trying to get in the middle of the two of you? Where's Letty?"

"She ran, I don't know where she went," I confess.

"She'll be okay. She's stronger than we all know."

"She lost our baby," I blurt out, unable to keep it in a second longer.

"Wait... what?" If the situation weren't so dire, I might laugh at the confused expression on Reid's face.

"The reason she left Columbia and started over at MKU was because I got her pregnant the night of Skye's party. She lost it at twenty weeks. She had to fucking deliver it and everything, man." My fingers curl in my hair until pain shoots down my neck, but it's nothing compared to that in my chest at saying the words out loud for the first time.

"Fuck," he breathes.

"I had no fucking idea," I confess.

"Shit."

"So her hearing that Alana is pregnant..." I trail

off because I don't really need to attempt to explain how Letty must be feeling right now.

"What's the plan?" Reid asks, draining the rest of his beer.

"I don't believe her. I smell a rat. The fact she's clearly gone after Letty to ensure she knows first. Fuck," I say, scrubbing my hand over my face. "Something isn't fucking right here."

"Okay. I'll make her squeal like a fucking pig," he promises, something dark flashing through his eyes as he does.

"Make sure she's not actually fucking pregnant first."

"Kane," he snorts. "What do you think I am, a fucking monster?"

I can't help but burst out laughing at the faux innocence on his face.

"We all know exactly what you are," I mutter as he pulls his cell from his pocket.

Picking up my forgotten beer, I tip it to my lips as he hits call. The ring of his loudspeaker fills the room before Ellis answers.

"Bro, I got a job," Reid barks instead of a hello.

"Shoot."

"Alana Murray. I need her medical records."

"Sure thing. Give me twenty."

Reid hangs up without saying another word.

"Shall we race him for the answer?"

"Thought you'd never ask," I say, draining my bottle and eagerly standing up, ready to face the bitch and discover the truth.

My lungs burn, fighting to drag in the air I desperately need when I finally come to a stop on a street corner.

Resting my palm against the rough brickwork, tears continue to track down my cheeks as the image of her curling her hand around Kane's upper arm won't leave.

Something inside me shatters all over again as I remember how she looked up at him like he was the most important person in her world.

I should have seen it coming.

I knew he was playing me. I knew it was all too good to be true.

You don't go from hating someone as viciously as he did me to suddenly wanting something serious.

I was just too fucking stupid to see it.

Looking up, I find a flashing neon sign for a store.

Knowing my fake ID is in my purse, I swipe the

backs of my hands across my cheeks and take off, needing something to numb the pain.

I swipe a bottle of vodka from the shelf and walk toward the register with as much confidence as I can muster. My fake is good, it's always worked before but today is not the day for it to fail me.

My heart jumps into my throat when the young guy looks between me and the card. After a couple of seconds, he nods and hands it back to me before putting my bottle through.

The second I'm out of the store, I twist the top and allow the liquid to fill my mouth before swallowing down shot after shot until the burn becomes too much.

I stumble back against the side of the building, willing the nothingness of the alcohol to come faster but the warmth from my stomach doesn't fill my veins as quickly as I need it to.

With the bottle empty, I throw it down the alley behind me and revel in the sound of it shattering, much like the disaster that is my life.

That whore is carrying his baby. Kane's baby.

My arms wrap around my stomach as pain lashes at my insides. The memory of feeling him moving in my tummy hits me and my tears once again overflow.

I was supposed to have our baby. Not her.

Knowing that I can't lose myself alone in an alley, I push from the wall and make my way down the sidewalk as I call for an Uber.

I need to get away from here.

I need...

I need someone who can put me back together.

The second a car comes to a stop beside me, I pull the back door open, not even bothering to check that it's actually for me.

I repeat the address I want to go to and sit back.

The world is just starting to spin around me and I crave more.

"Can you go faster?" I ask, my voice starting to slur, knowing that when I get to the house, there will be more to drink.

My legs don't feel like they're attached to my body as I walk toward the front door. Hell, I don't feel like my entire body is my own as I swing the door open and scan the faces for the one—or two—that I want.

Everything moves around me in slow motion as I stumble through the crowd all here to commiserate the guys' loss tonight. They're so close to taking the lead. If only Kane had—a scream rips through my head at just thinking of his name.

"Letty?" I spin around but don't see who might have said my name.

I keep searching, stumbling my way toward the back of the house.

The deck. They'll be on the deck.

After what feels like an eternity, I get to the doorway and crash through, my eyes immediately landing on a pair of familiar green ones.

"Letty. Fuck."

In seconds, I'm wrapped in a pair of arms and I shatter.

"It's okay. It's okay. I've got you," he says into my ear as I press my nose into his chest, breathing in his scent and allowing it to ground me. "Come on, let's get out of here."

I feel him lean over as if he's grabbing something before he walks me inside.

I don't look up or at where we're going, I keep my eyes squeezed shut and trust that he'll look after me.

"What's wrong?" Leon says a second before I sense him come to a stop in front of us.

"I don't know. I'm taking her upstairs."

As he speaks, Luca's body trembles as he tries to contain his anger.

I don't think any of us needs to say his name out loud to know who's reduced me to this mess.

"Lee," I whisper, holding my hand out for him.

He takes it without a second thought, squeezing in support as Luca starts walking again.

The three of us climb the stairs, leaving the party behind and not long later, one of them closes a door behind us and the volume of the music muffles before I'm lowered to the edge of a bed.

I blow out a shaky breath, feeling both of their concerned stares on me as I keep my eyes trained on the floor.

"Here," Luca says, handing me a bottle of vodka. My head tells me that I've already had too much too fast, but my heart ruptures once again and I blindly reach for it.

"Whoa. Take it easy, Let," Leon says, taking the bottle from me after I've swallowed a few shots.

Luca's arm remains wrapped around my body, his fingertip digging into my waist where he's holding tight.

"What did he do, Let?"

I look up and gasp at the darkness in Luca's eyes as he begs me to tell him that Kane has fucked up, that he can say those magic little words 'I told you so.'

"He... He..." I swallow down the sob that wants to rip from my throat. "Someone else."

"Motherfucker," Leon barks before something on the other side of the room crashes to the floor.

Luca's silent but his jaw tics with frustration and a vein pulsates in his temple, silently showing me how furious he is.

"She's... she's preg—" I can't get the word out as the sob finally spills free.

My tears fall freely as I shatter into a million pieces in front of both of them.

"Shit, Letty." Luca takes my face in his giant hands, his thumbs wiping away my tears.

I close my eyes, waiting for him to say the words that I know are coming. But when he speaks, it's not what I expect.

"What do you need? Tell me how to make it better."

My eyes flick up to his. The darkness is still there, but there's a sparkle of something else that I can't get a read on as the vodka flows through my veins.

"Luc," Leon warns as he comes to sit on the other side of me.

"I-I—"

"Letty?" Luca growls as he closes the space between us slightly.

My heart rate picks up and relief floods me that the pain somewhat subsides with the way he's looking at me.

"M-make it go away. P-please."

"Luc," Leon warns again before the heat of his hand slides around my back, resting on my waist.

A shudder rips through me at his soothing touch.

"Please, I need—" I don't get to find out what the end of that sentence was going to be because Luca's lips find mine as his fingers slide back into my hair.

I move on instinct, parting my lips and allowing him to push his tongue inside to find mine.

A needy whimper rumbles up my throat as he licks deep into my mouth forcing thoughts of anything else from my head and utterly consuming me.

Or at least I thought he was until the light brush of fingers graze my neck as Leon moves my hair aside and presses his lips right on my pulse point under my ear.

Then I'm totally fucking consumed.

Heat floods my body as Luca's kiss continues and Leon's hands slide up my waist until he's cupping my breasts. His movements are more brazen, more confident and I can only put that down to the fact that we've been here before.

Lifting one hand, I wrap it around Luca's neck as I tilt my head to deepen our kiss even more. My other hand reaches back for Leon's thigh, needing contact with both of them.

"Fuck, Let," Luca pants when he finally rips his lips away, resting his head against mine.

His eyes hold mine for a beat until I moan as Leon's fingers pinch my nipple through my shirt and then he pulls back to watch what his brother is doing.

"Up."

At his demand, I stand, unable to do anything but follow orders. Leon stands with me, his front pressed to my back, his hands firmly on my hips.

Reaching behind him, Luca pulls his shirt from his body, revealing inches of ripped perfection.

"Off."

Leon's hands slide up, gripping the fabric of my shirt and pulling it up. Luca's eyes lock on to every inch of skin that's revealed until my sight is removed momentarily as Leon lifts it over my face.

The second it's gone, Luca is on me once more. His bare chest pressed against my lace-covered one and his lips on mine.

I sag against him as the sound of fabric rustling behind me fills my ears before Leon's heat pins me between the two of them.

Holy shit, the rumors are true, I think as their expert touches and kisses make me forget everything other than this moment.

Luca breaks our kiss before I'm spun to face Leon.

"We've got you, Cupcake. Just let go."

I nod briefly before he kisses across my jaw and down my neck.

"Lee," I whimper, needing his lips on mine as Luca's hands explore my body in a way they never have before.

His solid length presses against my ass while I feel Leon's at my stomach. The thought of turning them both on sends heat to my core making my clit pulsate greedily.

Fuck. I need more.

Sliding my hands down Leon's stomach, his abs jump at my touch as I go for his waistband.

He lets me pop the button open but he pulls away when I go to slide my hand under the fabric.

"About you, Let. Not us."

"N-no, that's not fa—" I don't get to finish my argument before his lips slam down on mine.

Luca unclasps my bra, releasing my heavy breasts before his hands slide around my body to cup them. He teases my nipples making my hips roll, teasing them both in the process if their simultaneous growls of approval are anything to go by.

"You could come from this, couldn't you, Let. Pinned between us and with us barely touching you," Luca growls in my ear.

My response is a full-body shudder as his hands skim down my stomach to the waistband of my skirt.

He opens it and allows it to fall to the floor before running his fingers around the lace trim of my panties.

Oh fuck.

Tucking his fingertips under the lace, he kisses down my spine as he pushes them over my hips.

"Oh my God," I cry, ripping my lips from Leon's as Luca's fingers find my swollen clit.

"So wet for us, baby."

Squeezing my eyes closed, I rest my head back on his chest as he expertly plays me while Leon drops his lips to my breasts.

Faster than I thought possible, I'm racing toward what I already know is going to be an intense release with both their hands and mouths working in unison to please me.

"Oh God, oh God," I chant as my orgasm begins to appear before it explodes within me, making my knees go weak and my body sag.

But neither of them allow me to fall.

I'm still blissed out from my high when my back hits the mattress and Leon drops to his knees between my legs.

Our eyes meet for the briefest moment. I gasp at the desire and pain that's staring back at me.

"Lee," I breathe, needing to know he's okay, but all he does is shake his head as he parts my thighs, spreading them wide.

Ripping his eyes from mine, he trails them down my body. My skin burning as he does before Luca drops down beside me and claims my mouth once more, his fingers tickling over my ribs until he tugs at my nipple right as Leon's tongue flattens against my clit.

My back arches off the bed as Luca swallows my cries.

Still on the edge from my last release, I fall over once again long before I'm ready to.

"Leon," I cry, my fingers threading through his hair as I ride out wave after wave of pleasure.

It's not until a loud slam echoes around the room that I realize something is wrong.

Leon pulls back from me at the same time I rip my eyes open and look around the room to see Luc is gone.

"Luc." His name falls from my lips as my heart tumbles once more.

Scrambling from the end of the bed, I pull at his sheets to cover up my naked body as Leon falls back onto his ass.

"Fuck," he grunts, wiping at his mouth with the back of his hand, giving me the reminder that I didn't really need about what just happened.

"I just got sober really fucking fast," I say as a shiver works its way through my body.

"That probably shouldn't have happened," Leon confesses, climbing from the floor and swiping up his shirt from the carpet and handing it to me.

"Thank you," I whisper, taking it from him and tugging it over my head to cover up.

He drops to the bed beside me and lets out a loud sigh.

"I'm sorry. I shouldn't have let—"

"Lee," I say, reaching for his hand. "None of that was your fault. Please don't—"

"I didn't need to encourage it, or continue. You just looked so sad, Let," he says, reaching for my face, cupping my cheek and turning me to look at him.

"I just wanted to help."

My heart aches for the broken boy before me.

Reaching out, I place my hand on his thigh, wanting to support him in the same way he does me. Only, I don't just meet his thigh, instead he sucks in a sharp breath when my fingers connect with his still hard length.

"Shit," I gasp, quickly moving my hand lower. Averting my gaze from his, I mutter, "I guess I should offer to return the favor, huh?"

The sound of his laughter forces me to look up at him again, and I can't help but smile then I find him with his head thrown back and a wide smile on his face.

"As much as I'd love that, it's probably not the best idea." He pushes from the bed and starts picking up my discarded clothes.

"Well, what kind of a friend would I be if I didn't at least o-offer," I stutter when I look up to find him holding my panties out for me to pull on. "Thank you," I whisper, swiping them from his fingers.

"Come on, let's get out of here before he gets back."

"We should go find him."

"No, we shouldn't. Come on."

Trusting that Leon knows exactly how to deal with his twin, I take his outstretched hand and follow him across the hall to his own room.

"Bathroom?" I ask, pointing at a door opposite the one we just walked through.

"Yeah." With a smile that I really don't feel, I leave Leon standing in the middle of his room looking totally lost.

My chest aches as I close the door behind me and lean back against it.

The room around me continues to spin from the vodka I've consumed, but it's no longer numbing the pain. I fear nothing is going to do that now.

Coming here was a mistake. Not only am I hurting after the revelations of today, but now I've hurt Luca. Again.

"Argh," I cry, my hand tugging at my hair in frustration for all the fucking mistakes I'm making. And as ever, they all lead back to Kane fucking Legend.

The memories from the parking lot threaten to come back to me once more but I stuff them back down. I'm afraid that if I think about her words or the way she looked at him again that I won't come back from it.

"Let, you okay?" Leon calls, concern evident in his voice.

"Yeah, I'll be out in a minute."

Pushing from the door, I make use of the toilet before washing my hands. I splash my face with water, attempting to sort out the mess that is my makeup after all the tears and... kissing.

Fucking hell.

Realizing that I can't hide in his bathroom all night, I reluctantly pull the door open and face Leon.

Thankfully, he's pulled on a new shirt so I'm not faced with his insane body forcing me to remember just how it felt pressed up against mine.

Walking over to where he's sitting on his bed, I curl my legs up under me and sit opposite him.

"I shouldn't have come here. I've made everything so much worse. I just... I just needed you."

"It's okay, Let. You know we're here if you need us."

"But—" I look over at the door, wondering where Luca has run off to and if he's okay.

"He'll be okay."

"I never should have asked him to—"

"This isn't your fault."

"No, you're right. It's *his*," I hiss, not even wanting to say his name.

"Do you want to talk about it?"

I blow out a long breath as I stare into Leon's kind eyes.

"He's been sleeping with someone else. She showed up after the game."

"You said she was preg—"

"She is." I tell him about the random woman in the coffee shop, who I now know wasn't random at all. She'd planned it. She was waiting for me.

"And she just blurted it out in the middle of the parking lot?" he asks when I tell him how it ended.

"Yep."

"And he had no idea?"

"I didn't hang around long enough to really take in his reaction."

"Jesus, Let. I knew he was an asshole, but I really hoped it was real, you know. Despite how I feel about him, I wanted it for you."

Reaching for his hand, I squeeze it. "Thank you, Lee. I really appreciate you not jumping off the deep end with it all."

"You know I love you, Let. I just want the best for you, whatever that may be."

"Thank you," I whisper.

"There's more, isn't there?"

I stare at him for a few seconds, wondering just how he can read me so well.

"Yeah. I—"

"Wait, you don't have to tell me." I see panic fill his eyes and I remember our deal from a few weeks ago.

"Let's make a deal. When you're ready to talk, come and find me and we can have it out. Lay all our truths on the table."

"Lee, you don't need to tell me anything. That's not why I'm talking."

He releases a long breath showing just how relieved he is.

"It's not that I don't want to tell you, Let. I just... I don't think I have the words to even begin."

"It's okay," I say, smiling at him, wanting him to know that I don't expect anything in return for sharing my own secrets. "Eighteen months ago I was at a party in the Creek—"

A loud crash sounds from somewhere in the house before shouts and screams fill the space around us.

"What was—"

Both our eyes widen at the same time as the realization hits us.

"Kane."

"Fuck."

I'm pretty sure neither of us has ever moved faster in our lives as we fly toward the door.

I follow Reid down to his basement, it's not the first time I've been down here but even still, it shocks me.

He's had the entire place fitted out like a prison with a special extra open space at the end where he carries out his... experiments, shall we say.

Walking to the very end of the long row of doors, he pulls a set of keys from his back pocket and pushes it into the lock. The sound of metal hitting metal echoes through the eerie space.

He marches inside the small cell leaving me to peer in from the doorway.

Alana is curled into one corner with her arms wrapped around her knees.

A trickle of guilt runs through me at the sight of the tear tracks down her cheeks but then I look into her cold blue eyes and I remember who she is. The games she's trying to play.

"Let's go," Reid demands, lifting her from the floor

by her arm and pulling her from the enclosed, dark space.

He places her in a chair that's secured to the floor and ensures she doesn't move from it by the death stare he gives her alone.

"Now," he says, pulling another chair over and sitting right in front of her. "Are you going to ruin all my fun by telling me what the fuck you're playing at? Or do I get to play some unexpected games tonight?"

Her lips twist and her eyes narrow as she stares back at him.

Fair play to her, most people in her position right now would piss their pants.

I don't know anything about her, about her past. All I know is that she's married to a man who for whatever reason refuses to fuck her and I'm the one left to entertain her when her old man is busy. But from the way she's staring back at Reid like he isn't one of the scariest fucking men on the planet, I start to wonder what she's been through in her life to seem so unfazed.

"Right. Good. I'm glad that's your decision," Reid says, rubbing his hands together as if he's a kid who's just been given free rein in a candy shop.

He stands from his chair and walks over to a floor-to-ceiling closet and pulls the doors open.

Alana's eyes follow his every move before she scans the contents of the closet. But once again, there's no sign that she's nervous in any way as she looks at the array of torture devices Reid has at hand.

"So, Alana..." he muses as he looks over his options. "Tell me about your pregnancy."

"I'm not telling you fuck-all," she snaps. "I have no reason to be here."

"No?" he asks, looking over his shoulder at her. "Well then you can tell me everything, can't you? Give me all the details, prove to us that nothing is wrong and we can let you walk out the front door unharmed."

"I hope you know that my husband will kill you for this," she hisses.

"Your husband, really? The man who doesn't give a shit about you. Who hands you off to others so he doesn't have to deal with you. The man who works under my orders."

"Under your father's orders, not yours."

"Hmm... how confident are you on that? Enough to risk your life, your baby's life?"

Alana pales slightly as Reid pulls a switchblade from the closet. It's pretty tame considering all the things he has in there, but then I guess he wants to start easy and build up to the bigger stuff.

"So, I'll ask you again. Tell us about your pregnancy."

"I'm thirteen weeks. Had my scan last week," she says, staring me right in the eye as she does.

"Scan picture?"

"In my purse."

"Legend," Reid says, nodding toward the cell he placed her in.

Grabbing the purse from the floor, I throw it over to him.

Immediately, he starts rooting through it without a care in the world until he pulls out a small, familiar square piece of paper.

He stares at it, scanning all the details before he passes it over to me.

My stomach twists painfully as I look at it. It's so similar to the one Letty has of our little boy, only as I stare at this one, I feel nothing.

The baby is obviously smaller and not as easy to make out but it's there and the details printed on the side show Alana's name and last week's date.

"Due date?" Reid barks and she immediately rattles off a date six months in the future.

He takes a seat in front of her again, his eyes never wavering from hers.

"And the night you conceived the baby?"

"I'm not telling you that," she snaps. "It's personal."

"So personal that it'll save you from death?"

Her lips part ready to speak.

"No, I didn't think so."

She rips her eyes from his and looks at me once again. "It was the night you took me to the Greek place in Maddison. We stayed in the Royal after in that incredible suite. You remember?"

I nod once, unfortunately remembering it all too well.

"That night."

"You're on birth control," I state. "And I never once came anywhere near you without protection."

She scoffs. "Don't be naïve, Kane. You know as well as I do that nothing is one hundred percent effective." She rolls her eyes as if the answer is so obvious but despite her pleading words, I'm still unconvinced by her.

I have no idea what it is. The detachment in her words, the complete opposite of how Letty talks about her pregnancy even a year after losing it. Something just isn't right.

The ring of Reid's cell phone cuts through the silence as Alana and I stare at each other, her waiting for me to call Reid off and me waiting for the truth.

"Yes," he barks into the phone which isn't on speaker this time. "Okay, great. Thank you so much. You've told me everything I need."

He hangs up, the tension only becoming thicker now he knows the truth.

My heart pounds and my head starts to spin.

"Reid?" My voice sounds desperate and I hate that she can hear the vulnerability but I need to know she's lying. I need to be able to go to Letty and tell her that it's bullshit, that she's the only one to have ever carried my baby.

"Go back upstairs, Kane."

"No, I want to be here," I argue.

"Go upstairs. Now."

"But—"

He turns and stares me dead in the eye.

"Fine. Fine." I throw my hands up in defeat.

Turning my back on them, I march past cells. I wonder if anyone else is inside them, and if they are, how much they can hear before I climb the stairs and go back to his kitchen for another beer. But before the door to the basement slams closed behind me, I hear her shrill scream.

I pause, listening to it ring out, praying that it means she's a lying cunt and is about to get everything that's coming to her.

I'm fucking desperate to reach up into his liquor cabinet and grab something stronger, but I know I can't. The second he confirms what I knew from the moment Alana opened her mouth in that parking lot, I'm going for Letty.

I'm still pacing back and forth with the half-empty bottle of beer in my hand when the door slams closed once more and he appears in front of me.

His torso is speckled with blood and he's got a satisfied, evil smirk playing on his lips.

"So?"

Without saying a word, he pulls out a bottle of whiskey and a glass, pouring himself a generous measure before throwing it back.

"How much do you know about that bitch?"

"Nothing."

He nods as he pours another drink.

"She was abused as a kid."

"From watching how she stood her ground with you, that doesn't surprise me."

"It was so bad that she was admitted to a hospital with serious internal damage."

"Right?" I ask, not understanding where he's going with this.

"She's infertile, Kane. There are no records of her being pregnant or ever being pregnant. The damage was so severe that she's unable to conceive."

"Fuck," I breathe, relief filling me. "So why?"

"I don't know. She still refused to talk. But I'll find out."

"She's still alive?"

"Of course. What do you think of me? There's no way I'd kill her without enjoying her first."

"You're fucking sick, you know that?"

He throws back one more measure of whiskey. "You wouldn't have me any other way. Now what the fuck are you still doing here? Go get your girl."

"Call me when you find out."

"Sure thing. It might not be quick though. Something tells me she's going to make me work for it." His smile is wicked as his eyes focus on a spot over my shoulder as he imagines all the things he's going to do with her.

"Well, enjoy that, you twisted motherfucker."

He belts out a laugh as I place the bottle on his counter and head for the door.

"You said that like you're a fucking saint, Legend."

"Angel fucking Gabriel, bro."

He's still laughing when I get to the front door and slip through it, leaving him to his evening of torture.

I rev my engine and floor it down Reid's long driveway. I'm more than happy to get away from that lying bitch and leave her to *play* with the Devil and discover where her limits really lie and what makes her finally confess.

I knew something was up the second she looked at me.

She's always got a conniving look in her eye. I had a feeling from day one that she was up to something. I mostly assumed that she wanted me to fall in love with her and take her away from her sham of a marriage, but she never once said anything about us being together. Well, until she claimed to be carrying my child.

Maybe that's what it was all about, her way of forcing us together.

But why now?

Letty.

If she knew enough about Letty to go after her and spill her secrets, then she knows how much Letty means to me, which means the bitch has been following us.

My hands wring the wheel, not liking the feeling that thought stirs within me. It only solidifies Letty's words of wanting to stay out of this world. I understood them at the time, no one other than brainwashed kids want to be a part of this world, but to walk-in voluntarily because of me, no.

Only fucking idiots would sign up for this life knowing exactly what it entailed, the risks.

I shake my head as I think of a younger me looking up at the Hawks, at Victor, like they were gods. Sadly, it's still how shit works in the Creek. It's how they get new junior members wanting to initiate in every single year. They're told they're safer on the inside. That their families are safer if they join—that's if their daddies aren't already senior members, which most are. It's expected of the boys to join, follow in their father's footsteps. And if they don't... well, it's time to get the fuck out of the Creek before Victor and his band of merry men find you and force your hand.

The gates open as I approach to let me escape and I head straight back toward Maddison.

Pulling my cell from my pocket, I find the person who's going to know exactly where I need to be and I hit call, putting it on loudspeaker and dropping my cell to my lap.

"You fucked up." Is Ella's greeting the second the call connects.

"It's not how it looked."

A bitter laugh crackles through the line. "That's what they all say."

"I'm serious. How much do you know?" I ask, not wanting to tell her shit that Letty hasn't already.

"That she showed up going out of her mind. But don't worry, she's got plenty of friends who want to comfort her, make her feel better."

The exact thoughts she's trying to imply fill my head, making my grip on the wheel tighten and my foot press down that little bit harder on the accelerator.

"Where is she?" I growl down the line.

"Enjoying herself away from you," she spits.

"Ella," I warn, my voice menacingly low.

"Kane," she seethes back, not backing down from my threat.

"Fine, I'll find her myself. She's clearly not sitting beside you, so I know exactly where she is. I pretty much already knew, I just needed it confirmed."

"Kane, no. P-please don't."

"She's mine, Ella. Mine. You can try to stop me all you want but I'll plow right through you," I warn.

I'm back in Maddison and pulling up to the Dunn house not long later.

I stop on the street a little down from where I parked the first time I came here for her and briefly think of the outcome of that night.

A wicked smile threatens my lips at the memory of taking her in that motherfucker's bedroom. But then reality crashes down and I remember why she's here, why she ran to them.

If they've fucking touched her...

Throwing the car door open, I climb out and make my way toward the house. Unlike last time, I don't hide and people immediately recognize me.

More than a few try to stop me to tell me how I almost turned the game around earlier but I don't stop to chat with any of them. I've got a target—or two —in mind, and I won't stop until I know they're nowhere fucking near my girl.

If she's upset thinking I've fucked up, then she needs to have it out with me. Not them. Never fucking them.

I blow through the house forcing more than a few

sets of eyes on me but none of them approach. Only one is brave enough and assumes he knows how to handle me.

"Kane, what the fuck are you doing?" Micah asks, coming to stand in front of me.

"Get out of my way, Lewis."

"No, not if you're here to start a war."

"Fuck that, I'm here to fucking end it. Where is she?"

"I-I um..."

"Fuck it." I push past him, sending him stumbling back as I march through the house looking for any sign of Letty or either of the Dunn twins.

It seems luck is on my side when I get to the kitchen because I find Luca shirtless with his back to me, his head hanging low as he leans forward on the counter.

I should probably take note of his stance, of the defeat in it, but I don't. My adrenaline is pumping too fast with my need to take him out.

She fucking ran into his arms. She turned her back on me and ran to him.

Storming up behind him, I wrap my fingers around his waistband and haul him back, throwing him down on the counter full of liquor bottles. The glass rattles with the force of him colliding with it and they topple over like dominoes, each one hitting the floor seconds after the last, smashing and filling the room with the scent of alcohol.

Gasps and screams sound out around me but I keep my focus on the man before me.

Stepping up to him, I stand right in his face, my eyes boring into his.

"Where is she?" I bellow in his face as his jaw begins to tic.

"None of your fucking business."

My hand wraps around his throat, squeezing in warning.

"It fucking well is. She's mine. Where the fuck is she?"

"Fuck. You," he spits.

Pulling my arm back, I finally get to do what I've been so desperate to do all this time.

Something settles within me the second my knuckles connect with his cheek, the sound of skin on skin, of bones connecting is just like music to my fucking ears.

"Motherfucker."

With aggression I was not expecting from him, he takes me by surprise and forces me back, pinning me against the wall with his forearm against my throat.

"Go on then, pretty boy. Fucking try it," I taunt.

Luca pulls his arm back, his face pulled tight, anger and hatred swirling in his eyes as he stares at me.

We're similar in height and size, but I know for a fact that I've got speed on my side when it comes to fighting.

I've been trained by the best. While I spent hours in the ring with multiple Hawks members training, Posh Boy was in the gym and out on the field running plays. It might have made him a kick-ass quarterback, but it's going to do nothing for him right now.

"What are you waiting for, pussy?" I hiss, waiting for him to throw his punch so I can get the upper hand.

A growl rips from his lips right before he moves, but he doesn't get the chance because a voice fills the silence around us.

"Luca, no," Letty cries.

Ripping my eyes from his, I find her fighting through the crowd to get to us.

The second she emerges, my heart drops into my feet and all the air rushes from my lungs.

"Scarlett?"

My eyes plead with her to tell me there's some other reason she's standing before me in only a man's shirt, while a shirtless man has me pinned against the wall.

"No." I shake my head, refusing to accept that she ran here and literally straight into his arms. "No, tell me you didn't."

She doesn't get to say anything because another Dunn appears behind her, his eyes trained on his brother.

"Luca, don't do this. Your arm," he says quietly but it's enough for Luca's grip on my throat to lessen.

I look between the two brothers, my chest heaving with anger.

Guilt shines in both of their eyes but no one says anything.

"Princess?"

When my eyes land on her once again, hers are full of unshed tears but it's not them that make my blood boil once again because it's the state of her messed up hair and obviously swollen lips.

"No," she screams, clearly as angry as I am right now. "You don't get to show up here after everything and look at me like I'm the one in the wrong. You got her fucking pregnant, Kane."

A loud gasp ripples through our audience.

"Right, everyone get the fuck out," a familiar voice booms from somewhere behind Letty but I don't take my eyes from hers to see as the small blonde clears the room like a pro with Leon's help.

"You can fucking let go now," I mutter to Luca but he just presses harder against me. "Get out of my face, asshole."

"Fuck you."

I move faster than he can anticipate and my fist lands right in his eye socket, sending him stumbling back and colliding with the counter I first had him against.

"Kane," Letty screams, running for Luca who's slid down, so he's sitting on the floor, his eye already swelling along with the bright red mark on his cheek and his face like thunder.

She drops to her knees beside him, gently pulling his hand away from his face to inspect the damage.

"You need to leave," she barks, briefly looking over her shoulder at me. "No one wants you here."

"Letty, please. What she said, it wasn't true."

"No?" She stands, turning on me, her eyes narrowed. "Prove it."

"W-what?"

"Prove. It."

My lips part to say something but I don't have any words, how the fuck am I supposed to do that right this second.

"You can't even stand there and tell me that you haven't slept with her. You're a fucking joke, Kane."

The anger and pain within me collide and I drop my eyes down her barely-clad body once more.

"Me? You're standing there dressed in one of their shirts and accusing me of being with someone before I even started here. Which one of them did you fuck tonight, Letty? Which one did you go running to in an attempt to forget about me? Was it Luca this time, or did you use Leon again to make you feel better about yourself?"

"A-again?" is growled from behind her, and when I look over Letty's shoulder, I find Luca looking between Letty and Leon with his brows pulled together.

"Oh, isn't this night just getting better and better? He didn't know. He didn't know you've already fucked his brother."

"Enough," Leon barks, coming to stand behind Letty.

"Lee?"

"Not now, Luc."

A smile pulls at my lips before a manic laugh rips from my throat.

"You're a fucking hypocrite, Scarlett Hunter." I take a step toward her as Leon wraps his arm around her shoulder. "I'm not going to fucking hurt her," I spit.

He scoffs. "Bit late for that."

"Didn't fucking stop you taking what's mine at the first opportunity." My lip curls in disgust. "Or have you been fucking her the entire time I have?"

I had no idea Luca had hauled his ass from the floor until I'm forcefully shoved away from Letty and Leon, my shoulder slamming into the wall, sending a sharp pain down my arm.

"Get out of my fucking house." He continues pushing me toward the back door and I allow it until we get there, then I stand my ground.

"Get your hands off me." I hold his eyes for a few beats before looking back at Scarlett. "She's a lying cunt, Letty. She's not pregnant, she just wanted to hurt you. But you, you were the one to do this." I nod between the twins. "I hope they enjoy you because they might not get another chance when I get my hands on you again."

Both Luca and Leon take a threatening step forward as if I'm actually fucking scared of them.

"This isn't over, Princess. Not by a long shot," I warn before spinning on my heels and marching from the house.

4

LETTY

Silence fills the Dunn's kitchen as we all stare at the door Kane just stormed through.

My heart thunders in my chest and my hands tremble.

There's a part of me that wants to believe him, to run after him and tell him all of this was a mistake. But then I remember the way she looked at him. What he's saying might be true, she might not be pregnant, but he's still fucked her and she still wants him.

"It's okay," Leon says, wrapping his hand around the back of my neck and pulling me into his chest.

"No," I say, pressing my hands against him and taking a step back.

His eyes stay on me as I turn to Luca who's standing only a few feet away, leaning back against the wall as if his body won't hold him up. His shoulders are dropped in defeat and his eyes are clouded over as if he's not even really here.

"Luc," I breathe, taking a step toward him.

He was already freaking out, he really didn't need Kane to blurt out that this wasn't mine and Leon's first time together.

He expels a long breath before his eyes finally lift. When they find mine, a gasp rips from my lips as I find them full of unshed tears.

"I'm sorry," I whisper, taking another step closer to him, needing to comfort him, to tell him that everything is going to be okay. But the longer I look at him, I start to doubt if that's even going to be the case. He looks utterly devastated.

"When?" he finally asks, his eyes never leaving mine.

"Y-years ago. It was just one time, we were drunk. You were with..." I rack my brain but really, Luca's a player and it could have been anyone. "A cheerleader probably."

An indecipherable noise rumbles up his throat before he lifts his hand to run his fingers through his hair.

"I-I don't... I can't—"

He pushes from the wall and disappears into the hallway and then either upstairs or out of the house, I have no idea.

I stand there, my body sagging in defeat as I wonder just how today turned into such a shitshow.

I turn, my eyes immediately finding Leon's.

'I'm sorry,' he mouths, and I nod, accepting it. Not that it's his fault.

"Me too."

"We should go back to the dorms," Ella finally says, reminding me that there was someone else to witness this nightmare.

"Y-yeah."

"No, Let. Stay, please. I need to know—"

"I can't, Lee." I look at the door Luca went through only a minute ago. "He doesn't need me here."

"But I want—"

"She'll be okay with us in the dorms," Ella says, pulling me into her body and wrapping her arms around me. "I think allowing everyone to cool off is probably for the best."

Leon's lips part to argue once more but he must realize that Ella is right because instead of arguing, he takes a step back and says, "I'll go grab your things."

The second he also disappears through the door, I turn to Ella and with one look into her concerned eyes and I break down.

She gathers me up and lets me cry on her shoulder.

I have no idea how much time passes, but I don't even realize that Leon has rejoined us until she thanks him and smooths her hand down my hair.

"Let's go, sweetie."

"W-wait, I need—" I reach for my Chucks before pulling them on my feet.

She nods at someone through the small window in the kitchen door and not a second later, Micah steps through.

"Ready?"

"Yeah," Ella answers for us before leading me toward the same door Kane blew through not so long ago.

The late summer evening air chills my skin the second we step out and I wrap my arms around myself in an attempt to keep warm as we head toward the road.

"Here," Micah says, shrugging off his hoodie and draping it over my shoulders.

"Thank you," I whisper.

The second we step onto the sidewalk, I can't help myself and I look up to see if Kane's car is here.

I hate myself for the move but I can't help wanting him even after everything that's happened tonight.

Guilt-ridden that I'm looking for him and not Luca, I look back at the house and toward his window. It's dark with no movement inside so with a sigh, I turn back toward Micah's car and climb in after Ella opens the door for me.

We're all silent as Micah starts the engine and sets off on the short journey back toward the dorms.

Ella sits beside me and reaches for my hand, squeezing it in support.

Resting my head against the window, I stare at the darkness outside.

Both of them escort me to my room, once again not saying anything and I couldn't be more grateful for the silent support. I think enough words have been said tonight.

Ella takes a seat beside me on my bed while Micah hovers.

"Do you want anything to eat, drink?"

I shake my head.

"I'll get you a bottle of water," he says anyway and slips from the room.

"I'm sorry I ruined your night," I mutter quietly to Ella.

"Don't be silly. The guys lost. The party wasn't exactly banging."

"Not the point."

Micah walks back in and places the bottle on my nightstand.

"Can I do anything? I'm sure I could get Ellis to get the others to kick his ass for you."

A small smile pulls at my lips.

"Thank you, but it's okay. I think I might actually be the one who really fucked up tonight."

"What happened, Let?" Ella asks quietly.

Blowing out a long breath, I fall back onto my pillows as tears pool in my eyes once more.

"I-I think he's been sleeping with someone else."

"Asshole," she hisses. "I'll fucking kill—"

"Ella," I snap, cutting her off. "We weren't official, we haven't laid down any rules or anything—"

"But even still, that's not—"

"I ran straight to Luca and Leon and... shit. I'm not exactly fucking innocent either."

"Twin sandwich?" she asks before all three of us snort with laughter.

It's so wrong. So, so wrong, but after all the tears and the pain, it's so fucking welcome.

Sitting up and scooting back against the wall, I stare down at my knees.

"I fucked up. But... shit."

"They that good?" Ella asks, her eyes sparkling with excitement.

I sigh, wishing the situation were different. "Yeah, that good."

"Jesus," Micah mutters, running his hands through his hair. "Is that what you really want? Is it? Two at a time?"

To anyone else, he might look like he's just asking a normal question, but I see more. I see it slowly killing him.

"It's just a fantasy," I answer for Ella in the hope of helping him out a bit. "I'm sure you wouldn't turn down two girls at once."

"One would be fine," he mutters, pushing from the chair while his eyes remain on Ella. "If you need anything, I'll be in my room."

"Thank you, Micah. You're a good friend." He smiles at me before disappearing and leaving me alone with Ella.

"Jeez, what's his problem?" she asks once he's far enough away he won't hear. "He needs to get laid," she says, answering her own question.

"Hmm..." I mutter, not waiting to get in the middle of anyone else's life when my own is such a mess. "I need to take a shower," I admit before she starts digging.

"Want me to wait?"

I glance at the clock and my eyes widen when I see that it's not even that late. Today feels like it's lasted a week.

"It's okay, I'm probably just going to crash," I lie. The reality is that I'm going to spend all night staring at my ceiling thinking of all the things I could have done differently as my regrets about what did happen threaten to drown me.

"Okay, if you're sure. I'm all up for a night of cheesy rom-coms and a tub of ice cream each as you drown your sorrows."

"I just want to sleep."

"Okay. I'll wait for another day to dust off my old DVDs."

"Deal."

"Call me if you need anything."

She disappears and the second the door closes behind her, my entire body sags in defeat and I stumble into the bathroom.

Really, I don't have the energy to shower, but every time I move I can smell Luca and Leon on me and I need it gone. I need the memory of how badly I fucked up tonight gone.

The effects of the vodka seems to have long disappeared now just leaving a lingering thud behind my temples.

Dragging Leon's shirt over my head, I drop my panties and step under the stream of water hoping that it won't only wash away their scents but also the memories of every bad decision I made tonight.

I shouldn't have run.

If I didn't freak out at the thought of someone else being pregnant with Kane's baby then maybe all of this could have been avoided.

I fall back against the tiled wall and slide down until my ass hits the floor.

The anger that covered Kane's face as he realized what I'd been doing with the Dunns fills my mind. Then the utter devastation on Luca's when he discovered that Leon and I have been lying to him for years.

A sob rips up my throat as I drop my head into my hands and finally let myself drown in my regrets and the pain that comes with them.

The sound of people moving around outside my room wakes me the following morning long before I'm ready to face reality.

My eyes are swollen and sore from crying long into the night, and my body is heavy with exhaustion.

Turning over, I grab my cell and look at the time, not missing that I have no calls or messages from either Kane or Luca.

I get it. They must both hate me right now.

"Ugh," I groan into my pillow, knowing that I need to do something about my disaster of a life but really, would be more than happy to hide in my room all day and not talk to anyone.

Refusing to act like the victim in all of this, I drag my ass from bed and get dressed.

There's one person in all of this mess who's done nothing wrong and that's where I need to start.

Pulling on a pair of jeans and a sweater, I tie my hair up in a messy bun and apply a light layer of makeup before pulling my door open.

All eyes turn on me as I step out, reminding me that every single person here is aware of what went down last night. My cheeks heat as the image of Leon between my thighs hits me.

What the hell was I thinking?

I wasn't. I was fueled by anger and vodka.

No one says anything as I make my way through the room and I hate that they're walking on eggshells because of me.

"It's okay, you can continue as if I never walked in."

"You caused quite a scene last night," Brax says after another awkward few seconds.

"Sorry if I killed the party."

"We weren't really in the mood anyway," West adds.

"You sure brought the entertainment though."

"I would say you're welcome but..." I trail off.

"How are you feeling?" Ella asks sympathetically.

"Better than I should." I guess I sobered up before falling asleep so I've managed to avoid the worst of my hangover.

"Hungry?" Violet asks, pushing a plate of pastries in my direction.

"Thank you," I mutter, picking one up.

"I'm... um..." I point to the door. "I need to try to fix a few things."

I can see curiosity as to who exactly I'm heading to see on all their faces but none of them ask, they just nod or smile sadly as I leave them to it.

By the time I pull up at the Dunn's house, I'm a nervous wreck. Not only am I going to have to face them after what happened between us all, but I'm also going to have to look all their roommates in the eyes too.

Blowing out a long breath, I climb from the car before I convince myself to go back to the dorms and hide.

Not wanting to wake anyone, I forgo the doorbell and just invite myself in. There's a good chance they wouldn't let me in anyway if they saw it was me.

The sound of talking comes from the living room, so I head that way in the hope of finding Luca in there.

I come to a stop in the doorway, the sight before me literally rendering me speechless.

I must make a noise because after a second, every set of eyes turns to me.

"Letty!" Shane, the twins' younger brother, announces happily as my eyes remain locked on Luca, who's cradling his baby niece.

Luca's eyes lift to mine but I see no happiness within them and my heart shatters all over again. His eye is black and swollen and his cheek has a nasty bruise on it from Kane's fists last night. My stomach turns over at the thought of them fighting because of me.

"Hey," I say, finally looking at Shane when the tension in the room begins to get heavy. "She's gorgeous."

Shane's smile lights up his face as he glances over at his daughter.

"Thank you." He reaches to the woman beside him. "You remember Chelsea, right?"

"Of course." I smile sweetly at her as I stand awkwardly, feeling Luca's eyes burning into me.

"What do you want, Let?" he barks, making Shane gasp in surprise.

"I-I um... was hoping we could talk," I say, awkwardly, wringing my hands together as everyone stares at me.

"Leon's upstairs if you need someone to talk to. You two seem to be close these days."

"Luc, please. It's not like that."

"No? Then what's it like because the last time I saw you two together he had his head—"

"Luca," Leon booms from behind me, cutting off his words.

I don't turn to look at Leon, although I do feel the light touch of his fingertips on my lower back as he passes me. I appreciate the support but I don't think it's going to be anywhere near enough.

"We were about to have breakfast, would you like to join us?"

"She can't," Luca answers for me.

"Luc, please. Can we just talk?"

"You've had years to tell me the truth, Let. Time's run out."

My lips part to respond but I soon find I have no argument.

"There was nothing to talk about," Leon answers for me. "It was years ago and we put it behind us. Just like all the high school girls you spent time with."

Luca's jaw tics as Shane and Chelsea look between the three of us, I assume putting all the pieces together.

"Yeah, difference is, they meant nothing. They were nothing. Not my best friend," he says, narrowing his eyes at Leon. "Or my brother." He pins me with the same look.

"Luca, I—"

"No," he snaps. "I'm not talking about this now. You need to leave."

All the air rushes from my lungs at his words. Never has he ever spoken to me like that before. Tears burn my eyes as I silently beg him to just hear me out.

"Scarlett," he hisses.

"Fine. Fine." I throw my hands up in defeat. "But this is bullshit and you know it." Turning to Shane and Chelsea, I smile sadly at them. "I'm sorry I interrupted. I hope you have a nice morning together."

With one final look at a heartbroken Luca who's still cradling his beautiful niece, I spin on my heels and run to the front door. I accept for the first time what a massive mistake it was to come here and try to talk to him.

"Letty, wait."

"Of fucking course you want to talk to her. Might as well just take her upstairs and continue where you left off last night," I hear Luca mutter, but I don't stop, I can't.

Clearly Leon ignores him as well if the pounding footsteps behind me are anything to go by.

"Letty," he calls when I'm almost toward my car.

"No, Leon. I need to leave."

"He's just angry."

"I know."

"He'll come around, just give him some time."

He finally catches up with me. His hand wraps around my upper arm and he spins me to face him.

His breath catches when he takes in the wetness on my cheeks.

"He's never going to be okay with this, Lee. I'd already hurt him enough with Kane. Add last night and I—" A sob erupts as I consider the possibility that I might have permanently fucked things up with my best friend.

"It'll be okay. It's just the pressure of the season and everything."

Leon wraps his arms around me, but unlike usual, I don't melt into his hold. I'm too broken right now to even accept his comfort.

"I need to go." I drag myself from his hold. Without another word, I make my way to my car.

The second the engine comes to life, I slam my foot on the accelerator and speed away from the house, feeling Leon's eyes on me the entire time. But I don't look back. I can't. I'll only shatter faster if I take in the look in his eyes.

5

KANE

The front door to the house crashes back against the wall alerting anyone who might be here that I've arrived home. Although I take one step inside and realize that no one probably noticed because there's music booming from the living room.

The knowledge that I've just walked in on a fucking party only adds to my already uncontrollable anger as I head toward where it's coming from.

Swinging the door open, I find it's not so much of a wild party as much as a private one.

Devin and Ezra are in the middle of the room with two girls each as they grind against each other.

"Ah, look another to join the party," Devin shouts, ensuring his two girls turn toward me. Wide smiles light up their faces as their eyes eat me up.

"Nah, you can fuck off," I bellow over the music as I storm past them into the kitchen.

"Still got your panties in a twist over Letty?" he calls back.

I stop dead and spin around to him.

"What did you just fucking say?" I shout, pushing the girl at his front to one side and getting right up in his face.

"I said—"

My fist curls in his shirt as I push him backward, forcing the second girl to stumble out of the way.

"What the fuck, Legend?" he barks when he hits the wall with a thud.

"Get your fucking nose out of my business," I seethe, leaning right into him so our noses almost brush.

"What the hell happened?"

My heaving breaths fan his face as images from the past few hours flicker through my mind like a fucking movie.

"Fuck," I bark, releasing him with a hard shove. "FUCK."

Spinning around with my hands in my hair, I find Ellis running into the room with a panicked look on his face.

"Let's go," he says to me, holding the door open and nodding toward the stairs.

"I need a fucking drink."

"I'll get one."

"What the fuck happened?" Devin asks again, beginning to sound desperate.

"Just get back to your whores," Ellis mutters as I

storm past him, taking the stairs three at a time until I'm on the top floor.

My bedroom door slams back on itself as I begin pacing, desperately trying to get the image of Letty sandwiched between the Dunn twins out of my head.

"FUCK," I bellow once more before Ellis joins me, closing my door behind him and throwing a bottle of vodka at me.

Without missing a beat, I twist the cap off and lift it to my lips, swallowing down the liquid as if it's water.

"Start talking," he demands, dropping into the chair on the other side of the room.

"Fucking Alana."

"I got that when Reid called. She claims to be carrying your baby?"

"Yeah, although she fucking told Letty first."

"Shit."

"You have no fucking idea. She went running to the fucking Dunn's to get her rocks off."

"Shit," he says again.

"I need to get out of this shit, E. I can't keep fucking doing this." I stare out the window into the darkness as I pull at my hair. I wish I could somehow walk away from Victor and everything he continues to demand from me.

"I thought Reid was working on it," Ellis repeats what I told him after he demanded to know where I disappeared to last week when I didn't show up to classes.

Truth is, I have no fucking idea what Reid is up

to, other than he's up to something. The bullshit with the shipments has his name all over it, I just have no idea what his game plan is.

I'm hoping that he's planning on wiping Victor from the face of the Earth but we know that it's not just as easy as pulling a trigger. He has his fingers in too many pies, too many allies in places we're not even aware of. It would be fucking suicide to take him out without proper planning.

"Yeah, well, he's not doing it fast enough. I can't live both lives. It's not going to work."

"Is it the two lives or Letty that's getting to you?"

"She fucked them. Both of them the second she thought I screwed up," I say, the words falling from my lips without instruction from my brain. The emotion in my voice makes me wince. It makes me sound weak and I'm anything but fucking weak.

"You went out with Alana Wednesday night. You took her to a hotel," he helpfully points out, making my stomach churn with the memory. "Don't you think it's a bit hypocritical to judge her when she thought you'd gotten someone else pregnant?"

"I don't—fuck. I don't know anything right now, E."

"Well, she's not actually pregnant, so that's something, right?"

I stare at him for a beat, feeling the weight of the devastation Letty must have felt when Alana landed that blow press down on my shoulders.

"Letty got pregnant the night of Skye's party last year."

Ellis's chin drops.

"She lost it at twenty weeks."

He scrubs his hand down his face as my words sink in. "Fuck, Kane."

"Her hearing that Alana was pregnant would have slayed her."

"Shit. How long have you known this?"

"She told me the night of my crash but she never got out that she miscarried. I accused her of aborting it and stormed out."

"A miscarriage at twenty weeks. That's like—"

"Hell?"

"Yeah."

"She didn't tell anyone. She went through it all alone."

He's silent for a few seconds as he stares down at his hands before he lifts his eyes to me. "Kane, you need to talk to her. What she did tonight, fuck. I get it. Can you even imagine how she must have felt?"

I shake my head, emotion clogging my throat at the thought alone.

"She ran to them, E. Both of them."

"Can you blame her? They've always been there for her. All you've done is make her life hard."

"Thanks," I mutter, dropping down onto my bed and tipping the bottle to my lips once again.

"What happened to Alana?"

"I left her with Reid."

"So she's dead then," he deadpans.

"I don't know. He looked quite excited to get the chance to play with her."

"Of course he did. She's totally his type."

"What, a whore?"

He throws his head back and barks out a laugh. "I was going to say blonde but yeah, whore works just as well."

With Ellis's help, I eventually drink myself unconscious. When I wake again, the sun is streaming through the open curtains and I've got the hangover from hell.

"Jesus, fuck," I mutter as I roll over, shoving my face into the pillow to block out the light.

I'm just drifting back off into oblivion when everything hits me once more.

She slept with the fucking twins. Pain slices through my chest.

It shouldn't hurt this fucking much. I shouldn't care this fucking much.

Especially when I'm just as bad.

Reaching down, I realize that I'm still wearing last night's clothes. I slide my cell from my pocket and hold it in front of my face to see the time.

"Fuuuck," I groan when I see how late it is before I notice the number of missed calls I have from Reid.

Tapping the screen, I move it to my ear as I call him back.

"Afternoon," he booms through the speaker.

"Shhh," I hiss.

"Went out celebrating that you're not having a kid

with the devil incarnate?" he asks, amusement filling his voice.

"Something like that. What's she saying?"

"Fuck all but I'd put money on it all being a setup. She might be a stubborn bitch but I don't think she did this alone."

"What are you thinking?" I ask, but I think I already know what he's going to say.

"Victor."

I groan as he says the name I was dreading.

"I need out, man. I can't fucking do this anymore."

"I know. It's gonna happen. I just need a bit longer."

I groan into the phone again, rolling onto my back and throwing my arm over my eyes.

"I'll call you when I find more out. Just trust me, yeah?"

"I know, I know. I just..."

"I'll get you out."

I hang up, not feeling as confident that he's going to manage it as I probably should. I want to trust that he can do it, but I fear it's going to take too long. I need to focus on classes and football if this is going to be my life or I might as well just walk away and become a senior member of the Hawks.

Maybe that was always my destiny and this was just a pipedream. Something I'd almost be able to have but just not quite. A little like Letty. I'd get a taste before my fucked-up life gets in the way and ruins it all.

Needing to get out of the house and away from this place, I shower, dress, and jump in my car.

I don't have a destination in mind but when I pass the sign to Rosewood, I can't say I'm surprised. After moving here to give Kyle a fresh start after he got out of juvie it became something of a sanctuary for me. Somewhere away from the bullshit life I was being forced to live in the Creek and away from the Hawks.

Here, no one knew who I was. They had no idea about the things I'd done, the people I'd hurt, the lives I'd ruined. I was just a man looking after his younger brother, giving him the second chance he deserved after being screwed over by Victor Harris's devil child.

I think about Gray and what might have happened to him after he tried to take Harley away from my brother as a way to teach him a lesson for screwing him over. Victor doesn't seem to care that his youngest is MIA. I never even got the chance to see mine on a screen and I already know that I'd have given my life for him in a heartbeat. I can't comprehend how you can so easily turn your back on your own flesh and blood.

The more I think about it, the more I come to the conclusion that there's got to be more to the story than meets the eye.

I blow out a breath as I pull up to the beachfront parking lot and kill the engine. I sit back, watching the waves crash onto the shore and the families that are making the most of the late summer sun.

What would life have been like now if Letty did have our baby? Would we have found a way to be a family? Could that have been us down there teaching our little boy how to build sandcastles and dipping his toes into the warm ocean?

Pulling my cell from my pocket, I search for her number and hit call. I don't know what I'm expecting after what happened last night but I can't help the disappointment flooding me when it finally goes to voicemail.

The second I lower my cell, the disappointment gives way to my anger. The image of her with the Dunns coming back full force and making my fists clench with the memory of my knuckles connecting with Luca's face.

That hit was a long time coming but fuck if it was nowhere near enough.

I sit there staring out at the ocean as the sun descends under the horizon.

6

LETTY

I pull up at Mom's only to find Harley's car sitting in the driveway. Killing the engine, I rest my head back and look at the house. It feels like a safe haven right now. It's away from him, away from everyone who knows what happened last night.

I'm dreading tomorrow, walking into class knowing that the majority of the students will know how badly I fucked up.

"Argh," I scream into the silence of my car, wishing like hell that I could turn the clock back and handle that bitch's revelations differently.

With my regrets pressing down on my shoulders, I get out of the car and head for the house. I find Harley immediately in the kitchen making herself something to eat.

"Hey, Sis. How's it going?" I take one look at her and burst into tears, unable to contain it.

"Oh, crap. Shit." She comes rushing over and pulls me into a hug.

My little sister is almost eighteen now, we're exactly the same height and build. Gone is the annoying little girl who used to follow me around like a shadow and in her place is a beautiful young woman.

My stomach rumbles as she holds me, making us both laugh.

"I was going to make a sandwich," she says. "But I've got a better idea. Come on."

She takes my hand and leads me back to the front door.

"I-I can't go out, I look like a mess," I argue.

"You don't have to leave the car. But I think you need more than a sandwich right now." She lifts a brow as she stares at me. "Then you can tell me everything."

"Okay," I whisper, knowing that I don't really want to talk about it but feeling the burning need to be honest with my sister. Hell knows I've kept enough back from my family in the past eighteen months to last a lifetime.

She immediately turns toward the ocean and I can't help but feel lighter. The beach makes everything seem that little bit better.

"Aces?" I ask, assuming where we're going.

"Bill's milkshakes fixes everything."

"Can't argue with that."

By the time we pull up into the oceanfront lot, I'm feeling better than I was when I first saw her.

"We can go inside. I'll be okay."

"Are you sure? I don't mind having a car picnic if you don't want to do people."

"No, it's okay. A burger in the car wouldn't be the same."

"True. Come on then."

Together we walk from the end of the lot and toward Aces. This little diner is the best thing about Rosewood. I have some fantastic memories of hanging out here with Luca, Leon and the rest of our school friends back in the day.

I sigh, images of the years gone by playing out in my mind as Harley leads us to a booth in the back so we can hide away.

"You sure you're okay?" she asks, clearly hearing my loud sigh.

"Yeah, I'm good. This place just brings back so many memories."

We take a seat not a second before Bill comes rushing over with a wide smile on his face wanting to know everything about MKU and how I'm doing. The man knows everything there is to know in this town. Fuck knows how but he does. He also knows exactly what not to say, evidenced by the fact he doesn't so much as mention Columbia, for which I'm grateful.

We give him our orders, of which he'd already guessed because all the kids here order the same thing, and he rushes back to his kitchen almost as fast as he arrived.

"So... how's Kyle?" I ask, more than willing to focus on the younger Legend brother for a few minutes before the inevitable questions come from Harley.

Her eyes soften and a smile starts to play on her lips as she thinks of him. The sight makes my heart ache but I'm so happy for her. They both deserve some happiness after everything they went through.

"He's really good."

"I can tell by the look on your face," I point out, making her entire face heat. "Where is he? I thought you were practically living together these days."

"He's got Ash and the boys around. Strategizing and watching old games or something. I spent the day with Ruby before heading home thinking Mom would be there."

"Where is she?"

"I have no idea. She's being a bit elusive. I think she's got a man."

My heart sinks as I remember Dad's words last week about always loving Mom. If she's seeing someone else, even after all these years, it'll kill him.

"Have you seen Dad?" I ask, mostly assuming she hasn't.

"We were going to go yesterday but he said he was busy. I haven't seen him in ages."

"I saw him last week. He's good," I say, hoping to stop her worrying.

"Oh? Did you go back with Kane?"

All the air rushes out of my lungs at her mention of his name.

"So this little trip home has everything to do with him then, I'm assuming." She raises her brow at me and sits back to continue staring at me. "Out with it, Sista!"

I want to laugh at her attitude but I can't find it in me.

"It's a mess," I admit, resting my elbows on the red table before me and dropping my head into my hands.

"I wouldn't have expected anything else with you two. So..."

"I thought it was real," I whisper, not really wanting to say the words out loud. "I'd told him everything and he... he said all the right things, did all the right things. I thought him knowing and accepting the truth meant things were finally going to turn around..."

"But?" she asks.

"I don't even know what's true and what's not right now. This woman turned up claiming to be pregnant with his kid—"

"What?" she screeches so loud that half the diner turns our way.

"Har," I snap.

"Sorry. Sorry. I just... I didn't see that coming."

"You're not the only one."

"So, what happened?" she asks eagerly, leaning forward to mirror me as she waits for the next installment.

"I ran straight to Luca and Leon. Made a few mistakes as they comforted me."

"Let?" Her eyes widen at my vagueness.

"The less you know, the better."

"I'm not a kid," she snaps, assuming her age is the reason I don't want to go there.

"I know, Har. I'm just... mortified. It's all such a mess."

"Okay. Continue please."

I very briefly summarize what went down in the Dunn's kitchen while she stares at me, eating it all up as if she's watching her favorite TV show.

"He said she's not pregnant?"

"That's what he said, but how can I trust that after everything?"

"Who was she?"

I shrug. "No idea. Blonde woman. Bit older than him, maybe. Beautiful. Like totally flawless."

"Alana," Harley seethes.

"Wait. You know her?"

"Yes," she hisses, her distaste of the woman clear on her face. "She's a conniving bitch. I can't stand her."

My lips part but I can't decide which one of the million questions that are spinning around in my head to ask first.

"They're not a couple. They've never been a real couple, if that helps at all."

"So what are they then?"

"I mean, I don't really know. Some weird kind of arrangement. Every time I bring it up, Kyle tells me to keep my nose out of it," she sulks.

"But they've been seeing each other for a while."

"Yeah," she admits with a wince. "But I really

don't think he likes her, and I'm not just saying that because she's an annoying bitch."

"But he's been sleeping with her?" I ask, unable to hide the hurt in my voice.

"Yeah, but not very often. Well, not at the house all that often."

My stomach turns as I think about him being with another woman. Taking a woman to a house that he's never taken me to. It shouldn't hurt as much as it does, but I can't stop it.

"Letty, do you..." She trails off as if she doesn't even want to say the words she's thinking.

"Spit it out, Har," I demand as one of Bill's servers brings over our milkshakes.

She pauses as he slides them across to us.

"I think... I mean, I don't know for sure but..." I raise a brow at her, wishing she'd just cut to the chase. "I think he's a Hawk," she whispers.

I can't help myself, I throw my head back and laugh.

"You think? Jesus, Har."

"What?" she whines, looking totally put out.

"He is a Hawk. That's no secret. He's worked for Victor for years, he sold his soul to him in return for help getting Kyle back."

"He... shit." Harley falls back into the bench. "I mean, I suspected but... shit. Letty, you need to be careful if he's tied up with Victor."

Don't I fucking know it.

Bill brings our burgers over and our conversation

comes to a grinding halt as we fill our faces, although at no point does it leave my head.

"If it helps at all, I wouldn't trust that bitch as far as I could throw her."

I stare at my sister's serious face for a few seconds.

It's not that I don't believe her. That bitch introduced herself while having a conversation about cheating on her husband. Her loyalty has never been in question. But...

"And I can trust Kane?" I ask, that's the real issue here.

"Letty," she sighs, pushing her half-eaten burger away. "Kane is... Kane. He's a lot of things, he's done bad shit. But he's not a liar. If he's telling you that she isn't, then I'd be inclined to believe him." My eyes hold hers, shocked that she's rooting for him here. "What?" she asks with a laugh as if she can read my mind. "I know how to handle a Legend. And I know Kane likes to look like he doesn't care about anything, but I think that's far from the truth when it comes to you."

"You haven't seen us together for years."

"True, but I've seen his face whenever your name comes up at home. You got yourself under his skin years ago, Let. And I'm pretty sure you never got out."

Her words take me straight back to the restaurant he took me to last week and his words ring out in my mind.

"You need to talk to him."

"I know," I mutter, my stomach dropping at just the thought. He was so angry last night. I can't imagine him willing to sit down and having a rational conversation about this.

Kane Legend doesn't do anything the rational way.

"I need to move," Harley says after a few silent minutes. "I think I'm going to explode otherwise."

"Come on, let's go."

We pay for our meals and wave to Bill who's in the kitchen before we head out. Without saying a word, we both walk toward the beach, it's as if we're drawn to the ocean.

Dropping down the steps, we both pull off our sneakers and walk down to the water's edge.

"I missed you, you know, when you went to college."

"I'm sorry I wasn't in contact more."

Harley must read more than I want her to in my tone because she looks over at me, her steps faltering.

"I didn't say that to make you feel guilty. I totally understand why you did what you did. I was just saying, it's nice having you close. Getting to do this again."

"Yeah, it is. I missed you too, Har Har."

"We need to stick together now anyway."

"Why do you say that?"

"We've both got Legends to tame." After a beat, she bursts out laughing and I can't help but follow.

"Do you think it's weird that we're with brothers?" I ask once we've calmed down.

"There are no rules, Let. Well, unless you wanted to bang Zayn."

"Ew," I say, swatting her shoulder.

"Just shows we've got similar taste."

"Dangerous bad boys with wicked intentions?"

"Yep, that's the one. Although I must admit, I think you got the short end of the stick. Kane is going to be harder work than Kyle."

"Christ, I draw the line at comparing notes, Har."

"That's fair. Can you just tell me one thing?"

"Shoot."

"Is it true that Kane's pierced... you know... down there."

"What do you think?"

"I think he looks just like the type who would be."

"Then you have your answer."

"Oh my God. You think you can get him to talk Kyle into it? I mean, I've heard it's all kinds of awesome."

"You're in high school, Har. Who the hell are you talking about cock piercings with?"

"Oh, pipe down. Just because I'm the little one, it doesn't mean I don't do the exact same shit you and Zayn did in high school."

"But you're meant to stay sweet and innocent forever," I mock in a baby voice to piss her off.

"Too late for that. Kyle has well and truly ruined me."

"I need to have words with that boy."

"Don't you fucking dare," she warns, making me laugh again.

"I might just for my own amusement. Hell knows I could use some right now."

"Go back and talk to him."

I shake my head. "Not today. It's all still too fresh."

"You can't go to classes with this hanging over you."

I know she's right, but the thought of standing in front of Kane right now kinda terrifies me. He was so angry last night, I'm not sure I'm ready to deal with that wrath without the back up of others.

We walk until we have no choice but to turn around and head back. Harley talks away about school, about cheer and about Kyle and the football team. I listen to everything, glad to have something else to focus on for just a little while before I have to head back to reality. As much as I might want to remain hidden here and push everything I left behind from my mind, I know I can't. I spent the last eighteen months avoiding the truth, it's time I started dealing with my issues head-on. You know, like the adult I'm supposed to be.

By the time we get back to the parking lot, the sun has almost set behind us casting a stunning orange glow on everything.

Looking back over my shoulder, I take one final look at the ocean and suck in a deep lungful of salty air, grounding myself and preparing for what drama my week might hold.

"Ready?" Harley asks me, pausing beside me for a few minutes while I soak up the last of the peace.

"Yeah. Time to pull up my big girl panties."

"You've got this, Let. I've got faith in you."

"Thanks," I whisper, turning back toward the lot and heading for her car. "Wait," I say, my hand landing on her forearm as the back of a very familiar gunmetal gray car disappears from the lot. "Was that..." I trail off, not believing my eyes.

No, it couldn't have been. He wouldn't have... he wouldn't have followed me here. Right?

"Was that what?" Harley asks, clearly missing the back end of the car by the time she looked up. "I didn't see anything."

"It doesn't matter. I was probably imagining things," I say, trying to play it off like it's nothing but the speed of my racing heart tells me that's not the case.

That was him. Something inside me knows it was.

But why?

"You really need to deal with all this, Let. It's making you crazy. Well, crazier than you've always been."

"Thanks, Har."

"So, any chance you could come back for a little longer, and with a little warning next time. It would be great to spend the weekend together or something," Harley asks as we head home.

"What about the weekend?" I ask, already keen to leave again and I haven't even returned yet.

"Isn't it homecoming? Won't you want to be there for the game and the party?"

I think of Luca and Kane. Neither of them are

going to want me at the game. But their next couple of games are away, and I won't get the chance to go.

I blow out a breath, knowing that no matter how much they might hate me right now, that I'm not going to be able to miss the game, to miss seeing them kick ass on the field.

"I could come back after the game. Have a girly night in?"

"That sounds perfect. I'll tell Kyle he has to spend the night with the guys, and we can have the house to ourselves."

"Or we could just stay home," I suggest, not really wanting to be in Kane's house.

"I'll sort something out. Eeek, I'm excited," she says, jumping from the car. "You coming in or heading straight back?"

I sigh. "I really should get back."

"Letty, just go and talk to him. Lay everything out on the table and see what happens."

"When did you get so wise, Harley Hunter?" I ask, pulling her in for a hug.

"You need to be wise to tame a Legend."

"A lion might be easier," I admit, knowing just how wild Kane can be.

"It's worth the ride."

I burst out laughing the second I hear her words. "Please, please tell me that my little sister did not just say that," I beg.

"I only speak the truth," she says with a shrug.

"Come here, trouble." I pull her back into my

arms and hold her tight. "Thank you. I really needed this," I whisper in her ear.

"I'm always here, Let. Whatever you need."

"Thank you," I say, pulling back and taking her hands in mine.

"Everything will work out. You'll see."

With one more smile, I release her and head to my car ready to make the journey back to Maddison County.

I take it slow, wanting to put off what I need to do for even longer. But eventually, I end up exactly where I don't want to be, parked on the street outside the Harris's house.

Kane's car is parked out front along with another two and the lights are all on. Any hope I had that he might not be here is diminishing fast.

Telling myself that it can't be as bad as this morning's attempt to talk to Luca, I climb from the car and make my way to the front door.

I shake my arms out at my sides as I come to a stop. The door is black with a really menacing skull knocker on it. Just the sight of it sends a shudder through the entire length of my body.

Lifting my hand, I knock it once in the hope no one hears and I can go running back to my car knowing that I at least tried to do the right thing.

Sadly, that's not what happens.

7

KANE

I had the best of intentions for when I got back to the house. I was going to lock myself in my room and attempt to make some headway on my lit assignment. Then call it a night so that I could show up to practice in the morning not looking like those two assholes turned my world upside down on Saturday night.

But when I walk into the living room, I find Devin and a six-pack of beer and those intentions go straight out the window.

"How's it going?" he asks as if the night before never even happened.

"It's..." I trail off, not having an answer. "I'm sure someone's filled you in on all the details by now."

"I've heard a few things. I can't believe she tried to claim to be carrying your kid. That's fucked up," he barks, throwing me a can.

"Yeah. She'd been trailing Letty too, ensuring she found out before me."

"I always knew that bitch was crazy but fuck."

"So what now?"

"Fuck knows. Reid's trying to find out the truth but this has your dad's name written all over it."

"Don't fucking call him that," he growls, his face twisting in anger.

"What have I missed?"

"We're still not getting what we fucking need. He's screwing us."

"I thought Reid sorted your shipments."

"Yeah, you and me both. Something's up and I'm going to have to fucking talk to him about it."

"Victor?"

"No, fucking Santa Claus," he deadpans.

"You should go to Reid with this," I say, going with my gut.

"Why? Victor is the one in charge of us."

"I know, I just... I've got this feeling that Reid is up to something," I admit with a wince.

Devin sits forward, resting his elbows on his knees.

"Explain."

I drain my can before crushing it and dropping it to the table. "I don't know. Something just isn't adding up. Vic set Letty up to bug this place because there was an issue with supply. But you're saying there are shipment issues."

"Why the fuck didn't you tell me this before?"

"I thought it would sort itself out." I shrug like it's not a big deal. In reality, I wanted Reid to continue whatever the fuck it is he's planning in the hope my release is a part of it. It was probably selfish of me not to say anything but I really don't want to get in the middle of something that's going on within the Harris family. I'm already in deeper than I ever wanted to be.

"What the fuck is he playing at?"

"No idea. Don't you trust him?" I ask, knowing full well that he does, just like I do.

"Yeah, with my life. But if he's planning something then he should have fucking told me."

"There'll be a reason he didn't," I tell him, pulling off another beer can, cracking the top open.

Devin does the same, his jaw ticing with frustration. He doesn't need to tell me why. I know how irritated he gets being in Reid's shadow all the time.

I'm about to say something, fuck knows what, mind you, in the hope of distracting him when there is a knock at the front door.

"Expecting someone?" I ask, wondering if he was waiting for a chick to appear and instead ended up with me.

"No. You?"

"Who the fuck comes here for me?" His eyes catch mine and I know he's thinking of the exact same person I am because anger flickers through his eyes. "It won't be her. And you need to let it go."

"Whatever." He climbs from the couch and heads to the front door.

I hear the rumble of his voice before the door shuts once more, I assume after whoever it was has been sent on their way. What I'm not expecting is for him to appear in the doorway with a wicked smile playing on his lips.

"You were wrong. You've got a visitor."

Devin stands aside but no one appears for a second. But then she steps forward and all the breath races from my lungs as I stare at her.

Her hair is piled on top of her head, her face almost free of makeup showing just how dark the circles under her eyes are and how pale her usually glowing bronzed skin is.

"Come to apologize, Princess?" Devin asks, stepping close to her and picking up the tendril of hair that's hanging around her face.

She doesn't react to him at all, instead keeps her eyes on me.

"C-can we talk?" Her slight hesitation gives away how she's really feeling right now.

Devin shoots me a look, his eyebrow quirked with a silent suggestion.

The thought of him touching her makes me want to cut his fucking hands off but I can't help his idea beginning to sate the twisted need within me to make her pay for last night.

Sitting back and stretching my legs out wide, I run my eyes down the length of her body.

"You know, I'm not really in the mood for talking, Princess."

Her eyes narrow on me as I bite down on my bottom lip, imagining all the dirty things I'd like to do to her right now just to prove who she really does belong to.

She gasps when Devin tugs harshly on that small lock of hair and her eyes fly to his.

"Kane's always been more of an action over words kind of guy. I thought you'd know that after all these years, Princess."

Her hand flies up to knock him away from her. Before she manages to connect with him, he wraps his hand around her wrist and pulls her into his body, dropping his lips to her ear and whispering something to her. Something I really fucking wish I could hear.

She jolts, trying to pull away from him but she's no match for his strength.

"Come on, Princess. Rumor has it you're up for anything."

If I weren't so pissed, I might laugh at the look on her face.

I know Letty, and I know she's not like the girls Devin usually spends time with, even with knowing what went down last night with the Dunns.

"Fuck you, Devin," she seethes, pushing at his chest with her free hand.

"Aw, Princess. The fun is only just starting," he growls, backing her into the wall and pinning her there with his hips.

She shoots a look over at me as if I'm going to come to her rescue.

"What?" I ask, fighting to keep how I'm really feeling off my face at the sight of Devin touching what's mine. A bitter laugh falls from my lips when anger twists her face. "You think I'm going to rescue you?" I shake my head, tipping my beer to my lips. "Have at it, Dev. She clearly doesn't care who touches her."

"What the fuck, Kane?" she seethes. "Get the fuck off me." Her hands start flying at Devin as she tries to fight him off. He lets her land a few hits before he takes her wrists once more and pins them against the wall above her head.

"Keep fighting, Princess. The wild ones always get me the hardest."

"You need to get the fuck off me."

Devin growls at her, baring his teeth in a way that should terrify her. But despite the fact she's fighting him, I know she's not scared. My girl is stronger than that.

Ripping my eyes from them, trusting that Devin won't take things too far, I pull my cell from my pocket pulling up a playlist and hitting play so it fills the room.

I have no idea if Ellis and Ezra are upstairs but we really don't need Letty's angry cries alerting them and dragging them down here. I'm all for messing with her but we don't need an audience.

Draining my beer, I slam it down on the coffee table and walk over to where Letty is still trying to free herself.

"What's wrong, Princess?" I ask innocently, tucking that lock of hair behind her ear. "I thought two men at once was your new thing. You know damn well that Devin and I could take you to places those two cunts could only dream of."

"No," she cries as I trail my fingertip down her cheeks. "I-I just came to talk. To e-explain."

"I'm not sure it's necessary. Like Dev said, actions speak louder—" I lower my fingers to her breasts and pinch her nipple, making her gasp. "Don't you think?"

"Kane, please. Don't do this," she pleads.

"Oh come on, Princess. Don't pretend that you're not enjoying this."

Devin stands aside and allows me to press my thigh between her legs. She might be wearing jeans but the heat of her pussy almost immediately burns through my sweats.

His hand slips around from her waist and disappears under her sweater. He stops on her stomach knowing that I'd take him to the fucking ground should he go any higher.

"Look." I nod down to her chest. "Your nipples are begging for more. You want us both to suck on them?"

"No," she cries, her voice holding a hardness that makes me believe her. It doesn't mean I'm going to stop though.

I lean in, my lips brushing her ear much like Devin's did not so long ago. "And I already know you're soaking wet."

"No," she repeats.

"You came here to apologize, right?"

"Kane, please. I do, I want to explain. Not... not like this."

"Hmm... how desperate are you to tell me

everything, Princess?" I squeeze her breast hard enough to make her whimper as I press my hard cock against her hip. "Desperate enough to get on your knees and show me just how sorry you are?"

Her eyes widen in shock but I don't miss the flash of gold that only appears when she's turned on.

"Maybe you'd blow Dev too, just to show me how much you really mean it?"

Her brows pull together. She wants to argue but she also has no idea what I'm going to say next.

Running my nose down her cheek, I look into her eyes.

"I like this look on you, Princess. Now tell me, did they give you what you needed?"

She shakes her head so slightly that I'm not sure if she's aware that I feel it or not.

"No?"

She gasps, giving me my answer.

"Need two real men, huh?"

"No. Kaaane," she cries when I drop my hand and cup her pussy, pressing my finger against that seam of her jeans so it grazes her clit.

"You're a dirty little whore, Scarlett Hunter. But we've both always known that, haven't we? You fucking gush every time I whisper it in your ear." Lifting my hand, I push it inside her jeans and part her folds. "Fucking soaked."

I circle her clit as I hold her eyes. I can see she's desperate to close them as the sensations take over her body, but I won't allow it and she knows it.

"Were you this wet for them, Princess? Did you come as hard for them as you do for me?"

"Kane," she cries once more when I push lower and spear two fingers inside her. I curl them until I hit her G-spot.

"Fuck, that's hot," Devin grits out. He's still innocently touching her stomach but when I glance over at him, I find he's got his hand in his sweats slowly working himself.

I expect Letty to follow my lead and look at him, but when I look back up, I find her eyes are still firmly on me.

"Are you going to come for us, Princess? Let Devin see just how fucking wicked you are when you come all over my fingers."

Her head thrashes from side to side as I rub at her harder, pushing her closer to release.

"He's so fucking hard for you right now, Princess. He thinks you're a dirty little whore too. That get you off knowing that we all know who you really are, doesn't it?"

"Oh God," she whimpers, unable to stop my onslaught before she crashes.

Her pussy clamps down around my fingers as pleasure floods her body, but even still, her eyes never leave mine.

"Good girl," I breathe, holding her eyes. "Now get on your fucking knees."

Pressing one hand to her shoulder, I force her down. Her knees are so weak from her release that she goes easily.

Lifting my fingers to my mouth, I suck them clean as she watches.

"You taste like betrayal, Princess."

Reaching for my waistband, I push my sweats down my hips, letting my cock spring free.

A growl erupts from beside me and for the first time since I stepped up to her, Letty looks at Devin.

Her eyes widen as she realizes that I want her to do this with an audience. But that slight bit of fear in her eyes affects me in a way I wasn't expecting.

"Get the fuck out, Dev," I growl.

"Wait, what?" he barks, confused and lost to the moment.

"This is between me and Letty. Get the fuck out."

"Fucking spoilsport," he mutters, taking a step back before the living room door slams a few seconds later.

"Where were we?" I say, looking down at Letty who's sitting on her haunches with my cock bobbing in front of her face. "Oh, that's right. You were going to apologize."

Her large dark eyes stare up at me as I rub the head of my cock against her lips.

"Open up, Princess. You've got a lot of making up to do."

I don't wait to see if she's going to do it willingly, instead I thrust forward, filling her hot little mouth in one move.

"Fuuuuck," I groan as she sucks on me. "Damn, that's fucking good. Tell me you didn't do this to them. Tell me."

Her eyes continue to hold mine as she pulls almost all the way off me. I expect her to pull all the way back and to reply, but she surprises me by just shaking her head and taking my length back into her mouth once more until I hit the back of her throat.

"You like sucking my cock, don't you?"

Her eyes flash with desire once more as I lift my hand to rest against the wall and thrust deeper into her throat.

"Fuck, Letty."

My hips move faster, fucking her mouth, taking everything I need from her as drool drips from her chin and tears spill from her eyes.

"You look so fucking beautiful, Princess. So fucking beautiful and all fucking mine. You got that?"

She nods before taking me again and sucking until I have no choice but to come down her throat with a loud growl.

The second she pulls back, I tuck my hands under her arms and lift her up the wall.

Her lips part to say something but I hold her face in my hand and press my thumbs over her lips.

"No."

Her eyes hold mine, her brows drawing together in confusion.

Confident she's not going to say anything, I move my hands, sweeping the tears from her cheeks and the drool from her chin.

"Not even close to being enough, Princess," I breathe. It's not a surprise, I already knew that a fucking lifetime with this woman would never be enough.

She squeals as I drag her from the wall and throw her over the arm of the couch.

"Ow, shit," she cries when my palm lands on her denim-clad ass.

"Quiet," I bark. "Unless you want the others down here to watch you get fucked."

She slams her lips shut as I wrap my fingers around the waistband of her jeans and drag the fabric over her hips, quickly followed by her panties.

Cupping her pussy from behind, I push two fingers inside of her.

"Mine," I growl. "This pussy is fucking mine. You got that, Princess."

"Yours," she whispers.

Ripping my fingers from her, I line my cock up and thrust so hard into her that her feet leave the floor.

"This." Thrust. "Is." Thrust. "Fucking." Thrust. "Mine."

Running my hand up her spine, I free her hair and twist the length around my fist making her back arch, causing me to hit her even deeper.

"Tell me they didn't fuck you. Tell me they didn't get this."

She shakes her head violently. "No. Yours, Kane. Yours," she cries as I slam into her over and over, hitting her cervix every time I bottom out in her.

"Fucking right, Princess."

The couch slides across the floor as I fuck her

hard and fast. The sound of our skin slapping sounds out over the music as she moans beneath me.

"I want to hear you scream my name, Princess. I want to know you know who's ruining your pretty little cunt right now."

Pulling on her hair, I stand her upright, my lips moving down her exposed neck. I suck the sensitive skin beneath her ear into my mouth and sink my teeth down.

"Kane," she cries, her pussy rippling around me as the pain washes through her.

"Tell me what they did. Tell me what they did to you."

She hesitates and I bite her again, harder this time until the taste of copper fills my mouth.

"T-touched me. K-kissed me."

"Here?" I ask, running my fingers over her lips.

"Yes," she breathes.

Twisting her face to me, I push my lips against hers.

"Mine," I growl against them.

She nods.

"What else?"

"F-fingers."

A possessive growl rumbles deep in my chest at the thought of them putting anything inside her.

"Who?"

"L-Luca."

"Motherfucker."

"What else?" I demand, my hips continuing to thrust in and out.

"Tongue," she whispers, turning her face away from mine in shame.

Dropping my hand down the front of her body, I part her pussy and press two fingers against her swollen clit.

"They tasted *my* pussy?" My voice is rough even to my own ears as she whimpers and shudders in my hold.

"I'm sorry," she whispers. "I'm sorry. I'm so sorry."

"Who?"

"L-L-Leon."

All the air rushes from my lungs as relief that I wasn't expecting floods me. I hate what she did, that they got a piece of what's mine, but I'm so fucking glad it wasn't Luca.

With one hand cupping her pussy, I lift the other to her throat and squeeze enough to ensure she listens to every word I'm about to say to her.

"If you run to them again. If you let them touch you again. I will fucking kill them."

She nods quickly, taking my warning seriously.

"You're mine, Letty. Fucking mine. Have you got that?"

"Yes," she cries.

"Good. Now let me show you."

Releasing her throat, I grip the nape of her neck and push her back down onto the couch. I slam into her over and over until I feel the familiar tingles start up at the base of my spine.

"Come, Princess. Milk my fucking cock like a dirty little whore."

Exactly as I knew she would, she cries out her release, her body locking up as pleasure takes over. I thrust two more times, filling her to the hilt before my own release slams into me, my cock jerking violently inside her.

The moment I'm done, I pull out and right my sweats.

Taking two huge steps back, I stare at her bent over with the evidence of what we just did running out of her.

"Now you can leave." My voice is cold and void of any emotion. Her entire body goes rigid for a beat before she stands, keeping her back to me and pulls up her jeans.

"Fine," she spits. "But tell me something."

I don't respond. I already know what she's going to ask me. I'm actually surprised it's taken her this long.

"When was the last time you fucked her?" Her voice quivers as she speaks but she still doesn't look at me.

"Before I started here. I've taken her out twice since but I didn't fuck her."

"But you touched her, didn't you." It's not a question. She already knows.

"Yes. Just like they did to you."

A sob erupts from her.

"The difference is, my life depends on it. You made the choice."

"Goodbye, Kane."

A manic laugh falls from my lips as she walks

toward the door and she stops with her fingers around the handle.

"You're not stupid, Letty, so don't try and act it. This is far from over and you know it."

She sucks in a shaky breath and lowers her head.

"This. Us. It'll never be over and you know it."

Her chin drops but no words come from her as she finally rips the door open and takes a step through.

"Until next time, Princess. And you can bet your life that there will be a next time."

The front door slams behind her and it takes every ounce of restraint I have not to follow her and drag her ass up to my bed.

___

8

LETTY

By some miracle, I manage to keep my sobs inside as I speed across town toward the safety of my dorm.

Only Micah is in the living area when I fly through. I don't look at him and he doesn't say a word, just watches me with what I can only imagine is concern in his eyes.

But if he's as close to the Harrises as I'm beginning to think he might be then I'm sure he's aware whose name is written all over this.

I pause in the doorway and suck in a breath.

"Please, don't tell the others."

"Whatever you need."

"Thank you," I whisper before locking myself into my room.

I fall back against the door with a thud as my first sob erupts.

Lifting my hands, I cover my face and cry for everything that's happened.

The loss of my friendship with Luca, the end of the good times with Kane. The fact he touched another woman and the knowledge that I so easily allowed both Luca and Leon to touch me. But mostly, I cry because of the pain in my chest from not fighting Kane earlier when he told me to leave.

I shouldn't have followed orders. I should have turned around and looked in his eyes and told him how I really felt. Explained how much it fucking hurts that he was with someone else but that even knowing that, that I can't walk away.

But I didn't. I said goodbye and I left as if I didn't care.

I don't remember when I finally climbed into bed last night or at what point I passed out but I know it was a long time after I locked myself in. Long before I'm ready, my alarm sounds, dragging me from my sleep where things are much easier to deal with.

I groan, rolling over to find my cell and shut it the hell up.

Cracking my eyes open, I stare at the screen waiting for it to become clear and find messages from Leon.

A sigh rips from my lips. At least I haven't ruined every relationship with my mistakes.

> Leon: I'm sorry about earlier. Are you okay?

Leon: Let, please talk to me. I'm
worried about you.

Leon: Scarlett Hunter, don't make
me come over there.

I can't help but laugh at his final message although I do wonder what happened because as far as I know, he never came here. Or if he did, he didn't wake me.

I look at the time of the messages and realize that it wasn't all that late. I must have passed out earlier than I thought.

In a rush, my thumbs fly over my screen to reply.

Letty: I'm so sorry, I crashed. I'm
fine. Please don't worry. I'll see you
in class. x

Knowing he won't reply right away because he's at practice, I roll out of bed and head for the bathroom to get ready for class.

My stomach is in knots knowing that I'm going to face other people, mainly Kane and Luca. I have no idea how either are going to react to me.

"Jesus," I mutter the second I look in the mirror and find dried blood on my neck.

Lifting my fingers to the mark, I cast my mind back to last night as Kane latched on to me. No wonder it hurt, he actually bit me.

Tracing my fingers over the wound, I think back over the events that occurred in the Harris's living room.

I should not have enjoyed that as much as I did. Even having Devin there didn't really turn me off.

Kane is right. I am just a dirty little whore.

My body heats from the inside out as I hear him growl those words in my ear as if he's standing behind me.

Shaking my head, I try to banish him from my thoughts. I strip out of yesterday's clothes and stand under the hot spray of the shower.

When I emerge, Ella, Micah, and Violet are sitting around the table with coffee and breakfast.

"Bacon?" Vi asks and I shake my head, already knowing that I'm not going to be able to stomach anything. "Just coffee would be great."

"You need to eat, Let," Ella says, concern evident in her voice.

"Maybe later. I can't right now."

All three of them watch me as I pull out a seat and lower my ass into it, my neck burns as they all find the mark I was unable to hide.

"Leon was here last night," Ella blurts and my head flies up from the table.

"He was?"

"Yeah, but Micah said you'd come in and gone to bed so we convinced him not to disturb you."

I glance at Micah, silently thanking him for letting me have my time alone. A small smile pulls at his lips in acceptance.

"Yeah, I crashed."

"Where did you go?"

"I... um... I went home. Spent the day with my

sister down at the beach. It was nice." *Until she convinced me to deal with my issues and I went to Kane.*

"Okay, are we all going to ignore the fact it looks like she's been attacked by a vampire or what?" Vi asks, finally addressing the elephant in the room.

Lifting my hand, I cover up the angry mark left behind from my latest mistake.

Was it a mistake though?

My punishment last night was inevitable, I just sped the process along a little by turning up and making it easy for him.

"I saw Kane," I admit with a wince.

"He fucking bit you," Ella balks. I'm not sure if she's horrified or impressed. "I guess it would be stupid of me to ask if he was angry."

"That doesn't even begin to explain it. I fucked up, I deserved it."

"Bullshit, Let. He hurt you first with that skank. Did you at least find out the truth?"

Did I? Our hazy, lust-fueled conversation fills my mind, but it's patchy at best.

"I-I don't know."

"Christ, Let. Maybe try and have a conversation in public next time so you can actually talk," Violet helpfully suggests.

I can't help but wonder if it would have made any difference. Something tells me that he'd still have unleashed his fury on me exactly as he had inside the house last night. And I already know that I'd have let him.

Christ, I'm screwed up.

"So what's the plan now?"

I shrug because the reality is that I don't have one. Chances are, the only one out of the three of them who will talk to me today will be Leon. Something tells me the other two will just shoot me death stares from a distance. Luca planning how best to get away and Kane scheming how best to get his hands on me when I least expect it.

"Well, can I suggest you get one because something tells me that Kane isn't going to let this lie," Ella says, her eyes holding a seriousness I feel all the way to my toes.

"I know."

The sound of the guys barreling into the room cuts off anything else she was going to say.

They're both joking around until their eyes land on me when they both instantly stop.

"Don't stop on my account," I bark, pushing my chair back and dumping the remains of my coffee in the sink.

"Hey, no, that's not—"

"We just didn't expect—"

"I live here, assholes," I snap, instantly feeling bad when their faces drop. "I'm sorry. That wasn't fair."

"Hey, girl. Everything's cool. We're just worried about you." Both West and Brax gather me up in a hug, squeezing the life out of me. "And if it makes you feel any better at all, you look a hell of a lot hotter than Luca and Kane this morning, even if you've been attacked by a vamp."

"Jeez, you spotted that fast," I mutter, pulling away from them.

"You've looked in a mirror, right?" West asks, staring down at it.

"Yes," I hiss. "I'm going to class." Swiping my bag from the floor, I throw it over my shoulder and head for the door.

"Wait, I'll walk with you," Ella calls.

"Okay. I'll meet you outside. I need some fresh air."

The second I step into the hallway that leads to our lit class, Leon pushes from the wall and races over.

I smile at the sight of him but his own joy soon falters when his eyes fall to my neck.

"What the fuck did he do?" he growls.

"Forget it, Lee. It doesn't matter."

His fists curl in frustration as I close the space between us.

"Forget it, are you fucking kidding. He hurt you, again."

"I deserved it," I mumble, averting my eyes from his intense stare.

"No, no, you fucking don't."

"How's Luc?" I ask, trying to change the subject, although it's no less painful.

Leon lets out a long sigh. "He's... he's a fucking mess. I left without him this morning after Coach pulled him in for a chat."

"Was Kane there? Did the two of them..." I trail off, not needing to spell it out.

"They stayed away from each other, but we were just training. It might be a different story later."

"Jesus," I mutter, lifting my hands to my head.

"They need to have it out. It's the only way they'll get it out of their systems."

"You want them to fight?"

"No, obviously not. But it's what's going to happen."

"I've messed everything up," I whisper, taking a step toward him and dropping my head to his chest.

Leon wraps his arm around me and holds me as I suck in some shaky breaths.

"I never should have come here."

"No, Let. You can't say that. This is where you belong."

I suck in a long breath, trying to find some strength to say the words I need to say.

Pulling my head from his solid chest, I look up at him, holding his green eyes.

"He knows," I breathe. "He knows what we... what you did."

He reaches out and tucks a lock of hair behind my ear. "He barely even looked at me this morning. It'll be fine, Let."

"But—"

"I knew the risks, Cupcake. I did it anyway." He wiggles his brows, a smirk appearing on his lips.

"Leon Dunn, you're wicked."

"It was worth it though, right?"

"Oh my God," I mutter, hiding my face in his chest once again.

I know the second Kane joins us in the hallway, not only does the air around me become charged with tension but Leon's hand tenses on my waist.

"We should go in," I say without looking over my shoulder.

"Hold your head high, Cupcake," Leon says, cupping my jaw and forcing me to do just that. "Don't let him see that he's affecting you."

"But—"

"You're strong, Scarlett Hunter. Show him."

I nod at him, grateful for his support.

"Come on then."

Without looking back, I take a step away from Leon and march toward our class with him following behind me.

We take our usual seats, leaving an empty one at the end of the row for when or if, Luca appears.

I'm already settled when Kane finally joins us. He doesn't so much as look at me as he makes his way across the room and then up the stairs to his usual seat at the back despite the fact my eyes stay on him the entire way.

Leon leans over and whispers in my ear. "Have faith. Everything will work out." He squeezes my thigh in support before Professor Whitman joins us and immediately begins our lecture.

We're ten minutes into the lecture when the door opens and a familiar face steps inside. Leon stiffens beside me. I know he's trying to play it down, but I can see the concern for his twin every time I look at him.

Without looking up, Luca finds the closest empty chair and drops into it.

My heart sinks as I watch him pull his notebook out and slump back in the chair as if he's got the weight of the world on his shoulders.

I want to talk to him. I want to fix everything but I'm not sure anything I can say will make any of it any better. He's chasing something that doesn't exist.

Blowing out a long breath, I glance at Leon who gives me a small encouraging smile before focusing back on Whitman.

Ella meets us after class and the three of us head toward the coffee shop. Once again without Luca who slipped out of our lit class the second it ended. Unlike Kane who remained at the back of the room, waiting for us to leave—or at least, that was what I assumed he was doing. I wasn't going to wait around to find out otherwise.

"Are you going to be okay?" Leon asks before he leaves us to go to his afternoon class.

"Of course she is. She's got me watching her back," Ella says as if she's not barely five feet tall and able to hold her own against the likes of Kane.

"That's what I was worried about," Leon mutters, amusement glittering in his eyes.

"Oh hush. I got this."

"I am standing right here, you know, and I don't actually need a bodyguard."

"We know," they say in unison before Leon gives us a little wave and heads off to class.

"So psych and then...?"

"Then I'm locking myself in my room and getting some work done."

"But—"

"But nothing. I'm so behind. I'm forgetting about everything this week and just doing classes and assignments."

"That doesn't include homecoming, right?"

I shrug. I've already planned to spend Saturday night with Harley, so I only need to find a way out of Friday night's party.

"Yes."

"Letty," she whines.

"I'm not going to the bonfire, El. You can just forget about it."

She looks over at me, a smirk appearing on her face.

"Ella," I warn, already able to see a plan forming behind her eyes.

"What? You're going to that bonfire. It's tradition and it's your first year here, so you've got to go."

"No, I really, really don't."

"But everyone will be there."

"Even more reason for me to hide. Everyone already knows more than enough about my life, I don't need to give them any more."

"They'll all have forgotten by the weekend. Some other drama or scandal will have taken over your Dunn sandwich gossip."

I groan. "You had to go there, didn't you?"

She shrugs, a smile playing on her lips. "Well, not all of us would regret it."

"You're a nightmare." I wrap my arm around her shoulders as we head toward the Anderson Building. "So any Colt gossip, or have you been too busy worrying about what I've been up to?"

"Nothing to report. I barely even saw him Saturday night."

Ella chats away about everything else I've missed while I've been drowning in my own nightmare of a life. She manages to keep me from my depressing thoughts all the way back to our dorm after class.

"You really locking yourself in there?" she asks when I'm in my doorway with a bottle of water and a bag of chips in my arms as sustenance.

"Yes, and if anyone wants me. I'm not here. Got it."

"You want me to lie to all the hotties that are fighting after you?" she asks as if talking to them will actually be hard work.

"Yep. Just bat your eyelashes at them and send them on their way."

"Ugh, it sucks but I guess someone has to do it."

"You're a nut."

She shrugs.

"Thank you, Ella. I really appreciate everything."

"Anytime. Call me if you need me."

I smile at her before slipping into my room and flipping the lock with the intention of not emerging until class tomorrow morning.

9

KANE

Thankfully, I managed to get to my room last night before Devin appeared and demanded to know more about what the hell that was all about. Not that he was complaining as he got his rocks off to my girl writhing against the wall.

The thought of him seeing her like that, on top of Luca and Leon already experiencing it this weekend makes my fists curl as I sit on the bench in the locker room after our afternoon practice.

Most of the guys have already left. I know I need to follow them but I'm struggling to find the motivation to head home. All I want to do is go and find her for a repeat of last night.

A door opening on the other side of the locker room drags my gaze from the floor. My teeth grind the second my eyes lock on to Luca's angry ones.

Not only was he dragged into Coach's office after our session this morning but his barely restrained anger as we ran plays this afternoon ended with him having another visit.

I take in the bruise on his cheek and he doesn't miss the move.

"You wanna go again, Legend?" he asks, holding his hands out to his sides.

"Like you wouldn't fucking believe. But, you've already got Coach on your ass," I say, choosing to see him as my captain not my enemy at that moment.

He quickly looks over his shoulder and lets out a breath as the tension between us mounts.

The few guys that are still in here all seem to have stopped what they're doing to watch us.

"You're wrong for her, you know that, right?" he growls, taking a step toward me.

"That's not for you to decide."

"You're hurting her."

I push to stand when he closes the space between us needing to be eye to eye with him.

"And you're not?"

His lips part to respond but he must realize that I'm right.

"You're fucking ripping her apart right now. You can blame this all on me as much as you like but you claim to be her best friend and you've been anything but since she came here. You don't like me, fine. I won't lose any fucking sleep over that. But she fucking needs you, you asshole." It pains me to say the words, but it's the truth. "You don't even know why she's here. You're too focused on what's up here—" I slap him across the head, unable to keep my hands to myself.

His jaw tics as he steps closer again, putting us nose to nose.

"Luc," a familiar voice says from behind him. "It's not worth it."

"He fucking deserves it."

"What about the rest of the team? They deserve you getting benched because you can't keep your fucking head?"

Luca doesn't hear a word of his brother's warning because he pulls his arm back, fist clenched with a determined look on his face.

The only thing he forgets is just how fast I am because I move long before he throws the punch and he ends up stumbling forward before colliding with the wall.

"You're not going to win this fight, Dunn," I mutter, finally throwing my bag over my shoulder and taking a step toward the door. "Letty is mine. It's time you get that into your head and move the fuck on."

I stare at him for a beat as he leans against the wall with his head hung in defeat before ripping the door open and marching through it.

I don't stop until I'm in my car with the engine running. Then I rest my head back and close my eyes for a beat, still trying to convince myself to just go home. Sitting forward, I move my arm to put the car in drive when my passenger door opens and a body drops into the seat.

"What the fuck?" I bark, looking over at my uninvited visitor. "Get the fuck out."

"We need to talk," he says, keeping his eyes focused on the building in front us.

"If you're gonna sit there and tell me just how sweet she tastes, then I'll save you the fucking bother because I already know. I had her last night."

His fists curl in his lap but he doesn't bite, unlike his brother.

"I know, you left your mark."

"Oh good, you saw. You need—"

"That wasn't for my benefit though, was it? You might know that I..." He trails off, probably knowing that I really don't need to hear the fucking words. "But you don't seem pissed at me."

Reaching out, I squeeze the wheel, my knuckles turning white with the force.

"He's in love with her." The words spill from my lips before I've even realized that I've thought them.

"He thinks he is, yeah," Leon mutters.

"He thinks?"

"Yeah, it's complicated."

I finally look over at him and raise a brow. He sighs, clearly not wanting to give away his brother's secrets. But I don't let up and after a few tense seconds, he starts talking.

"Letty showed up right when Luca needed a distraction."

"The beginning of the season," I guess, and he nods.

"We took the championship last year, now the

pressure is on. And our dad... well, he doesn't make it any easier on him."

I know of their dad, everyone does. Brett Dunn played in the NFL, he's got a stellar record and a legacy he wants to pass down to his boys, no matter the cost, it seems.

From what I've heard, their younger brother, Shane, didn't sign to a college team and has instead become a father. I can't imagine that went down very well with Daddy Dunn.

"None of this is my problem, Dunn."

"Maybe not, but he's your captain and if you want a successful year, the best way to do it isn't to piss him off."

"I wasn't the one who threw the first punch."

"Today you weren't but the bruises on his face suggest otherwise."

"She doesn't want him, what do you want me to do about that exactly?"

"Stop rubbing it in his fucking face."

I want to argue with him, but it's pointless.

"He thinks she can make it all better. He needs something to focus on. But it's not her."

"Right," I say, rubbing my palms down my thighs and stretching my legs out. "What exactly are you trying to tell me, Dunn? I already know she isn't his because she's mine."

His jaw drops in shock and he seems to forget everything he was about to say.

"That woman," I confess. "She's not pregnant. She's just a bitch I've had the displeasure of spending time with, and not by choice. The only woman I want carrying my kid again is Letty."

His entire body stills at my words and I immediately realize my mistake.

He doesn't know.

"A-again."

I scrub my hand over my jaw as I figure out what to say next. "Shit."

"Letty was pregnant?"

"Y-yeah. She miscarried our baby at twenty weeks. She was alone, grieving, and pretty much suicidal. It's why she left Columbia. I had no fucking clue," I add quickly before he turns this on me.

"Sh-she... fuck," he breathes, sinking down in his chair as my words hit him.

"If I knew, man. I would have—"

"It's okay. I know. Fuck, man." Leon leans forward, dropping his head into his hands as he absorbs what I've just told him.

I let him have his moment and stare out at the building before us.

"I didn't want any of this. I just want to play football, you know? Have a life outside of my past, make something of myself." The words fall from my lips.

"Do you love her?" he asks, damn near giving me whiplash.

I turn to look at him and he nods, clearly seeing the answer in my reaction.

"Fight for her, Kane. If she's really what you want, prove it to her. Put her above everything else because if she's the one, then that's all that matters, right?"

My lips part to respond, but I don't have any words.

"And you're okay with that?" I finally ask.

"Hell no, I think you're an asshole. But Letty is one of my closest friends and I want her to be happy. And if that's you, then so be it."

"Right."

"Just... sort your fucking life out. She's been through enough already."

He's got the door open and is half off the seat when I speak.

"Please don't tell anyone."

"Kane, I'm not fucking stupid," he snaps. Although I think we both realize that he might be, seeing as he's basically just given me his blessing to go after her. I know in the grand scheme of things, it means nothing. But right now, hearing those words from him, it feels kinda big.

He stands, wraps his hands around the roof of my car and leans in.

"Stay away from Luca. Prove to Letty that you can actually be fucking trusted, and I think we might just have something."

"I don't swing that way, man. But thanks for the offer," I deadpan.

"On the field, you fucking asshole."

I throw my head back and laugh as he slams his hand down on the roof and swings the door closed. And hell if it doesn't feel fucking good to do it.

"Wait," I call after dropping the window as he starts walking toward his own car. "You're going to see her, aren't you?"

"Yeah. But I'm not putting a good word in for you. You want her, you've got to do all the work."

"Thanks," I mutter, not expecting anything different.

Luca emerges from the building while we're still obviously having a conversation and he looks between the two of us with a hard expression on his face.

"We can take it all the way again this year and you know it," I say to him.

"We'll see," he grumbles before stalking toward his car and not paying his brother an ounce of attention.

Leon doesn't seem fazed as he drops into his own car and starts the engine.

I wait for them both to disappear before I throw mine in drive and set off to do what Leon suggested. Start getting my fucking life together.

***

"Evenin'," Reid says when I walk into his kitchen to find him at the counter cooking something.

It's a bizarre sight but then that's Reid Harris all over. Totally fucking bizarre.

"Hey. You got any answers for me yet?"

"Funny you should ask that," he says, washing his

hands and turning to me. "I was going to call you this evening."

I stare at him, waiting for him to come out and say whatever it is he's got to tell me.

"Come on, she can tell you herself."

"She's still alive?"

"Of course. What fun is she to me dead?"

"Psycho," I mutter as I follow him toward the basement door making him laugh.

The warmth of the house diminishes as we descend the stairs and the scent changes to one much less pleasant than whatever he was cooking up there.

We pass all the doors once more, making me question again if there's anyone inside them.

"How many guests do you currently have?" I ask, unable to keep the question in.

"A couple. This one is certainly my favorite."

"That means all the others are men then," I deadpan as he pulls the same door open that he'd thrown Alana behind on Saturday night when I had the pleasure of coming down here.

"Yeah, boring motherfuckers too. They scream like little bitches. Ain't that right?" he bellows, startling me as he slams his fist down repeatedly on the door next to Alana's.

No sound comes from it, I assume because they're soundproof, so I can only imagine the reaction of whoever might be inside.

"I gave my new pet a makeover. What do you think?"

With his hand on her lower back, he leads her from the small space.

My breath catches in my throat when I take in her short blonde hair. But even more shocking than the loss of her long locks is just how good it looks.

"You did that yourself?"

"Yeah. I think I might have missed my calling in life," he says, encouraging her to sit on the chair again.

I look around his torture chamber and then into his wild eyes as he looks over his 'pet.'

"No, no. I think you're exactly where you should be."

He chuckles as he passes Alana a glass of water, giving me a chance to study her.

Aside from the new haircut, I can't see any other evidence of him doing anything to her. There are no cuts, bruises, or missing fingers. My brows draw together as I remember the blood splattered on him when he emerged from talking to her Saturday night. Was that not her blood?

"Come on, Pet. Don't keep my boy waiting. Tell him exactly what you told me," Reid demands.

Her tired eyes find mine, and I see the real changes in her. The sparkle in her eyes is long gone. She looks tired and gaunt. It's what she deserves after what she did to Letty but still, I can't help feeling a little bad for her. Aside from her recent shitty actions, she'd never actually done anything to make me think she's a bad person. And after seeing the way she stood up to Reid Saturday night, I'm now wondering what her real story is.

She certainly isn't the weak, lonely little woman that Victor claims she is.

"H-he made me," she whispers, although her eyes don't waver from mine.

"He? Who's he?" I ask, ensuring my voice is low and deadly.

"V-Victor."

"He made you tell me that you were pregnant?"

She nods.

"Why?"

"He wants to keep you."

Her words are no surprise. Deep down, it's what I was expecting but exactly what I didn't want to hear.

"He wanted you to fall for me, to come back to this life and forget about college."

I fall down in the chair that's behind me and let her words settle in my head as my fists clench.

Anger swirls within me like a storm but it's not directed at Victor, well, not all of it, most of it is at myself. At myself for believing that all of this could actually be a possibility. That he would stand by his word to let me go and to allow me to have a future outside of the Hawks and Harrow Creek.

I was so fucking stupid for believing him.

Standing once more, I lift the chair from the floor and throw it against the wall with a roar that echoes off the bare concrete around me.

"Why, Alana? Why did you do it?" I bellow, getting right in her face.

"Because I didn't have a choice," she replies without missing a beat or even flinching.

"Didn't your husband have something to say about it? About you being sent to fuck me?"

"I told you, we don't—"

"Why, Alana? Why doesn't your husband want to fuck you?" I drop my eyes down her body. She's still wearing the Panther's shirt and short denim skirt she was on Saturday. Her goose bumps are the only sign that she isn't perfectly happy being down here as Reid's prisoner.

My eyes flick to his, curious as fuck as to what he's done to her to make her talk. He's usually pretty quick with his fists or his knife but she looks to be in perfect condition right now.

"Because he won't. It doesn't matter. The less you know, the better."

"What the fuck does that even mean?"

"It means that I'm as much as a fucking puppet as you are, Kane. I don't fucking want this," she says, throwing her hands out. "I never fucking wanted this."

"You married in. You didn't have to be a part of this."

"Didn't I?" she scoffs.

"What are we missing?" I ask her before looking up at Reid, suspecting he knows more than he's letting on about this.

"It doesn't matter. Not knowing is safer."

I take a step back, my eyes back on her.

"Your medical records true?"

"Yes. I can't... I can't have—" Her voice cracks before she looks down at the floor. It's the first and only time she's appeared affected at all by any of this.

"I need you to tell Letty. Because you are going to apologize to her and you are going to tell her the truth."

"Okay," she whispers.

My eyes widen in shock.

"Believe it or not, Kane. I never actually wanted to hurt you, or her."

"I'll believe it when I see it."

Turning my back on her, I march toward the stairs.

"We need to talk," I throw over my shoulder, my eyes locking on Reid.

He nods. "I'll be right up."

I take the stairs three at a time, my muscles pulling from Coach's hardcore session this afternoon, but I don't look at Alana again.

I pace back and forth in Reid's hallway as I wait for him to appear.

"I need out, Reid. I need out fucking now," I bark the second he emerges through the door.

"You think I don't fucking know that. I'm trying but he's not letting go, man. He's going to rip everything away from you if we're not smart about it."

"I don't give a fuck. Let him take it. It's not worth it."

"You don't mean that."

"Don't I?" I ask, coming to a stop in front of him. "I'm done, Reid. I'm done with the demands, the deals, the fucking bullshit. If he pulls everything from beneath me then so be it."

With one last look in his eyes so he can see just how serious I am, I turn and leave.

"Just give me a little more time," he calls when I'm at the front door.

I don't respond, I can't. The thought of walking away from everything I've ever known terrifies me, but not as much as losing Letty for good does.

I might have only had her for a few days in reality, but she's always been there, even when she wasn't. Even when she was Riley's, there was always an us. It was always meant to be us. That I refuse to give up on.

The slam of his front door rings out in the silence of the night before I drop into my car and head for home. My home, for now at least.

LETTY

I ignore the banging on my door, assuming that it's just one of the guys who are trying their luck again.

They attempted to convince me to come out for dinner, and then again an hour later for a drink with them, but each time I've refused, telling them that I have too much to do.

It's not a lie. After the start to the semester I've had, I'm behind before I've even started. I've got deadlines approaching and I'm not even close to having any of my assignments ready to hand in.

Sitting there with music playing, surrounded by textbooks and class notes is the exact distraction I need.

I can push Kane and Luca from my mind for a few hours and just lose myself in work, in my own words.

It's a welcome relief. And one I don't want distracting from now that I've found it.

"Go away," I call when whoever it is won't go away.

"Letty, let me in. Please," a familiar voice begs.

Anyone else and I would have held strong but there's something about the tone in Leon's voice that forces me to climb from my bed and flick the lock to let him in.

"Lee, what's wro—" My words are cut off the second he walks in and pulls me into his body. "What the hell?" I ask, although my words are muffled against his chest as he holds me tightly.

He must kick my door shut behind him because the sound of it closing fills my ears as he remains motionless holding me.

"Lee, you're scaring me. What's wrong?"

"I'm so sorry, Let. I'm so fucking sorry."

"Why? What have you—" He lets me pull back and it's not until I look into his eyes that reality slams into me. "He told you?" I sigh.

"He didn't mean to, it kinda slipped out."

"What were you even doing talking to him?" I ask, walking back to my bed and clearing a space so we can sit. "I thought you hated him."

"He's not my favorite person, no, but..."

"But?" I ask when he trails off and comes to sit down beside me.

"He's important to you and—" I can't help but burst out laughing, cutting off what he was going to say.

"Important. Yeah, so important he's been fucking around."

Leon looks at me and raises a brow before dropping his eyes down my body.

"Yeah, alright. I haven't forgotten."

"Of course you haven't," he says with a smirk and a wink.

"You did not just—fucking hell, Lee."

"Sorry, sorry. Couldn't help myself."

Silence falls between us and I scoot back until I'm resting against the wall with my knees pulled up in front of me.

"I wish you'd have told me, Let. You could have called me, turned up at my door, anything. I'd have been there no matter what, you know that, right?"

He looks over his shoulder, his concerned green eyes capturing mine as they fill with tears.

"I do, I do know that. Trust me, I didn't call because I didn't think you wouldn't be. I just... I thought I could get through it and move on as if it never happened."

"Let, you lost a—"

"I know," I say, holding my hand up, not needing him to say the words that will rip my heart out all over again.

"He said you did it all alone."

I nod. "I didn't tell Mom until I came back for Zayn's graduation. It was make it or break it by that point then. If I didn't confess then I really don't know what would have happened next."

He drops his head into his hands and it physically hurts to see how much this is ripping him apart. It's exactly why I didn't want to tell him —them—now.

"I'm okay, Lee. I'm stronger now. I'm in a better place and I'm able to deal with it all."

"You couldn't even bear to hear me say the words."

"Just because I'm doing better, it doesn't mean it doesn't hurt."

He nods in understanding and scoots back to sit beside me, wrapping his arm around my shoulders and pulling me into his body.

"I guess I owe you now," he whispers.

"What?"

"A secret for a secret, right?"

"No, Lee. Just because you know it, doesn't mean I expect anything. I'd have told you when I was ready no matter what."

"Really?"

"I really like to hope so, although I have no idea when that would have been. I don't expect anything from you, and I know that when the time is right, if you want to, you can come to me. I'll never hold it against you that you don't want to talk about whatever it is."

"Fucking hell, Let. He doesn't deserve you."

"Something we agree on."

Leon drops his lips to my hair and holds me tight.

"I never thought I'd say this, but... he needs you, Let. And I think you just might need him too."

"It doesn't matter. How can I trust him?"

"The same way he can you."

"You're never going to let me forget that, are you?"

"It's not about that. You both screwed up. But equally, neither of you knows the truth about what really happened. Just talk to him."

"He doesn't want to talk. He just wants to punish me."

"Make him, Let. He's hurting just like you are. Only, he deals with it differently."

"Okay," I breathe.

"What are you working on?" he asks after long minutes of comfortable silence.

"A psych paper."

He picks up my notebook and looks at my notes.

"I did this class last year. Want some help?"

A smile twitches at my lips. "That would be nice."

Walking into sociology the next morning, I couldn't shift the nerves that were making my entire body tremble knowing that Kane was going to be in class and I didn't have anyone else around me.

I didn't need them. I could handle Kane alone, they're just a nice security blanket.

With my head held high, I found a seat knowing that his eyes were on me, and I did my best to focus before walking out before he got a chance to get near me.

Leon's words from the night before about him needing me rang out in my ears. I told myself that I tried to be the bigger person, I took myself to his house to talk it out and he took what he wanted and sent me on my way.

If he needs me, if he wants to attempt to move forward with this then it's on his head now.

Not looking back as I walked from the room was hard, really fucking hard, but I forced myself to stay strong.

Our afternoon was similar, only I had the added protection of West and Brax. They'd ensure I didn't do something stupid like take myself to the back of the room and sit beside him just so I can feel him next to me, have his scent filling my nose.

Everything was different this morning because I walked into the Anderson Building with Ella at my side ready for our psych class. I knew I didn't have any classes with him and that as soon we were done here, I was heading home to continue working. Then I could finally take the weekend off with Harley.

"Can't I even tempt you with a cupcake?" Ella asks as we walk out of class after everyone else seeing as she wanted to talk to Professor Collins about her paper.

The hallway is quiet as we make our way toward the exit and my guard is totally down. Probably exactly how he planned it.

"Nope. I'm going back and working all afternoon."

"Fine, I'll just have to hope there's a hot boy in there who'll invite me to join him."

"I have everything crossed for you, El," I joke as a door just ahead of us opens and a body emerges right before me.

"Do you—fuck," I bark in fright when his hand goes around my throat and I twist into the doorway he just emerged from.

"What the fuck are you doing, you psycho?" Ella screams at Kane as I'm rendered useless by his touch alone.

My heart thunders in my chest so hard that I feel it in every one of my limbs.

"Go and enjoy your cupcake. Letty is otherwise engaged," he growls, letting us know he heard everything we just said.

"I'm not leaving you with her, not after everything—"

"I-it's okay, El," I say when I finally find my voice but I don't look at her, I'm too lost in Kane's heated stare.

"No, no, it's really not. This asshole doesn't get to use—"

"Do as you're fucking told, Ella," Kane snaps, his voice cold and deadly. It should scare me, I'm sure it does most people. But that's not the effect Kane Legend has on me or my body because I melt at his vicious demanding tone.

It's my ultimate weakness, and I'm beginning to wonder if it's always been the case.

I don't hear her leave, I'm too focused on the heat of his fingers against my sensitive skin and the wicked intent in his heated eyes.

The door slamming makes me squeal in fright as Kane steps closer to me.

"Scared, Princess?"

"Of you?" I ask with a smirk. Leaning in, I stop right before our noses touch. "Never."

"Wrong fucking answer, baby."

His fingers tighten a beat before his lips slam down on mine.

My fingers claw at the hand that's still holding me around the throat as I keep my lips together, refusing to give into him. We need to talk. We need to act like grown-ups, not sex-crazed teenagers.

"Open your fucking mouth, Princess," he demands, his lips brush mine and make my mouth water for a taste of him.

Keeping my lips firmly closed, I shake my head.

A growl rumbles deep in his throat causing a surge of heat to flood my core. "Where's my dirty little whore, huh?"

His hand skims my waist before cupping my breast and pinching my nipple hard.

Exactly as he intended, I gasp and he plunges his tongue into my mouth.

I still resist but it's futile because we both know I'm not going to be able to keep it up.

"Fight all you like, Princess. You know how hard it gets me." He grinds his cock into my stomach and my body sags against the wall.

"Yeah, baby. I've missed you too."

His lips kiss and his teeth nip down my jaw, his hand releases my throat, instead wrapping around one side and holding me tight with his fingers in my hair.

"You smell like sin, Princess."

"Funny, because I was thinking that's just how you taste."

"Match made in hell, Princess. I thought you already knew this."

One second he's there and the next he's gone.

Dragging my head from the wall, I find him on his knees before me.

"Kane, what are you—fuck."

He pushes my skirt around my waist before my panties practically disintegrate in his hands. He throws one of my legs over his shoulder, leaving me wobbling around on one as he dives for my pussy.

He growls the second he sucks my clit into his mouth and I cry out, forgetting where we are and losing myself to the sensation of his mouth on me.

"Kane," I cry as his tongue circles my sensitive nub, my hands threading through his hair and holding him firmly in place.

"So fucking wet for me, Princess," he says against me, ensuring I feel every single vibration of his deep lust-filled voice.

Lifting his hand, he slides two fingers deep inside me, curling them until he finds the spot that makes me see stars.

"Oh God, oh God," I chant as my release surges forward faster than I thought possible.

"Imagine if someone walked in right now. They'd see you getting fucking owned, Princess. Is that what you want?"

"Kane," I cry, my leg beginning to tremble and threatening to give out.

"You fucking love it, don't you? You're mine, Letty. I fucking own you and this pussy."

He licks me as if he's going to die without it until I shatter all over his face, my cries echoing around the empty lecture hall that he dragged me into.

The thought of a class starting in here any moment causes aftershocks to rack my body as he slows his pace and gently sucks my clit.

Finally, he pulls away from me but not until the beginnings of another release makes itself known with his gentle caressing.

Standing, he cups my jaw in the way I love before slamming his lips down on mine and letting me taste myself on him.

"See how fucking sweet you are?" he asks into our kiss.

"Kane," I moan, needing more of him.

"What's that, Princess? Your greedy pussy wants my cock too?"

"Oh God," I sigh as he once again kisses down my neck, running his tongue over the bite mark he left me with on Sunday.

"I like this. I like everyone knowing that you're mine," he whispers possessively against the wound. "One day soon, you're going to have a permanent reminder of me, Princess."

The thought of him branding me shouldn't make my core clench for him, but it fucking does.

The sound of his belt opening makes my mouth water and I drag my head from the wall to look as he pushes the fabric of his pants around his waist, releasing his hard cock.

I have no idea I move until Kane looks at me and my tongue is halfway along my bottom lip.

"Next time," he growls. "I'm too desperate for your pussy right now."

Without another word, he lifts me from the floor, forcing my legs around his waist and he drops me down onto him, filling me in one swift move.

"Kane," I scream, as he immediately pulls out before slamming back inside me, not giving me a chance to register what's happening let alone adjust. "Oh God, fuck," I cry, my nails digging into his shoulders as he fucks me into oblivion.

"Tell me you're mine," he growls.

"Kane."

"Tell me, Princess," he demands. "Tell me this is mine, that you are mine and mine fucking only."

"Yes, yes. Yours," I cry as his thrusts into my body get even more erratic.

His lips attach onto my neck, the other side from my existing mark, and he sucks the skin into his mouth.

My pussy floods around him and a low growl rumbles in the back of his throat.

"Dirty little whore. *My* dirty little whore," he whispers against my flushed skin.

"Yes, yes."

Pulling my lower half from the wall, he holds my ass in one hand and takes my throat in the other.

"Come, Princess. Come all over my cock."

He pounds into me, the sound of skin slapping skin covering our heaving breaths.

"Fuck, fuck, fuck. Kane," I scream as I fall over the edge.

His hand around my throat tightens before he explodes, his cock twitching violently inside me, filling me with his seed.

Stepping forward once again, he rests his forehead against mine as we fight to catch our breaths.

"Mine," he pants.

We stay like that for what feels like the longest time. But in reality, it's probably only a few minutes before his cell starts ringing and ruining the little bit of silence we'd carved out in all this chaos.

"I need to get that," he says regretfully, lowering my feet to the floor and pulling out of me.

He makes quick work of tucking himself away and pulling his cell from his pocket. But he doesn't turn fast enough because I see the name of the person who's calling and it's like a giant bucket of water has been dumped over me.

"You're never going to get out, are you?"

He pauses with his finger almost on the accept button. "I can't talk about this right now, Let."

Before I know what's happening, he's blown through the door he dragged me through not so long ago. I'm left alone in an empty lecture hall with only my regrets for company once again.

"This is an intervention," Ella says, marching into my room with Violet hot on her heels.

"No, no, no, no. I've already said I'm not going tonight."

"Yeah, and we're ignoring you and dragging you out of this room."

"No, I'm—" My argument is cut off when they each grab an arm and drag me from my bed.

"Get your sexy ass in the shower. We'll pick an outfit for you." Violet slaps me on my backside and pushes me toward my bathroom.

"No, I—" I try again but one look at the determination on their faces when I glance over my shoulder, my argument dies.

"You've only left this room for classes this week. You need to get out before you go crazy."

She's not wrong.

"Please," she begs, getting this sappy look on her face that she knows I'm not going to be able to deny.

"Fine. But if he's there, I'm leaving."

"Deal," Ella says with a smile but I don't believe her for a second with the conniving glint in her eye. "Now quick, we don't want to be late."

Rolling my eyes at my friend as she excitedly bounces on the balls of her feet, I close the door to my bathroom and start stripping out of my clothes.

By the time I emerge a few minutes later wrapped in a towel with wet hair and a face free of makeup, I find them both on my bed waiting for me with a drink each and a pitcher of margaritas on my desk.

"Starting without me?" I ask, heading straight for the empty glass and pouring myself a very large portion of what I can only assume is a strong drink, seeing as every drink either Ella or Vi make are. "Oh my God," I cough as the tequila burns my throat. "Is this neat?"

"Not quite. Good, right? Should loosen you up a little."

"I'm not getting drunk." *Bad things happen when I get drunk.*

"Not suggesting you do. Just have one, let go a little and enjoy yourself."

They sit on my bed gossiping about all sorts as I pull on the outfit they helpfully selected for me—a black and white tartan, pleated skirt and a black sweater that shows a sliver of my stomach. I wouldn't usually put the two together because of the amount of skin I'm going to be exposing but I don't have it in me to argue with them.

I blow-dry and straighten my hair and let Ella do my makeup before we head out.

After two very strong margaritas, my body is warm, my head is buzzing nicely and I can't help thinking that they might have been right. I need this. I needed to get out of my room and get some air.

"We didn't think you were ever going to emerge," West says as he, Brax, and Micah all watch us approach with hunger in their eyes. I know that Ella and Vi are adamant that nothing will ever happen within their little dorm family but looking at the guys eat them up, I can't help but wonder if they have very different opinions on the situation. Especially Micah as he all but drools while staring at Ella in her little black dress that leaves very little to the imagination.

"It was worth it, don't you think?" Vi asks, twirling around. Her flared skirt flies out giving everyone in the room a view of her thong-clad ass.

"Ugh, put it away," West jokes.

She flips him off. "Come on. You'll never get laid hanging around here with us."

"Ain't that the fucking truth," he mutters as the three of them stand and follow us out of the dorm.

"How are you doing?" Micah asks quietly while the others bicker behind us.

"Oh, you know."

He gives me a smile that tells me he does understand to a point.

"Ellis told me they were coming tonight."

"That doesn't surprise me. It's the biggest party of the year, of course they're going to want to be there."

"I'm not sure about Kane though."

"Thanks for looking out for me, Micah, I appreciate it."

"No problem."

"I understand if you don't want to tell me but..." I look over my shoulder to see the others are still way behind us. "How are you connected to them? You're not a Creek kid, so...?"

"I'm from Seattle. My dad and his... acquaintances have connected with Victor and the Hawks." My brows pull together at his words.

"In a good way or bad?" I ask, my hackles rising for my friend. It's no secret that Victor has enemies everywhere, and way more of them than allies.

"I don't know the details, I was just given a job."

"Which was?"

"I'm not sure we should really go there. The less you know, the better."

"But you're working with Ellis, right? Not against him?"

"Yeah. But things aren't always as they seem."

My brow creases as I stare at him.

"Come on. Put all your troubles behind you for a bit and enjoy yourself. We've got your back."

He pulls Brax's car door open for me and I climb inside. The others follow, Ella practically launching herself onto our laps for the short journey to the woods for tonight's homecoming bonfire.

As we make our way in the darkness toward the

party, excitement and the need to just let go fills my veins.

The earthy scent of the forest fills my nose along with the smoky bonfire up ahead that's casting an orange glow through the trees, directing us, along with the low beat of the bass as to where we're going.

"I'm so excited for this," Violet hisses behind me. "Do you remember last year?"

"Yep," West answers almost proudly. "My first alfresco experience. I remember every single—ow," he complains.

"You're a dog," Violet mutters, ensuring the earlier bickering starts again.

"Are they always this bad after a few drinks?" I mutter, although seeing as this isn't my first party with them, I already know the answer.

"Yep," Ella sighs. "It's almost like they're siblings removed at birth with how they go at it sometimes."

Ignoring the voices behind, we make our way through the trees. Twigs snap underfoot and the smell of pine gets stronger as we get deeper into the undergrowth until it thins out and reveals a huge clearing.

"Oh wow," I breathe.

"It's something, right?" Ella asks when she pulls to a stop beside me.

The bonfire is huge, like massive. Its captivating flames flickering right up into the dark night sky.

"Come on, drinks are calling and then I want to dance the night away," Ella announces, dragging my hand and pulling me over to where a huge crowd is gathered. I soon find out why when we break through and find a row of trucks acting as a bar.

With drinks in hand, we make our way toward what appears to be the dance floor and allow the beat of the music to take over.

I have no idea if the others follow us, and right now, as I lose myself to the music, I don't care.

"I hate to say I told you so, but... I totally told you so," Ella shouts at me when one song comes to an end and everything quiets down a little.

"Yeah, alright."

"Drinks, ladies," Violet says, handing them over as she joins us.

Before long, the alcohol is buzzing through my veins and I find myself sandwiched between Ella and Violet as we move together to the music. It feels so good forgetting about everything, even if it's for the briefest of time and letting go with my roommates that are fast becoming my rocks.

"I need to pee," Violet shouts before her body heat disappears from behind me.

Her leaving drags me from the zone I'd lost myself in and for the first time in a long time, I open my eyes and look around at the students all enjoying themselves, and smile. This is how it's supposed to be. My freshman year at Columbia feels like a million years ago now, I barely remember how easy it had all been back then.

Before that party.

Before *him*.

My skin tingles as I think about him and

everything we've been through. Even with all the pain, I still find myself searching through the sea of people in the hope of finding him.

No matter what my brain tells me, my body is always on another page when it comes to Kane Legend.

I find the guys with the rest of the team, Luca and Leon included. My heart aches when Luca turns into the light from the bonfire and I get a quick look at the dark shadows under his eyes. I know I'm not the only one to put them there, I know just how much he's feeling the pressure, but the fact I haven't helped doesn't sit right with me. I want to help, I want to go over and just give him the hug he looks like he so desperately needs, but I know I can't. Even if I did, he wouldn't accept it.

As if he knows I'm looking at him, he turns my way, his eyes immediately landing on mine.

My breath catches as the connection we've always shared passes between us.

Just when I start to think that he's going to come over then he suddenly turns his back on me. Pain rips through my chest at his dismissal.

"He'll come around," Ella shouts in my ear, having clearly watched the whole thing.

"Yeah," I mutter sadly.

"You need more alcohol?"

"No," I answer quickly. The last thing I need right now is to lose the sense of myself.

Ella takes my hips in her hands and spins me around. I have no idea if she's got a game plan—a game plan that involves a certain football player—but she moves seductively behind me, earning us more than a few heated stares from every guy in the vicinity.

"Ella, what are you playing at?" I shout over my shoulder.

"Just enjoying myself," she says innocently, although the wink she adds tells me otherwise.

Looking forward once more, I let her do what she needs to do, my eyes still scanning the crowd for him.

The longer we dance, the more my skin tingles. I tell myself that it's the alcohol but deep down, I know it's not. I know it's him.

My mouth waters as I think about our previous experience of being under the cover of trees and my thighs clench together.

Damn him.

I find Micah in the crowd talking to Ellis, a few feet behind them is Devin talking to some guys I don't know and then I find Ezra with some poor girl pinned up against a tree.

Their presence only confirms what I already know.

He's here and he's watching me.

Fighting my urge to keep searching, I rest my head back on Ella's shoulder and close my eyes as she grinds to the beat.

I don't realize that a shadow has fallen over us until Ella's hands on my hips tighten and her movement falters.

My heart begins to race as I lift my head. I try to

prepare myself for looking into his blue eyes, but when I finally drag my lids open and look at who's standing beside us, it's not him.

"Lee?"

"Hey, Cupcake. Wanna dance?"

"Y-yeah."

Lifting my arms so I can drape them over his shoulders as he steps into my body.

"You don't need to look so disappointed, you know," he whispers in my ear.

"What? No, I'm not—"

"It's okay, Let."

Blowing out a breath, I ask the question I really want to know. "He's here, isn't he?"

"Yeah, but I've warned him not to try anything."

"You've warned him?" I ask with a laugh. "No offense, but I'm not sure he'd take that very seriously. He doesn't take well to being told what to do."

"Maybe not, but he hasn't come anywhere near you yet, so I'll take it as a win for now."

"It won't last."

"We'll see." Leon's smirk tells me that there's way more to his story than he's letting on.

Leon starts moving with me, once again sandwiching me between two bodies. It's a situation I've found myself in a little too often recently. My cheeks burn at just remembering my time between Luca and Leon and then Kane and Devin only the day after.

Dropping my head to his chest, I blow out a long breath as my regrets threaten to swallow me whole.

"Hey," Leon says, tucking his finger under my chin and forcing me to look up at him. "Everything is going to be okay."

"Is it?" I ask, my party buzz suddenly gone.

"Dance with me, Cupcake," he demands.

"Is that a good idea with him watching?" I hesitantly look up at Leon.

"I'm not scared of him, Let."

"I-I know but—"

"It's okay," he breathes, pulling me closer and moving with me in time to the music. "Let go, Cupcake. Just enjoy yourself."

I stare up into his soft eyes and will myself to do as he suggested and just enjoy hanging out with my friend.

"Drinks," Ella calls a few minutes later before she rejoins us with Micah, West, and Brax, along with Violet, who's attached to a guy I've never seen before.

We all dance together for the longest time. The others look like they don't have any cares in the world while I fight to push all of my issues aside. The fact my skin tingles with awareness from his stare doesn't help but every time I try to discreetly look around, I never find him.

But I know he's there, hiding in the shadows, just waiting to make his move.

It keeps me on edge as I dance while ensuring my blood continues to run hot with thoughts of what will happen when he finally makes himself known.

Will he drag me into the darkness and do his worst while we're hidden in the shadows? Will he throw me over his shoulder and march me to his car for that second round of hood sex he still owes me?

I know I shouldn't be thinking of all these possibilities, I should be planning on how I'm going to say no to him.

But I already know it's pointless. It always is when it comes to Kane.

"You can't forget about him, can you?" Leon whispers in my ear as he catches me looking around.

"He's watching me, I can feel it."

He shakes his head, a smirk playing on his lips.

"You're really gone for him, aren't you?"

"N-no, I—" Ripping my eyes away from his knowing ones, I suck in a deep breath. "I can't stop it, Lee. No matter what I do. No matter what he does. There's just this thing between us, I can't even explain it."

"You don't need to," he says, cupping my cheek and staring deep into my eyes as if he actually understands. I've never known Leon to have a girlfriend of any kind, let alone one he's had a solid connection with but that's not to say he's never experienced it.

"You're a good friend, Lee." He smiles at me as a shadow falls over us and a shiver runs down my spine.

Leon's eyes lift from mine and he nods ever so slightly.

"I guess I don't need to guess where he is anymore, huh?"

Kane comes to stand beside the two of us. He's

dressed all in black and looks as dangerous as ever as his blue eyes sparkle in the dim lights surrounding us.

Our connection holds for a beat as my body begins to burn hotter.

"Can I cut in?" he asks, taking a step forward at the same time Leon takes one back.

Reaching out, I grab Lee's hand and pull him back toward me.

"No," I say confidently, holding Kane's stare.

"N-no?" he asks with a laugh as if I'm joking.

He's about to discover that I'm not.

"Exactly. No. I'm spending the night with my friends," I say, jutting my chin out. The stares of said friends behind me begin to burn into the back of my head as they notice what's going on.

Kane's amusement soon vanishes from his face, quickly replaced by frustration.

"Princess," he growls, making my body shiver at the warning in his low tone.

"No, Kane. I'm done following your orders, go and find someone else to dance with." The words taste bitter as they fall from my lips. The thought of him touching someone else fills me with jealousy but I refuse to do as he says once again. All it does is land me in trouble.

"You're serious? You want me to go and find another girl?"

"Whatever," I say with a shrug, which I hope like hell doesn't show just how much the suggestion really does affect me.

Turning away from him, I focus on Leon as I start moving again to the music.

The sound of his low growl rumbles through me, but I don't turn to look at him.

"What are you doing, Let?" Leon whispers.

"Not letting him dictate my life," I hiss back, knowing full well he's watching me.

"He's not going to let this go."

"He's going to have to."

"I just want to talk." Kane's low, angry voice makes me pause.

"Yeah, well, I don't," I shoot over my shoulder before moving farther into the crowd and away from him.

"I'm impressed," Leon whispers.

"What? You didn't think I could stand up for myself?"

"Under normal circumstances, I know you can. But against Kane, it's hard to tell. I hope you know what you're doing, Cupcake."

"No fucking clue, Lee," I admit as I run my hands up his chest and drape my arms over his shoulders so we can resume dancing.

I'm sure anyone outside of our circle would think our dancing was intimate. In a way, I guess it is, but we both already know it's not leading anywhere. Saturday night was a mistake and we both know it. I love Lee, and I know he loves me too. But it's not the same as what I feel for Kane and I know it's not the same for him either. Maybe in another life, we'd have been perfect for each other. Luca and me too. But that's not how it is and I know there are two incredible ladies out there somewhere just waiting to knock both of them on their asses. And, hell, I can't wait to witness it. They're going to be two lucky bitches to win over the Dunn hearts, I already know that.

One song changes to the next as I think about the kind of woman who would be perfect for my boys. I lose myself in thoughts of them instead of the man's eyes I can still feel burning into my skin.

"Shit," Leon curses, his entire body locking up with tension.

"W-what's wrong?" I ask, twisting around to see what's holding his attention, but I don't get a chance to move because his hands tighten on my hips.

"Don't," he warns.

"Lee, whatever it is I—motherfucker," I bark when he releases me, and I get a look at what's pulled his muscles tight.

Only a few meters away, Kane has fucking Clara pressed up against his body and is grinding into her as if they're alone.

Jealousy like I've never felt before surges through me.

"I need to go," I say and with one final look at Kane's hands on that skank, I rip myself out of Leon's hold and push through the crowd to get away.

"I hope you know what you're doing, Cupcake." Leon's words repeat in my head as I begin running through the trees to get away as a sob rips up my throat.

No, Lee. I clearly don't have a fucking clue what I'm doing.

"Letty, wait." My footsteps falter at the sound of his voice and I come to a stop, my chest heaving and my eyes burning with my need to cry. "Are you okay?"

Glancing over my shoulder, my breath catches at the look on Luca's face as he stares at me from a distance.

He looks like he wants to say something but he doesn't get a chance because branches snapping behind him soon reveals Leon hot on our tails.

Unlike his brother, he doesn't stop at a distance, he comes rushing straight to my side.

"Can you take me home, please?" I ask before he has a chance to say anything.

"Let's go," Luca barks, storming past both of us without saying another word.

"He really hates me, doesn't he?"

"Nah, Cupcake. It's himself he's having an issue with right now. Come on."

His hand slips into mine and we follow behind where Luca disappeared. After a few minutes, we emerge in the makeshift parking lot to find Luca sitting in his car with the engine already running.

I climb in the back and to my surprise, Leon follows.

Luca's eyes follow our every move in the rearview mirror and his jaw visibly tics when I rest my head on Leon's shoulder.

Not able to look into his pained eyes, I close

mine. I soon discover that the darkness isn't any better because all I can see is him with her.

My stomach turns over at the thought of him dragging her into the trees and touching her, talking to her the way he does me.

I have no idea how, I assume it's the alcohol flowing through my veins but the next thing I know, Leon is gently sitting me up. When I open my eyes, I find that we're in the parking lot behind my dorm building.

"Oh, we're here," I mutter like an idiot as images of Kane with that jersey chaser hit me all over again. My anger swells, my body heating as I wonder where it might have led.

"Want me to walk you up?" Leon asks but his voice fades off into the distance when I lock eyes once more with Luca in the rearview mirror.

"Uh... n-no, it's okay. You take off, you have a big day tomorrow."

"It's okay, Let."

"No," I say a little more firmly. "I'm fine. I'll talk to you in the morning."

I'm halfway out of the car when Luca speaks.

"You coming to the game?"

I pause and look over my shoulder, finding his eyes once more.

"Of course. I wouldn't miss it for anything." With a smile, I step forward and close the door behind me.

I don't hang around for them to leave, I already know that they'll refuse to leave until they've watched me walk into the building.

I give them a quick wave before slipping inside the door. I make my way up to my room to run the events of the night over and over in my head and remind myself why I never should have gone in the first place.

12

KANE

The second Letty disappeared into the tree line last night with both Luca and Leon hot on her tail, I sidestepped Clara, ripped her hands from my body and walked away without a word.

I had zero interest in her and she was even stupider—or even more desperate—than I thought she was if she actually thought I was interested.

By the time I got to the parking lot, only Luca's taillights could be seen.

That was not the result of my little stunt with Clara I was anticipating.

I thought she was going to be angry, furious, and storm over to claim what's hers—me. But she didn't. If it weren't for the crowd parting to let her through, then I wouldn't have even realized that she'd noticed what I was doing. She seemed more than happy to ignore me when I tried to do the right thing and talk to her, so I assumed a wilder gesture might get her attention. Hell knows it's worked in the past but last night she was not playing by her usual rules.

I hadn't had anything to drink seeing as we have a game today, so I jumped straight into my car and followed them.

I trusted her. I knew she regretted what happened last weekend. She never would have shown up at the house like she did on Sunday if she didn't. But my need to know that she wasn't going straight home with them once again because she thought I wanted someone else was too strong to ignore.

Even after it was obvious that they were heading for the dorm and not their house, I still continued to trail them.

I had no idea if they'd seen me or not, and quite frankly, I didn't care. I just needed to know she was going home alone and that she was safe.

I parked at the other end of the lot and fury exploded within me as I watched her climb from Luca's car and walk alone in the dark toward her building.

The second they disappeared, I got out of my car and ran toward the building, needing to know she was locked inside and safe. The fear that Victor would go after her before everything is settled is very real.

A couple of floors above me, the door slammed closed and I breathed out the breath I didn't know I was holding.

Every single inch of my body screamed at me to

go up there and say all the things I need to, to tell her exactly how I feel and what I want. But when I did finally move, it was in the opposite direction.

I don't want to go in there with just words, I want to go in there with answers. I want to go with proof so she has no choice but to trust me when I tell her what I want.

It's those thoughts that forced me back to my car and heading for home.

I just need to be patient and then I can take exactly what I want.

My girl.

Fuck everything else. She's the only thing that's important right now.

The team and the coaching staff are all buzzing when we get back to the locker room after a solid win for our homecoming game.

It was incredible, playing again in front of a crowd that size and killing our opponents was insane. Unlike everyone else around me, I don't feel like we've just turned our season around because, by the end of the weekend, there's a very good chance my season is over.

As I sat in my car outside the stadium before I came in here to get ready for the game, I made the call that's going to change my life.

I should have done it earlier this week. But I

wanted this. One more taste at the dream that I had in my hands if only for a few weeks.

It's the proof I needed that a better life can exist. Just because I was born in the Creek, it doesn't have to mean that I have a life sentence signed by the Devil himself.

I've done his dirty work. I've done my time. And now, I'm done.

I'm so fucking done being his little bitch and if that means I lose all of this, then so be it.

Kyle is fine now. He got his new start and he's got his own future to look forward to.

The guys around me chat excitedly about tonight's party but I zone them all out.

I'm not going. I'm going to slip away, probably unnoticed by most and much to Luca's delight and they'll most likely go on to have a solid season. They'll forget all about my short stint as a Panther, while it'll stay with me forever.

"Dude, you coming to the party?" Zayn asks with a solid slap to my shoulder.

I have no fucking clue why he's okay with me right now but he's clearly decided that his warning was good enough and he's keeping his nose out of his sister's business for once.

"Nah, I'm heading home for the weekend."

"What? No. Come on. You can't go back to Rosewood after a game like that."

"Watch me," I mutter.

Throwing my bag over my shoulder, I nod at Coach who's talking to Luca and the quarterback coach as a way of saying goodbye. I head out to find the one person who I know will be happy to see me.

"Bro, you fucking killed it," Kyle says, racing over to me.

"Thanks, man."

"It was fucking insane watching you down there. I can't believe you missed the first two games. Fuck, I want this," he says, looking around in total awe over everything.

"You can have it," I say, throwing my arms around his shoulders. "Now, you promised me a steak. That better still stand," I tell him, leading him away from the crowd.

"Legend, wait," someone calls.

Simultaneously, we both look over our shoulders, but I soon find that it isn't anyone for me.

Ashton, Kyle's friend and captain, jogs over. "You seriously heading back?"

"Yeah, I am."

"You can go party if you want," I tell my brother.

"Nah, not this weekend. Come on," he says to me. "Enjoy. And don't get too wasted," he warns Ash before turning back to me and walking toward where my car is.

"You can totally stay. I can go back to Rosewood alone, you know."

"I know but I kinda wanna spend some time with you. Missed you, Bro."

"Aw, missed you too, kid," I say, reaching over and messing up his hair.

We hit up a steak house on the edge of Maddison

County before we head for our home in Rosewood. The building itself isn't much but it's the first actual house we've had and despite its less than desirable appearance, I kinda love it.

It's a white and blue painted bungalow. Kyle's description of it being a granny house when I first took him there is quite an accurate description, but it's ours and that's all that matters. He got to restart his life there. He got to fall in love with Harley there, and be happier than I think he's ever been in his life, and that means everything to me.

"So what have you done with your girl this weekend?" I ask as we drive into Rosewood. The second we pass the sign welcoming us to town, I instantly relax. This place is like my safe haven. No one knows me, there are no Hawks, no Panthers or anyone who can judge me past my slightly rough exterior and the fact we live in a granny house. It's exactly what I need for a few days as I wait to discover what the outcome of my phone call this morning will be.

I pull up in the driveway, thanks to Kyle leaving his car out on the road and I let out a long sigh as I stare at our home.

"Glad to be back?" he asks with a laugh.

"You have no idea. I just need... peace."

He stifles a laugh at my comment.

"What?"

"N-nothing. Come on. I've got a surprise for you."

I narrow my eyes in his direction but climb from

the car when he does, too curious as to what he's talking about to sit here any longer.

I follow him up the stairs to our porch and my eyes land on the swing in the corner. Memories of sitting there with a joint hit me. I guess I can do that again now, seeing as I'm about to be pulled from the team. No one will give a shit what I put in my body again.

"This surprise had better include a shit ton of beer," I mutter as he throws the door open and I march inside.

My steps falter the second I step into the living area and my eyes land on Letty sitting on my couch alongside Harley.

"Right, well..." Harley says, jumping from the couch as if it suddenly just burned her. "This has been fun, Sis, but I've got a date with my man, and so do you."

Before I know what's happening, the two of them are gone, leaving me alone with Letty.

"Uh," I say, lifting my hand to my hair and dragging it away from my face as I try to get my brain to catch up with what just happened.

13

LETTY

I stare at my sister's message as I sit in the parking lot outside of the stadium that I just escaped from. The final whistle had barely blown before I was in the aisle and heading for the exit.

I was stoked that the guys won, of course I was. Especially after last weekend's defeat, but I was more than ready to get away from Maddison and chill out with my sister.

I roll my eyes at my annoying little sister and put my car into drive.

I find a space a little down the street from the

house, Harley is obviously waiting for me because she bounces out onto the porch excitedly the second my foot hits the sidewalk.

"You're here," she shouts down.

"It's where you told me to be," I call back, reaching back inside to grab my purse.

"The Panthers killed it," she says as I climb the few steps to get to her.

"They did. Luc will be happy."

"So how's things?" she asks, turning into the house.

"Um... why are we here?"

"I just need to wait for a delivery and then we can head out."

"Oh, okay," I say, accepting her words for what they are and placing my purse on the table.

It's not the first time I've been here, but it's the first time I've been this relaxed. Previously, I was always aware that Kane could show up at any moment, but right now, I know he's busy in Maddison and will be heading out to celebrate his success later. *With Clara,* an annoying little voice says in my head.

I shake the thought away. I don't need or want images of them dancing together last night in my head when I'm supposed to be relaxing.

"Drink?"

"Sure."

"Make yourself comfortable. I'm sure it won't be too long."

She smiles sweetly at me and I follow orders,

more than happy to curl into the corner of the couch and forget about real life for a while.

"So what's the plan?"

"Haven't really got one. Junk food, movies, vodka."

"Sounds perfect. Mom in?"

"No idea. I've barely seen her all week."

She brings over two cans of soda and sits with me. She puts some music on the TV and we turn to look at each other, catching each other up on our weeks and her digging to find out more about Kane.

It's almost two hours later when an engine finally rumbles out front of the house. I was starting to think this was all a big ploy just to get me here.

"Finally," she sighs, leaning forward and placing her can on the coffee table.

"Aren't you going to get it?"

"Of course. He's usually hella slow though."

"Right," I say, narrowing my eyes at her, feeling even more that something isn't right here.

A car door slams shut before another and my heart jumps into my throat.

"Har, what's going on?"

She looks at me and manages to keep her face straight for all of two seconds.

"I've organized a surprise."

My lips part to respond but the front door is pulled open and a very familiar voice fills the space around me causing goose bumps to erupt across my skin.

"This surprise had better include a shit ton of

beer," he says a beat before he appears in the doorway looking larger than life.

I gasp the second our eyes lock. My brain screams to get up and run as Harley hops up from the couch looking more than a little excited at her little surprise.

"Harley," I hiss but she's already tucked into Kyle's side and they're heading for the door.

Before I get a chance to move, they're gone and the door slams closed behind Kane leaving us alone.

Lifting his hand, he nervously drags his hair from his brow and I feel somewhat better about the fact he's just been blindsided by this as much as I have.

"Princess, I-I didn't know. I—" He looks over his shoulder as a car starts and then drives off.

"I can tell," I say but my voice lacks the lightness it usually has.

"Shit," he mutters, looking totally thrown by this situation.

"I need to leave."

"W-what?" he stutters, staring at me as I rise from the couch with deep frown lines forming on his brow. "No, please."

"No, Kane. This isn't happening." I march toward him, or more so the front door. "We're done. Excuse me."

I take a step to slip around him but—unsurprisingly—I don't get a chance because his hot fingers circle my wrist, stopping my escape.

"We're not done, Princess. Not even close."

"Kane, I can't do this. I told you, I refuse to be a part of this life. The games, the lies, the bullshit."

"Can we just talk, please? There's so much I need to tell you."

All the air rushes from my lungs at the sincerity in his voice.

My head tells me to say no and keep walking out the door and out of his life. But I already know that doing that would be useless. There's someone out there that clearly wants us together because the universe seems to keep throwing us together no matter how explosive it is when we collide.

"Kane," I sigh, already feeling myself giving in to his burning touch and the vulnerability in his voice.

"Please," he begs, and I crumble.

Turning back to him, I look up into his eyes. The blue I'm so used to is sparking with something I've never seen before. Emotion. Hope. Whatever it is, the usual anger is long gone.

"You've got ten minutes and then I'm out that door."

"Okay," he whispers, tugging on my arm so I have no choice but to step into his body.

I fight against him but he's too strong. His other hand lifts to cup the side of my neck and I melt into his familiar hold.

"I missed you," he breathes, dropping his head to mine.

"This isn't talking, Kane," I warn. "Your time is running out."

He blows out a breath and he reluctantly releases me.

I don't retake my seat on the couch, instead, I take

the chair, ensuring that he can't sit beside me and cloud my judgment with his burning touch.

"Ten minutes," I remind him as he sits in front of me on the couch. He perches on the edge, resting his elbows on his knees and looks up at me through his lashes. All his regrets are clear to see on his face and I can't help but soften to him despite the fact he hasn't said a word yet, well not one to make any of this better.

"She's not pregnant, Let. I fucking promise you that."

"Then why did she say she was?" I sit back in the chair and cross one leg over the other in an attempt to look nonchalant. I don't think I achieve it at all when his lips twitch into a smirk.

He blows out a breath as his hand once again goes to his hair.

"One of the things I did for Victor since Kyle went down was to... entertain people."

"People?" I deadpan.

"Women. Kyle got put down for drugs and I refused to go anywhere near them, so he made use of my other... skills."

I snort in disbelief. "Right."

"I met with a few different women at the beginning but after a few months, he set me up with Alana."

My body noticeably jerks as her name rolls off his tongue.

His fists clench in front of him as if he's

physically holding himself back from coming closer to me.

"I knew of her. She's married to one of his closest men."

"He wanted you to sleep with one of the wives of his members?"

"Yeah."

"Why?"

"Honestly, I didn't ask. I just did what I was told. He was making it look like I had a legit job for the authorities and as long as I wasn't on the streets dealing, then I just went with it. I figured he wasn't putting out or their relationship was over and they'd just not made it official or whatever. It wasn't really my place to question it."

"No, you just had to make her come," I deadpan and he pales.

"Anyway, it turned into a regular thing. I'd take her out to dinner when Victor called big meetings or him and his men went out of town to keep her entertained. Anyway, when Kyle was released, I told him I was done as per our agreement and walked away, hoping he would stay good to his word."

"I already know he wasn't, this isn't news," I snap.

"I've seen her twice since I started at MKU."

My teeth grind as he admits that and my nails dig into my palms.

"The first time, nothing happened. Actually, you messaged me, and I left. It was..." He lowers his gaze for a moment. "It was the night in the library."

I gasp. "Y-you were with her before you—fuck, Kane."

"I didn't touch her. I sat opposite her at a table and spent most of the time thinking about you."

My cheeks heat at his words and I fight not to react to that statement.

"And the second time?"

He tugs at his hair until I'm sure I'm about to witness him pull it from his scalp.

"Last Wednesday."

I stare at him. "The night you disappeared."

"Fuck, Let." He pushes from the couch and starts pacing back and forth. "I couldn't see you after that. I fucking hated myself but I couldn't see any other way. I needed time to figure a way out, I couldn't just say no. No one just says no to Victor."

Don't I fucking know it.

"What did you do, Kane?" I ask, my voice not sounding like my own.

"We went to dinner, and then... and then I took her to a hotel on the other side of town."

"Oh my God," falls from my lips as a whimper. "You slept with her?"

Pain and regret pour from him as I wrap my arms around myself in the hope I can keep my weakening heart from shattering right here, right now. Did he lie to me on Sunday?

"No, I didn't sleep with her," he says confidently, repeating what he's already told me. "But I did... I did give her what she needed."

The noise that rips from my throat isn't one I've

ever heard before as the shards of my heart I was desperately holding on to shatter.

"Princess," he breathes, pain twisting his features as I stare at him as if he's someone I don't even know.

"I need to leave."

Pushing to stand, my legs don't feel as if they're going to support me, let alone get me to the door or my car.

"No, please. There's more. Please just hear me out."

I turn my back on him and walk around the chair on weak legs as he continues to beg.

"Why, Kane? Give me one good reason why I should listen to any of this. All you've done all my life is fuck me over. Again and again. And this is just another one of those—"

"Because I'm in love with you."

Thank fuck I'm near a wall because I swear to God, if I didn't reach for it in that moment then I'd be on the floor.

"No," I whisper, refusing to hear the words, let alone accept them. "You hate me and that's how it should be. We're a disaster, Kane. All we do is hurt each other. This isn't l-love, it's a fucking nightmare."

My chest aches more with every word that spills from my lips.

"You're lying," he breathes, his body heat beginning to warm my back.

His fingers gently stroke down my arm until he twists them with mine.

"You're lying, Let. This is more and you know it. I know you feel it too."

His hot breath tickles over my neck as he talks and it sends a shiver racing down my spine.

"Victor set her up to make me fall for her, to keep me. He knew I was going to walk and he tried to use her against me. That's why she said she was pregnant. She's not. I've seen copies of her medical records which prove she can't even conceive."

I swallow down the messy lump of emotion that's clogging my throat.

"H-he's not going to let you go, Kane."

"He will but it's going to cost me my future." His lips brush the shell of my ear as he talks. "Before the game, I called him. Told him it was over. Told him he could pull all his favors, football, college, a place to live. All of it."

I suck in a sharp breath at his confession.

"He won't."

"He will. I've got something important to one of his men. He lets me go or I'll deliver Alana back in parts."

My entire body tenses at his words. I don't want to believe he would, but the venom in his voice as he says it makes me believe him.

"How is she important? Her husband doesn't even sleep with her?" I know it's the least of my worries right now but I need to try to focus on something other than the feeling of his body pressed against mine.

"That's not for you to worry about. All you need to know is that she's important enough to set me free."

I drop my head for a second, letting his words register in my mind.

He allows me the silence just standing behind me with my hand firmly in his.

"But... but what will you do?" I ask, my head spinning with everything he's just told me.

"I don't know," he answers honestly, his fingers squeezing mine tighter. "I don't care as long as I have you."

My breathing falters as I hear his words.

"Kane," I breathe. "You can't give everything up."

"I'm not. I'm choosing."

"No," I say, shaking my head sharply from side to side. "You can't."

"I did, Let. It's done."

All my breath rushes from my lungs when he spins me and pushes me up against the wall. He stands close, the length of his body lightly pressed against mine as his intense blue eyes stare down into my eyes.

"I made the call, Princess. Victor knows I'm done. It's over."

The lump in my throat grows until even breathing becomes almost impossible and my eyes fill with tears.

"But it was your dream to play college football," I force out.

"It was. I've got a new one." His hand lifts to that spot on my neck that I love so much, his fingers slide into my hair and his thumb brushes my cheek. "I want you, Letty. You gave me an ultimatum and I chose." He leans in, his nose brushing mine. "I choose you."

My chest heaves, my head spins and my body burns with his innocent touch as we just stare at each other in silence.

The only sound aside from our heavy breathing is that of a clock somewhere in the room that ticks with every second that passes.

"Say something, Princess."

"I... um... I don't—"

He searches my eyes as I stutter to find something to say.

"Tell me you want this, Let. Tell me that you choose me too."

My chest aches at the vulnerability in his voice.

"Kane," I sigh. "There was never a choice to mak—"

He's moved before I get the final word out. His lips claim mine in a scorching kiss as he pushes against me, pinning me between his hard body and the solid wall at my back.

My lips part the second his tongue sneaks out and I greedily suck it into my mouth.

His hand that's not holding my neck finds its way to my waist and slips under my Panthers jersey, his calloused fingers scratching my skin in the most delicious way.

"Kane," I sigh when he releases my bottom lip and kisses across my jaw.

He lifts me, wrapping my legs around his waist and pressing his hard cock against my core.

"N-not here," I force out when he sucks on my neck, darkening the bruising on the last one he left behind which had almost faded.

"No, Princess. Not here. This time, I'm taking my fucking time with you."

My fingers thread into his hair and I pull his face back to mine, slamming my lips down on his and taking exactly what I need from him.

"Bedroom," I mutter into our kiss and he immediately pulls me from the wall and begins walking down the short hallway.

Kicking a door open, I don't get a chance to look around before I'm thrown down on the bed and he launches himself on top of me.

"Kyle couldn't have found me a better surprise, Princess." His fingers wrap around the hem of my shirt and he pulls it over my head before throwing it behind him somewhere.

"The little shits played us," I moan as he kisses across my collarbone, his teeth grazing my sensitive skin, making my nipples harden to tight buds, wishing his mouth was on them instead.

Arching my back, I shamelessly offer myself up to him.

"Dirty little whore," he whispers and like always, his deep rumbled words do wicked things to my insides.

He sits up between my legs and drags his shirt over his head, throwing it over the side to join mine.

"Fuck, you're hot," I blurt as I run my eyes down his chest and to his abs.

"I'm glad you think so, but I'm nothing compared to you."

His fingers make quick work of the button on my jeans and in seconds I'm laid out before him in just my bra and panties.

"Fucking beautiful."

Leaning over me, his hands skim up my side until his giant hands cup my breasts. I gasp at the sensation and he makes use of my reaction and plunges his tongue into my mouth.

His kisses and his touch are intoxicating, and I quickly lose myself in him, forgetting everything that exists outside of these four walls and just drown in the pleasure.

He's right, I do feel this. I always have but even now, even after he's admitted what he did. It still terrifies me more than almost anything else I've ever experienced in my life.

Everything falls away when I kiss her. My reality, my fears, everything other than the most important thing. Her.

I lick across her chest, her addictive sweet taste flooding my senses.

She moans beneath me and arches her back once more, trying to offer herself up, desperate for me to take more.

But I'm standing by what I said, I'm making the most of every second of this. At any point, she could change her mind and walk straight out the front door. I couldn't blame her if she did, everything I've just laid out to her, it doesn't exactly make the prospect of a life with me desirable.

I have nothing. And if I can't find a decent job fast, even the roof over our heads right now could be in question.

Her moan as I brush my lips down to the swell of

her breasts drags me from my own head and I look up at her.

My breath catches when I take in the gold that's sparkling in her eyes as she stares down at me.

Something crackles and my heart tumbles in my chest as our connection holds.

"Mine," I breathe, my lips caressing her skin as I say the word.

She nods once. "Yours."

That one word fucking slays me.

I didn't mean to say what I did out in the living room, not to say it wasn't true. It is. I think I realized it the night I went out with Alana before everything went to shit, although really, I should have registered it a long time before that. But I'm a fucking idiot who can't see what's in front of his face. The past ten years are enough evidence of that already.

But watching her almost walk away from me. It made me face up to my feelings faster than I'd ever experienced and I knew I had to do something to stop her from walking out on me.

I need her. I need her so fucking bad that I'm not sure I'll ever be able to express it.

Slipping my finger under the cup of her bra, I pull the thin lace away, exposing her hardened nipple.

My mouth waters to wrap my lips around it and suck it deep, but before I do that, I lift my eyes to hers and blow a stream of air across her sensitive skin.

Her entire body quakes at the sensation.

"Kane," she half moans, half warns as her hips

grind against me in an attempt to find what she needs.

"There she is," I growl. "My." Kiss. "Dirty." Lick. "Whore."

"Yesss," she hisses as I pull her nipple into my mouth and sink my teeth into it. Her fingers thread into my hair as I lave at the sting with my tongue before switching sides, exposing her other nipple and giving it the same treatment.

"Fuck. You're so fucking beautiful, Princess," I say as I sit up and stare down at her.

Her dark hair is a mess against my light gray sheets. Her chest heaves, only highlighting all the bite marks I've given her before my eyes drop to her swollen breasts, her dark nipples begging for more.

Slipping my hand around her back, I unhook her bra and quickly pull it from her body.

"No hiding from me, Princess. Not now, not ever."

She shakes her head as I drop lower, running my lips over her ribs and down her stomach.

"Your curves are so fucking sexy," I murmur against her skin.

I'd have to be blind not to notice the differences in her since we first reconnected. Her breasts are fuller, her hips wider, her thighs thicker. She looks healthier, happier, and I know that she feels more confident. It's evident in her every move.

"It's all the pizza," she whispers, a smile pulling at her lips.

"It looks good on you."

Sliding my hands under her body, I squeeze her ass until she cries out.

"Looks even better on me."

"Kane," she warns as I begin pulling her panties down her legs.

"What, Princess. Am I not going fast enough for you?"

Her head shakes from side to side.

"Tell me what you need?"

"You, Kane."

"I'm right here, baby. You're going to need to be a little more specific."

She props herself up on her elbows and stares at me, holding me captive in her dark eyes.

"Make me come. With your tongue."

Desire floods me at her words, making my already hard cock damn near painful.

Pressing my hands against her inner thighs, I spread her wide before me and after a beat, I rip my eyes from hers and run them down her body, zeroing in on her pussy.

I suck my bottom lip into my mouth as I take in her swollen cunt.

"Do you know, you've got the prettiest fucking pussy in the world."

"Show me, don't tell me."

"Fuck, Princess," I growl.

This woman fucking kills me.

Sliding off the bed, I drop to my knees and drag her to the edge until her ass is hanging over, giving me the perfect access.

Repeating my actions from her nipple, I blow a long stream of air down her center.

She moans, lifting her hips from the bed in her desperate need for more.

"Getting impatient, Princess?"

I kiss down her thigh, breathing in her scent as I get closer to where she needs me.

"Kane, please," she begs, her voice sounding tortured as she pulls at my hair trying to force me into place.

"Just think how much sweeter it'll be after the wait," I whisper before laughing at her frustrated growl

"Kane, I—argh, fuck," she moans, falling back on the bed as I finally give her what she needs and run my tongue up the length of her pussy.

Her sweetness floods my mouth as I lap at her, teasing her clit with torturous strokes of my tongue before dropping lower and spearing it inside her.

"Yes, fuck. Fuck. Kane." Words fall from her lips as I work her, giving her everything she needs as her hips grind against my face.

"You close already, Princess?" I growl against her clit, knowing that the vibrations of my deep voice will drive her wild.

"Yes, yes. Fuck," she cries as I push two fingers inside her, bending them so I know I'll find her G-spot. "Yesssss."

In only seconds, she cries out my name. She twists her fingers so tight in my hair, I'm sure she's about to rip it out as she loses herself in wave after wave of pleasure.

Her pussy gushes with her release and I eagerly lap it all up, making every drop of it mine as my body screams at me to take her, to fuck her until no other man in the world exists for her.

It's not until she's stopped pulsating around my fingers that I finally pull away from her and throw her back up the bed.

Dropping my hands to my jeans, I make quick work of popping the button and pushing them and my boxers down my legs.

Letty's eyes follow my every move, taking in every inch of my body as I expose it.

When I look up, she's got her bottom lip pulled into her mouth with her teeth sinking down into it as she stares at my cock.

"Missed me?" I ask with a smirk.

"You have no idea. How long have you had the piercing?"

"Few years. You like?" I ask, taking my length in hand and slowly working it as I climb onto the bed once more, settling between her legs.

"Uh-huh."

She reaches out and runs her fingertip over the cool metal running through the tip.

I hiss when she makes contact, already embarrassingly close to release from just eating her alone.

"It feels..." She pauses as she thinks, her eyes

darkening as she remembers all our previous times together. "Incredible."

"I'm glad you think so." Falling over her, I place one hand against the mattress beside her head and look down into her eyes as I run the head of my cock through her folds. She gasps at the expression on my face and my lips twitch, glad she's able to read the seriousness behind the words I'm about to say.

"This is your last chance to change your mind, Princess. After this, there's no more running, no more bullshit. You're mine and I want the entire fucking world to know about it."

She nods ever so gently.

"Tell me, Letty. Tell me you want this."

She hesitates for a second and I panic. My heart jumps into my throat, my blood races past my ears as I think for that briefest moment that she's going to change her mind. She's going to have figured out what a massive fuck-up I really am and turn her back on me.

"I want this, Kane. I'm yours."

"Fuuuuck," I growl, feeling those words right down to my soul as I surge forward, filling her with every inch I have.

Her heat engulfs me and I drop to my elbows, resting my head against hers and staring down at her.

No words pass between us as we remain stock still, connected in the most intimate way but it's like a million promises are made in that moment.

Tears fill her eyes as I hold them captive.

Reaching out, I catch one that escapes with my thumb.

"Mine," I finally whisper when my need to move gets too much to bear.

"Yours," she agrees, making my chest puff out and my heart to ache in an entirely different way.

Flexing my hips, I push deeper inside her before slowly pulling almost all the way out. Her velvet walls rippling around me, making me grind my teeth in my need to get it together long enough to at least get her off again.

"You feel... fuck, Princess. Like fucking heaven."

She nods at me, understanding exactly what I mean as I push back inside her body.

My lips part to say more, although I have no idea what's about to fall from me when she presses her fingers against them.

"No more," she says softly. "Just show me."

Dropping my lips to hers, I push my tongue deep into her mouth, searching for hers as I kiss her as slowly and as deeply as I fuck her. Showing her with every swipe of my tongue and thrust of my cock just how much she means to me.

Despite the fact I know we both want to up the pace—if history tells us anything, then we both know we're fans of hot and dirty quickies—I never speed up. I want her to know this is different, that I am different, that this really is the beginning of something.

Something fucking mind-blowing.

With one more thrust of his hips, I shatter in his hold and moan out my release into his kiss.

As my body convulses and pleasure washes through me, emotion slams into me too.

"Princess," Kane growls into our kiss before his body stills and his cock jerks deep inside me. I don't think about the fact he's bare again, I'm too overcome with everything that's happened this afternoon, everything that he's confessed to me.

"I choose you."

A sob erupts from my throat and the tears that were burning my eyes spill over and run over my temples.

"Letty," he says softly when he comes back to himself and finds me crying beneath him. "What's wrong?" His brows pull together in concern and while it makes me feel lighter, it also only makes my tears fall faster.

Throwing my arms around his shoulders, I pull him down onto me so his weight crushes me into the mattress.

He holds me for the longest time as I try to get my head around everything that's happened since he walked through that door and told me everything I didn't know I needed to hear.

But as amazing as hearing those words fall from his lips were, it comes at a cost. A huge fucking cost. His future.

I can't let him throw everything away for me. I refuse to let him.

"You're scaring me," he says, taking his weight from me and rolling us so we're both on our sides. "What's wrong?"

It takes me a few seconds, but eventually, I find the courage to open my eyes and look into his concerned ones.

"I—" I blow out a breath. "I can't let you do this, Kane. I can't."

Lifting his hand, he cups my cheek, wiping away my tears.

"I'm not asking you to let me do anything, Let. This might surprise you, but I don't do anything I don't want to do."

A laugh erupts at his words because I may have experienced that to be the case a time or two.

"I know but—"

"There is no but here, Letty. I've made my decision and I've put it into action. I meant every single word I said out there."

But. The word is right on the tip of my tongue but I fight it down, sensing that he isn't finished.

"I don't expect you to say anything similar back. I know I've hurt you time and time again and for that, I can only apologize. I was a fucking idiot, Let. I couldn't see what was right in front of my face. But you're it for me, Princess. You're the only thing I want."

"It's not that simple, Kane," I argue.

"It can be."

"But it can't. You can't just walk away from the only life you've ever known and into nothing just because you've had this sudden epiphany."

"It's not all that sudden," he mutters, a smirk appearing on his lips.

"What about Victor? I know what you said," I add when he goes to argue. "You can't really believe that he's going to just let you go. What about my dad? If Victor knows you're walking away because of me, then what will he do to him?" I ask selfishly. "What about football? The team needs you—"

"I'm sure Luca will be more than thrilled that he no longer has to deal with me, Princess."

"That may be true but he needs you and he knows it. You're the best. With you and Leon on either side of him, you guys are unstoppable."

"You think I'm the best?" he asks, the most incredible smile spreading across his face.

"Don't let it go to your head, I know fuck-all about football."

"You've hung around the Dunns for years, how is that possible?" he asks like almost everyone does.

"It just is, trust me. But that's not the point. The team needs you. You can't just walk away."

"I won't have a choice, Princess. Victor will pull my scholarship funding and get the AD to pull me from the team by Monday morning."

Leaning forward, I rest my head against his chest, not believing that he's done this.

He had the kind of opportunity that no Creek kids get and he's just handing it back because of... because of me.

"There's got to be another way."

Tucking his fingers under my chin, he lifts my face from his chest.

"I love that you want to fight for me, Letty. I really, really fucking do." He rolls his hips allowing me to feel his hardness once more showing me just how much he loves it. "But there is no other way. I can't afford to go to college or to live without getting a job and I can't do that alongside football. But it's okay. I don't need that stuff." He laces our hands together and lifts my knuckles to his lips. "I'll get a job, build a decent life away from the Creek and the Hawks. Do something that you can be proud of."

All the air rushes from my lungs at his words.

"Oh, Kane," I sigh, wrapping my hand around the back of his neck. "It's not about that at all."

We fall silent once more, the weight of our reality pressing down on us.

"Can we put all this aside until tomorrow?" he

asks, nudging his nose against mine, his lips brush against the corner of my mouth. His hand skims down my back and cups my ass, pressing our bodies tighter together.

"I... uh... I guess we could."

His lips claim mine in another knee-weakening kiss and I once again forget about everything for the time being and just give myself over to him.

I don't remember falling asleep but as I drag my eyes open and look around Kane's bedroom, I realize that I must have.

The room itself is nothing like I expect from Kane. The walls are cream and the furniture is all light and mismatched. I figure that none of it is actually his choice, just what he inherited when he moved in here.

Finding the other side of the bed empty, I swing my legs over the edge and pull his discarded shirt over my head.

The house is in silence but confident that he wouldn't have left me here alone, I pull the door open and pad down the short hall.

"Hey," I say, finding him sitting on the couch staring at his cell, deep in thought. The frown lines that mar his brow make my stomach sink as I'm once again reminded that he's given everything up.

I might have wanted him to choose between me

and the Hawks, but I never expected it to end with him giving up his dream.

There's got to be something we can do.

"Hey, Princess." A smile takes over his face when he turns to see me standing in the doorway in only his shirt. "Hmm, you look good enough to eat."

"Pretty sure you already have," I say, attempting to ignore the flush of heat that assaults my body and failing miserably.

"I sure did. I have plans to do it again soon too." He winks and my cheeks burn as I remember watching his face between my thighs.

"C-can I use your bathroom?"

His eyes leisurely take in my barely-clad body before he nods his chin over my shoulder.

"The door behind you. I should warn you, it's blue."

"Blue?" I ask with a laugh.

"You'll see." I back away, keeping my eyes on his heated ones. "Use anything you like."

"Thank you."

"Are you hungry?" he asks before I push through the door.

"Uh... yeah."

"What do you want? I'll order in."

"Chinese?"

"Sure."

"You can pick." I disappear into the bathroom and shut the door behind me before he can argue. "Whoa," I breathe. It's really... blue.

I use the toilet, finger brush my teeth with his toothpaste and splash my face with water. I do the best I can to remove my smeared makeup but quickly give up when it doesn't budge. I need to get my things from my car, assuming he's planning on me staying here, that is.

When I return to the living area, the couch is empty but a crash comes from the kitchen.

"Beer?" Kane asks with his head in the fridge giving me a great view of his underwear-covered ass.

"Hmm... do you have anything else in there?" He bends over a little more.

"Soda, water, OJ?" It's not until he looks over his shoulder that he realizes what I'm doing. "Oh, you are in so much trouble, Scarlett Hunter." He swings the refrigerator door closed and races toward me. I immediately take off, running around the table so he can't get me.

"This will end better for you if you just come to me," he warns after we've done a few laps, both of our chests heaving and wide smiles across our faces.

"Who said I want it to be better for me? Maybe I want you to spank my ass for being a naughty girl."

"Oh, Princess. That can certainly be arranged," he growls.

He takes a step toward me, stalking me as if I'm his prey and I dart forward, but not before I pull at the hem of his shirt showing him my ass.

"Such trouble." I don't make it another step before he's on me, showing me that he was only playing with me before allowing me to run ahead. Asshole.

My front collides with the wall as the length of

his body pins me there. I feel him hard at my ass as his hand slips under the shirt and splays on my stomach.

"You have no idea how much I'm going to enjoy your punishment for that little stunt."

"I think I do," I whisper, pushing my ass back against his and grinding against his cock.

A gasp rushes past my lips as his hand wraps around my throat, squeezing lightly. Heat floods my core at his possessive touch.

"And to think, I was going to treat you right this weekend."

"What's the fun in that? I like you wicked."

He spins me, pinning me to the wall with one hand on my throat still and the other one on my hip.

"I know you do, baby. And I fucking love it."

His lips are almost on mine when there is a knock at the door.

"Saved by the bell," he breathes against me and I sag against the wall, disappointment flooding me that he's not going to take me right here.

He stares at me and as if he reads my mind, he bellows. "Just leave it there. Thanks, man."

The guy says something in return but I'm too lost in Kane's lust-blown eyes to register the words.

In a rush, he pushes his boxers down around his hips, allowing his solid length free before lifting me from my feet.

"Let's build up an appetite."

"Kane," I cry as he fills me, my head falling back against the wall as pleasure surges through my body as if he didn't already make me come a handful of times only hours ago.

By the time we retrieve the Chinese food from the doorstep, it's cold.

"You go wash up and I'll reheat this," he says, holding the bag up he's just collected.

Just before I head for the bathroom, my cell pings in my purse.

Walking over to the dining table, I pull it out and unlock it when I see Leon's name.

Placing the bag of food on the table beside me, Kane wraps his arms around my waist and rests his chin on my shoulder.

"Should have guessed," he mutters when he sees who's messaged me.

"I thought you two were besties now," I comment, thinking about Lee telling me about the little chat they had in Kane's car.

"I wouldn't go that far," he growls. "But at least he doesn't want to steal you from me."

"They're both good people, Kane."

"Hmm... we'll see. Jury's still out on Luca."

"Oh shush, you're just jealous."

"That you ran straight to them the moment I fucked up, yeah, I fucking am."

I tense in his hold.

"What does he want?" he asks, dragging my thoughts away from my mistake.

I pull up the message and read it.

"He wants to know if I'm coming to the party

tonight." I don't know why I say it out loud, he's looking over my shoulder and can read perfectly fine.

"Tell him you're busy at a party for two." His lips brush up my neck, sending goose bumps skating across my skin.

"I thought you were warming the food?"

"I was, but then I remembered that you taste better."

"Food, Kane," I demand, shaking him off. He complains but soon picks up the bag again and takes it to the counter while I tell Leon that I'm in Rosewood.

I also shoot my mom a message because if anyone can help right now, then it's her.

Placing my cell back in my purse, I head for the bathroom.

"I hope you're hungry," he says when I emerge and I get a look at the amount of food he's laid out on the table.

"I thought it was a party for two, not the whole street."

"I've got a long night planned," he deadpans, pulling my chair out for me like the gentleman he most definitely is not.

"Thank you." I sit down and take in the wine glass. "Wow, this is fancy seeing as you didn't even know I was going to be here."

"What makes you say that?" he asks with a smirk.

"Your face when you walked in was a dead giveaway."

"I thought I was spending the weekend with Kyle."

"They totally played us."

"I'm not complaining. I wanted to tell you all this last night," he says, reaching across the table to take my hand in his.

"Speaking of last night." I raise a brow in curiosity. "When I last—"

"I left about two seconds after you did." I stare at him. "Alone. I actually followed you all the way back to your dorm."

"To make sure I didn't go home with them?"

"Partly, yes."

"That was a mistake that won't be repeated. I swear. But you can't imagine how it felt hearing her say—" I swallow, trying to force the lump down that just appeared in my throat at the thought of someone else having his baby after everything.

"I know, Princess," he says, holding my eyes so I can see the truth within his. "I get it. I want to know something though."

"Anything," I whisper, reaching for my fork, suddenly ravenous now the food is in front of me.

"You and Leon."

I smile and shake my head. I've been waiting for him to ask this for the longest time.

"We were seniors, we were at the Dunn's house celebrating an epic win. Luca had disappeared off with one of the cheerleaders and Leon had dragged me over to dance with him because he had this really insistent cheerslut trying to get in his pants." I laugh to myself as I remember him asking me to help him. Leon was never like his easy brother, instead much more selective of who he spent time with. I totally had a crush on the wrong one, that was for sure. Plenty of times over the years I wondered how things might have turned out if it was Leon who made my little teenage heart beat as wildly as Luca's did.

"I had the biggest crush on Luca, not that he knew that. He'd friend-zoned me practically the first day he laid eyes on me. So seeing him constantly off with every other girl but me hurt.

"Lee and I were both drunk that night, I stepped into him and we danced to get rid of the other girl and one thing just led to another."

"You never wanted to take it further?" he asks, genuinely curious more than jealous.

"It was never that and we both knew it. We were just both lonely and... yeah. Lee and I, we understand each other on a level that Luca and I never have. Even more so since I came back after—"

"I didn't mean to tell him," he says, regret filling his features as he pauses eating.

"It's okay. I know you wouldn't do something like that maliciously."

"Do you?" he asks, genuinely shocked.

"I know you're not a monster, Kane. I know learning about all that hurt you and I know you wouldn't go around willingly telling everyone who cared about what I went through. The only reason I never told them was because of how painful it was to recall, and the fact you needed to be the one to know before anyone else. I'd already kept enough from you and you already hated them. I didn't need to make any of it worse."

He nods, shoveling more shredded chicken into his mouth.

"Leon came straight to you after I told him?"

I nod, picking up a spring roll but making no effort to actually eat it. "We made a pact when I first started at MKU to share our secrets, he came to tell me his after discovering mine."

"Oh?"

"I didn't let him. Whatever he's hiding, he's not ready to talk about it."

"You're a good friend, Let."

I shrug. "I dunno. We all lost touch when I left, and that was my fault."

"No, you all had the same responsibility and life just gets in the way sometimes."

"I guess," I say, finally lifting my spring roll to my mouth and biting off the end.

We sit eating in a comfortable silence for the longest time just lost in our own thoughts before Kane blurts out another confession.

"I know that Riley's death wasn't your fault. I just..." He blows out a pained breath, placing his cutlery on his plate and scrubbing his hand down his face. "I was still dealing with the death of my parents, looking after Kyle, school, football. I knew I fucked up the second Riley talked to me about asking you to that dance and I encouraged him. I didn't want to look like a pussy or have to confess to liking you by putting him off, but I should have."

"Kane," I say, reaching for his hand. "I'm sorry about your parents."

He pushes his hair back from his brow, his emotions from even mentioning them are clear to see.

Sliding my chair out, I encourage him to do the same and I sit in his lap.

"You've never had a chance to grieve them properly, have you?"

Yes, their gran took them in, and she was a wonderful woman, but I know from being there that Kane immediately took on the role as guardian to Kyle even though he was only a kid himself. He got himself involved with Victor early on because he felt he needed to provide and he juggled that and school and football for years. Everything he's ever done has been for someone else. Even down to giving Riley his blessing to date me. Kane has always put himself last and I think it's about time that ends.

Wrapping my arms around him, I rest my head on his chest. "I'm going to talk to my mom. We're going to fix this, Kane."

"No, Let. She's already done more than she should to help me with all the stuff for Kyle."

"Please, Kane. Let me help. You don't need to take all of this on alone now. Mom will have contacts, maybe we can find a way through this."

He drops his lips to my hair and kisses me. "I don't deserve you."

"After everything you've been through, I think you deserve the world."

"Fucking hell, Princess." He holds me so tight I swear something inside me is going to snap, but I wouldn't have it any other way.

16

KANE

Reaching over, I search the other side of the bed for Letty, but it's empty and the sheets are cold.

Ripping my eyes open, I look around the room, needing to find some kind of evidence that she didn't realize she made a horrible mistake yesterday and got up in the middle of the night and left.

I sigh in relief when I find her clothes and shoes still in a pile on the floor.

Falling back into bed, I pull the sheets up around me and think back to yesterday.

She was the last thing I expected when Kyle announced he had a surprise waiting for me but fuck if it wasn't exactly what I needed.

Talking things out, telling her what I'd done and how I really felt was like this massive weight lifted off my shoulders. Yeah, I've still got a hell of a lot to worry about seeing as I single-handedly just made my life implode with this decision. But I have no doubt that it'll be worth it.

Rolling over onto my side, I press my nose into her pillow and breathe in her scent.

I'd be lying if I said I wasn't worried about what comes next. I know I brushed Letty's concerns about Victor under the carpet but the fact of it is, his threat is still very real.

His warning of me walking away might've been him pulling the rug out from under my feet with MKU but he's Victor fucking Harris. Ruthless, blood-hungry, psychotic gang boss. There's no way he's going to let me walk away without a fight whether I'm dangling Alana's safety in front of him or not.

I'm going to need to do better than that if I'm going to convince him that I can turn my back while keeping everything I know about him and his men locked up tight.

No one walks away from Victor Harris and lives to tell the tale. Hell, I've been involved in ensuring that doesn't happen more times than I'm willing to count. But I'm determined to make this happen.

I will be the one who got out of the Creek, got away from the Hawks and made something of my life.

I will.

Throwing back the covers, I pull on a clean pair of boxers and head out. The house is silent but when I glance through the kitchen window, I spot Letty's hair and realize that she's on the swing on the porch.

Making use of the bathroom, I make us both

coffee and head out. The sound of her soft voice as I pull the door open makes my steps falter.

"Mom, I know. Yes. Yes. You didn't have to say it," she mutters with a laugh that makes something flutter in my stomach.

"Well, sometimes you just can't help it. I'm sure you're well aware of that."

"Do you think—" She falls silent as she listens. "Okay yeah. Okay. Sounds good." Pause. "I'm not sure. Tonight or maybe first thing in the morning. I have no idea if he's got any plans."

I take a couple of steps forward, my need to see her is too strong and I come to a stop at the corner of the house and run my eyes over her.

She's curled up on the swing in one of my hoodies, her entire body, legs included, is hidden beneath the fabric. She's got a soft smile on her face as she listens to whatever Jada is saying, her face is free from makeup and her hair is piled wildly on top of her head. I'm not sure she's ever looked so beautiful.

The cool morning air bites into my skin as I stand there, but there's no way I'm moving right now, not when the sight is so breathtaking.

How did I do this? I don't deserve for her to look at me twice, let alone for her to be here and fighting for me right now.

There's a part of me that wants to go over and rip the cell from her ear and demand she lets me handle everything, but I already know how that would go.

She's not going to let this lie. She wants to help, and I want to make her happy so...

Sensing my presence, she glances up at me. A small gasp passes her lips before the corners pull into a beautiful smile that makes my chest ache.

"I-I need to go, he's awake." Chemistry crackles between us as our eyes hold. "Okay, speak soon. Thank you, Mom."

She hangs up and lowers her cell, neither of us saying anything for the longest time as we just soak each other in.

"You're still here," I say, like an idiot when I finally feel the need to break the silence.

"Where else would I be?"

"Running back to Maddison because you realized you fucked up agreeing to stay here."

"Huh, that's funny because I don't actually remember agreeing to anything," she deadpans.

"You're right. You didn't have a choice. I'd have locked you up here and made you see the error in your ways eventually."

"Like kidnap me?" she asks, obvious excitement shining in her eyes.

"If that's what it takes." Images of Reid's basement and Alana in one of his torture chambers pop into my mind but I force it out.

"Locked in the house with only you for company, I can think of worse things to do."

"You're wicked and I love it," I say, placing the mugs in my hand on the small table in front of her before reaching for her, wrapping my hand around the back of her neck, and tilting her head up so she has no choice but to accept my kiss. "Morning, Princess."

"Hey," she whispers almost shyly as I brush my lips over hers, once, twice, and then take them in a scorching kiss that I feel all the way down to my toes.

"Did you sleep well?" I ask, dropping onto the swing seat beside her and pulling her legs from beneath my hoodie to drape them over mine, running my hand up her warm thigh.

"I did. That was my mom," she says, in case I hadn't figured it out.

"What did she say?" I ask hesitantly. I'm well aware of the number of favors that Jada Hunter has already called in for me when I was desperately trying to get everything sorted for Kyle, the last thing I want is to cause her more hassle. Especially after all the pain I now know I've caused Letty. It makes me wonder if she'd have done all she did if she knew the truth about Letty and me back then.

"She's going to make some calls."

How I feel about her asking for help on my behalf must show on my face because she reaches for my hand and squeezes it.

"She wants to help, Kane."

"She should hate me."

She chuckles. "So should I, but you don't seem to have an issue with me being here."

"Princess," I breathe. "It's different. I'm not in love with your mother."

Her breath catches at my confession. Her lips

part but no words come out. It's as if she's fighting to find the right thing to say.

"It's okay, Let. I don't expect to hear the words back. I just... I realized and I knew that after everything, I needed to tell you. I know it's fast, I know it's crazy—" I lace my fingers with hers and pull her onto my lap. "But I needed you to know."

"Kane, I—"

I press my fingers to her lips, cutting her off.

"I really appreciate you doing all of this, but please, if nothing comes of it, please don't feel bad. All of this, aside from you, is what I deserve. I'm not a good person, Let. The things I've done over the years..." I sigh as I think of just a handful of the things that Victor tasked me to do.

"Everyone deserves a second chance, Kane."

"You're something else, you know that, Princess?"

Threading my fingers into her hair, I pull her lips to mine and try to show her just how incredible she is.

"I missed you when I woke up," I admit when I pull my lips from hers in favor of her neck.

"Oh yeah?" she breathes, shifting herself so she's straddling me.

"Yeah, I was dreaming of all the things I wanted to do to you," I growl, pulling my hoodie away from her neck and licking over her collarbone as my hand slips underneath the fabric to find her bare breast.

"Kane," she moans as I pinch her already peaked nipple.

My cock hardens as she grinds her pussy against it.

"Need you, Princess," I say, skimming my hand down her stomach and slipping my fingers inside her panties, finding her soaking wet for me. "Fuuuck," I hiss, rubbing her wetness onto her clit before dipping lower and inside her. "You're so ready for me, baby."

"So what are you waiting for?" she asks, her voice no more than a breathy whisper as she stares down at me with dark, glittering eyes.

Shooting a look over her shoulder, I acknowledge that despite the fact we're on the front porch no one can really see us, well not unless they're really looking. Not that anyone's attention is going to stop me from taking my girl, I just don't want her uncomfortable.

But as I spear my fingers inside her once more and she throws her head back in pleasure when I find her G-spot, I don't think she gives a single fuck.

Shifting awkwardly, I shove my boxers down just enough to pull my length out.

"Lift up," I instruct, hooking her panties aside and sliding down a little so she can sink down on me. "Fuuuck," I groan as she does just that.

"Kane," she breathes as she grinds her hips when she's fully seated on my cock causing a small gasp to escape her.

Holding her hips to help her move, I sit back and watch her as she loses herself in this thing between us.

It's fucking electric and something tells me that it's always going to be the same.

I've never experienced this burning need with anyone else—and there have been a few. But even now, deep inside her, it's not enough. It's never enough. A lifetime won't be enough.

She keeps her pace fairly slow, and despite the fact I'm desperate to slam up into her, I let her have her moment. I allow her to take from me exactly what she needs, hell knows that almost every other time she doesn't get a say.

Sliding her fingers into my hair, she tilts my head and brushes her lips against mine.

"We should have been doing this years ago," she confesses.

I've had similar thoughts over the past few weeks as this thing between us has grown but I've always come to one conclusion.

"The time wasn't right. If we never knew how bad it could be, how would we appreciate how good it is now."

Her entire body stops moving as she registers my words. Her head tilts to the side and a small smile plays on her lips.

"You might be onto something there."

"You're definitely on something," I say with a smirk, thrusting up into her.

"Fuck, you feel good," she moans, her fingers digging into my shoulders.

"Yeah? Allow me to make it even better."

I forget all about her having control. I grip her

hips so tight I'm sure it'll leave marks. I thrust up into her tight pussy and totally taking over everything until she's crying out my name loud enough for our neighbors to hear.

Her nails pierce my skin as she falls over the edge. Her pussy clamping down on me so tightly that I have no choice but to fall over the edge with her and fill her with my seed.

Collapsing on me, she fights to get her breathing under control as I soften inside her.

"Let, are you okay with us not using condoms?" I ask, remembering how she freaked out about it in the past.

My question makes her tense and after a few seconds, she looks up at me with her lust-blown dark eyes and makes my world shift on its axis once again.

"Honestly—" She swallows nervously, I can only imagine what she's thinking. "It terrifies me. I never want to go through that again. But... this. Me and you. I don't want anything between us."

"Let," I breathe and hold her tighter to me. "I don't either, but if you need it to put your mind at ease... I'll do it. I'll do anything."

"We were really unlucky last time. I was on the pill, maybe it didn't work or maybe I screwed up taking it, I don't know, I can't remember but I'm on the shot now so no forgetting anything. If it were to happen again unexpectedly, we'd be really unlucky."

"Okay, if you're sure. I want you happy, Princess."

"I really appreciate you bringing it up, but the

thought of not feeling you against me." Her voice cracks, showing just how much it means to her.

"Okay. Wanna come shower with me, then we're going out."

"Where are we going?"

"Surprise." Lifting her from my lap, I place her on her feet and swat her ass.

"You know," she says seductively. "My ass is still lacking your handprint."

A growl rumbles up my throat at the image that pops into my head at her words.

"So now I owe you a spanking and hood sex?" I ask, guessing where she's going with this.

"Yep," she says, practically bouncing toward the front door.

She disappears inside for a second but emerges with her car keys before I get to join her.

"Could you grab my stuff from my car?"

I look down at myself. "Like this?"

She shrugs. "Might as well give the grannies of the street a show," she says innocently.

"You noticed that about the place, huh?"

She glances around at the other bungalows of all different colors. "Was I not supposed to?" she asks while fighting a smile.

"I think it suits me."

"Oh yeah, the street really screams 'a bad boy gangster lives here.' Shit," she says when my smile drops. "I know you're done, it's just... it was a joke."

"Come here," I say, pulling her into my arms. "I'll be your bad boy gangster any day. Hopefully, I'll be able to put my past behind us and it won't haunt me for the rest of my life."

"You can be whoever you want to be, Kane."

"We'll see." I've yet to see if I'm going to walk away from the Hawks with my life or not. It's something that I know Letty is aware of. She isn't an idiot, she knows how things work, she's just choosing not to voice her concerns about it right now, much like I am. "Go get the shower going and get naked."

"Bossy much?" she asks as I turn to and jog down the steps in only my boxer briefs.

"With you, always."

I know she doesn't move an inch, I feel her eyes burning into my skin the entire way to her car.

"In the trunk," she calls when I get there.

Shooting a look over my shoulder, I find her resting her elbows on the porch railing, watching me intently with her bottom lip pulled into her mouth.

"You think the grannies like what they see?" I call to her.

"Oh yeah, you're totally making their day, Legend."

I laugh to myself as I pop her trunk and pull out her bags.

"You were only coming for the weekend, right?" I ask as I place them both on my bed.

"Yeah, I wasn't sure what Harley was planning so..."

"Fair enough. Come on then." Snagging her hand, I pull her into my body, dipping down to capture her lips before peeling my hoodie from her body and ripping her panties from her hips.

"I didn't bring that many spare pairs."

"You don't need them," I whisper in her ear, making her shudder with desire. "Now, how about we dirty you up before getting clean."

"Kane, you're insatiable."

"Only with you, Princess. Only with you."

17

LETTY

It's long past lunch when we finally leave the house for wherever we're going. After our extended shower, Kane found some bacon in the refrigerator and made us a really late breakfast. Despite my argument that I was fine and could wait a little longer, my overly loud growling stomach made him pin me with that look that says he's either going to kill me or ruin me and I stopped arguing, instead, getting the privilege of watching him work the kitchen like a pro.

"So are you going to tell me where we're going yet?"

"Nope." I sit back in Kane's passenger seat and look out the window as he drives down the coastal road as if we're heading back toward Maddison. All of my bags are still in his house, so I'm assuming he's not taking me back there.

After a good twenty minutes or so, lights catch my eye up ahead.

"Is that a fair?" I ask, noticing the top of a Ferris wheel.

"Sure is, Princess. What do you say?"

"I say hell yes," I squeal, already feeling like a kid again.

The one thing we used to do every single year as a family was to go to the fair when it was in town. I have incredible memories of eating cotton candy with Zayn and Harley until we were all sick and scaring the crap out of ourselves on the rollercoasters that, looking back, were tame as fuck.

"Thank God for that because we've got a couple of people waiting on us."

I glance over at him and the wide smile on his face makes something sing inside me. Knowing that I'm part of the reason it's there and that he looks genuinely happy and relaxed right now means a lot to me.

"I'm excited," I say, bouncing on my seat, more than ready to get out and let my inner little girl free.

"You don't even know who's there."

"Do you think I'm an idiot, Kane?"

"Absolutely not. Can you just pretend to be excited when you see them then?"

"I am excited."

He glances over at me, still smiling before resting his hand on my thigh and squeezing gently.

"I don't deserve you."

"You're right, I'm way out of your league," I deadpan.

"Exactly my point."

"Oh shush, have you looked in a mirror lately? And despite recent revelations, you're a Maddison Kings freaking Panther. Starting Panther. That puts you right at the top of the eligibility list at college."

"Was a Panther," he mutters sadly.

"Nope, I refuse to accept that this is it. We'll figure out a way, Kane. You deserve your place on that team."

"I love you."

His words hit me right in the chest just like the previous times he's said them but despite how my heart aches, I can't say the words. Not yet. Too much has happened between us, too many things need fixing for me to dive straight in like he has.

"Come on." He kills the engine and I realize that we've come to a stop in the parking lot.

The second I'm out of the car, I see Harley and Kyle waiting by the entrance for us.

Taking my hand in his, the two of us walk over. Harley is smiling at us like it's the best day of her life, Kyle looks happy but a little more apprehensive and it physically pains me to keep my straight face.

"I can't believe you, Harley Hunter. You lied to me. You played me," I say, poking her in the chest once we're toe-to-toe.

"I'm... um..." She looks down at our joined hands with her brows drawn together. "So you didn't have a good night then?"

"You're in so much fucking trouble," I warn before my smile breaks and I pull her into me with my free arm. "Thank you," I whisper in her ear.

"You're welcome. I have no doubt you'd have done the same for me if you were here when Ky and I were fucking everything up."

"I got your back, always." I wink as I release her.

"Are we ready to do this shit then?" Kyle asks. "I want to pretend that I'm a kid again with no cares in the world."

"Hell yes," Kane agrees, and together we pay for the admission and walk through to join the happy crowds inside the makeshift fence.

We move from ride to ride, from game to game. The guys get more and more competitive with each one they try, although much to our amusement, they're pretty shit at most. Kane smashes Kyle on the shooting games which only confirms all the things he's been doing the past few years that I probably shouldn't want the details of. But I do. I want to know everything. Every single dark and dirty part of the enigma that is Kane Legend.

"You happy?" he asks me as we finally walk toward the Ferris wheel at the back of the park. I've got a stuffed dog under my arm and a bag of cotton candy in my hand.

"Are you kidding?" I ask, lifting both up. "I'm in heaven right now."

"I won't take that personally," he mutters with a smirk. "Thought I was the only one to take you there."

"You did bring me here."

He barks out a laugh and I can't help but join him.

Pulling some of the pink fluff from the bag, I lift it to his lips.

He parts them but leans forward so far that when he wraps his lips around the fluff, he takes my fingers with it. His tongue caresses over my digits, sending heat straight to my core.

His eyes darken as they hold mine, full of wicked ideas and filthy promises.

"Kane," I warn. "There are kids around."

"Don't tell me you've never enjoyed the dark corners of a fairground, Scarlett Hunter."

My cheeks heat as I remember one time with Riley. It was right before we moved and I was still holding onto the idea that we'd be able to make the long-distance thing work.

"So I thought. Tell me everything," he demands, putting his hands on my hips and walking me backward until I bump into the side of a baseball throw stand.

"You really want to know?" I ask, my brow lifting.

"Humor me."

"Riley—" Kane's eyelids lower at the mention of his name. It's clear after all these years that he hasn't dealt with it. It only confirms my thoughts from last night about him not having a chance to grieve for any of them. "We didn't go all the way or anything but... yeah."

"I miss him," Kane confesses quietly.

Reaching up, I cup his rough jaw. "I know. He was a good person. The world is a worse place without him."

"Is it really bad that I don't feel guilty about this when you were his first?" he asks, his lips brushing mine as he does.

"He'd be happy we finally found our way to each other," I confess.

"Yeah, I like to think so. But if he's looking down on us right now, it's probably better that he averts his gaze."

I laugh at his goofiness, but he makes use of my parted lips and captures them in a knee-weakening kiss.

When we finally emerge from behind the baseball throw, my body is burning from his kisses. I'm desperate to drag him off elsewhere to finish the job he started, sadly though, he seems to have other ideas.

"Come on, I want to whisper sweet nothings in your ear on the top of the Ferris wheel."

Tightening his hold on my hand, he pulls me toward the entrance.

"Sweet nothings? When have you ever whispered those?" I joke.

"Okay fine," he says, coming to a stop behind me in the line. Wrapping his arms around my waist, he brushes his lips against the shell of my ear. "I want to whisper all the wicked things I want to do to you in your ear until you're squirming in your seat and barely able to keep it together with how badly you need my cock inside you."

"Kane," I breathe, already feeling the effects of his dirty words.

"Oh look, we're next," he says as if the last few seconds didn't actually happen.

He drags me forward on shaky legs and we get secured into the car before being slowly lifted into the air. The view of the ocean emerges before us, the rippling waves catching the afternoon sun. The sounds of the fair beneath us begin to drift away until it's just the two of us.

I blow out a long breath as contentment settles within me. Kane pulls me to his side and wraps his arm around my shoulders, holding me tight.

"Can we just stay here forever?" I whisper into the silence.

Kane tenses for a beat, both of us more than aware that everything is going to change again tomorrow.

"Maybe he won't do anything," I suggest, hoping that by saying the words out loud that it'll come true.

"Princess, I love your positivity but he's not going to let this go easily."

"W-what do you think he'll do?"

"Honestly, I don't know. I've got Reid on my side, he's got some cards to play to ensure it goes as smoothly as possible, but Victor can be unpredictable at the best of times."

"You're... you're going to be s-safe though, right?"

"Of course, Let." He holds me tighter and presses a kiss to the top of my head.

He's lying and we both know it, but I don't say anything, I can't. The reality is just too depressing to even consider.

As we start descending on our final lap, I spot Harley and Kyle. They'd wandered off to go on a roller coaster a while ago. I wave at them to get their attention and when we find them once we're off the ride, we agree to head off and find some dinner.

"Are you heading back to Maddison tonight?" Kyle asks innocently as he slides his soda back across the table.

"Um..." Kane hesitates.

Leaning over, I whisper in his ear. "Tell him everything. He can take it."

"Shit," Kane mutters, scrubbing his hand down his face.

"What's wrong?"

Kane looks around briefly as if he's checking no one is close enough to overhear this conversation before he leans across the table.

"I-I can't go back. It's over."

"What do you mean it's over? You got into MKU on a full-ride. That doesn't just go up in smoke."

"It does when the one who helps secure it for you is Victor Harris," Kane admits.

Kyle visibly pales while Harley's face hardens.

"Fucking hell, man. I knew you were doing some dodgy shit. But Harris, really?"

"How do you think I did all this, Ky? Got us a decent place to live, ensured you could restart your life like you have. I can assure you that the money didn't grow on a fucking tree."

"I know, I know. I just... I convinced myself that you'd found another way."

"I'm a Creek kid, Ky. There is no other way."

Kyle's jaw tics in anger. "There is another way, we're living it right now."

"With Victor's blood money," Harley adds.

Silence falls over the table for a few agonizing minutes as Kyle accepts everything I assume he's been avoiding, and Kane drowns in the shame of admitting the truth.

"I've walked away and he's pulling everything he's organized for me. Come tomorrow morning, I won't have a place at MKU. It's done. Over."

"You can't just lie down and accept this, Kane. You deserve that place, this chance at a better life."

"Trust me, Bro. After the shit I've done the past couple years, I really don't."

"Kane," I sigh, reaching over and squeezing his thigh.

"Mom can fix this, right?" Harley asks hopefully.

"I've asked her to look into it. We don't know just how questionable the scholarship and everything was. It could be a simple reinstatement, or it could be trying to find new funding which is going to take time."

"But the season," Kyle gasps.

"The Dunns already hate me. This is just more ammunition for them."

"They need you, Kane. I watched when you didn't play. They won't get where they need to be without you this year."

"What can I do?"

"Fight. Find the funding. Anything. You can't let this opportunity slip through your fingers."

My stomach knots as we sit here debating the college issue when the massive elephant in the room watches over us.

You don't just walk away from Victor Harris and the Hawks.

Kane is lucky to still be breathing right now, let alone worrying about the Panthers season.

Our food is placed on the table before us, cutting off the conversation as we all begin to eat. I pick at my food, my appetite suddenly vanishes as I'm forced to face the reality of this situation.

"So when are you going back?" Harley asks me.

"Um..." I glance over at Kane.

"At the very last minute."

"I've got papers to write. I should probably go back tonight."

"Not happening. You can write them at home."

Home.

It's not my home though, is it?

"We need to make a plan," Kyle pipes up.

"Oh?" Kane asks, throwing a fry into his mouth.

"How much do we pay for our place? Could we find you something smaller in Maddison so you could be close to Letty and then I could find an apartment or something here? I can get a job—"

"Me too," Harley pipes up, which forces a smile onto my face.

"No," Kane states. "Neither of you are doing that. This isn't your problem to have to deal with."

"But it is, Kane. We're family. It's what we do."

"Let's go talk to Mom. She's got friends in all the right places. Plus Poppy's aunt is some kind of advisor at MKU, if you're lucky, she's in the finance office, but even if she isn't, she'll know people."

A little bit of hope flutters within me that even if we don't find a way out of this, then at least we've tried.

"I really don't think—"

"Come on, let's go," I say, pulling some cash out of my purse, enough to cover our bill and place it on the table.

The four of us head for our cars.

"He's getting his hopes up," Kane says sadly once we're alone.

"He wants to help, Harley too. I refuse to accept that there isn't a way to fix this."

He looks over at me, the hope in his eyes makes my chest ache.

He really wants this but I know he's battling with his conscience as to whether he does actually deserve the second chance.

"We've got to do everything we can. If nothing comes of it, then at least we know we tried. But I fully believe we'll find a way. The team needs you. I need you." I swallow down the lump in my throat as he reaches for my hand and squeezes tightly.

"Okay, let's do this."

The drive to Mom's house is short and when we pull up to the house, we find her car sitting in the driveway.

"Well, that's a good start," I mutter, glad that she's here.

The rumble of Kyle's car arrives beside us and the four of us get out together and head for the house.

"Mom," I call when we find the kitchen empty. After a few seconds, footsteps fill the space as she emerges from her office.

The smile that spreads across her face when she sees us makes my heart happy.

I had no idea how she was going to take to me calling this morning to ask for a favor on Kane's behalf. Any other person would have told me I was stupid for being anywhere near him knowing the things she does about him. But that's not the kind of person our mother is. It makes me wonder just how bad things really got with our dad back in the Creek for her to walk away from him like she did.

"This is a nice surprise," she says, coming to wrap her arms around me. "Missed you, baby," she whispers in my ear, holding a little tighter than usual.

"You too, Mom."

"We've come to talk about Kane," Harley blurts.

"I assumed as much." She pins Harley and Kyle with a look. "You two make coffee, and you two," she says, looking between us. "Follow me. I've been doing some digging."

We trail behind her down to her office before she closes the door behind us.

We both take a seat while Mom does the same and she turns her narrowed eyes on both of us before settling on me.

"How much do you know?"

"Everything," Kane answers for me.

"E-ev—"

"I know about Dad, Mom. If that's what you mean."

She drops her face into her hands for a beat before looking back up at me. "I tried so hard to get you all away from this life, Letty."

"I know, Mom, and I'm sorry. I didn't mean to—"

"It's all my fault," Kane interrupts.

"No. Victor didn't come after me because of you."

"Victor did what?" Mom balks.

"That's not important right now. I'm fine, Dad's fine. What we need to focus on is getting Kane back into school."

"Right. Okay." She blows out a long breath. "Right now, nothing has changed, he's still enrolled and everything is fine."

"I only made the call to Victor yesterday morning. It won't have gone through the system yet."

"Kane," she says, pinning him with a look that will ensure he agrees to whatever comes next. "Please, start from the beginning, I want to know how this exactly played out."

So he does, he talks about how he first got tangled up with Victor after his parents died, how he felt the need to be able to care for Kyle despite the responsibility falling on their gran. He talks about Kyle going away and the deal he struck up with Victor that would finally end with Victor ensuring he gets his place at MKU, the one he should have had the year before. And then he tells her about everything that's happened since the beginning of the semester, including what happened to me and how I found out the truth about Dad.

Mom listens to all of it, zero judgment on her face. I guess it helps that she grew up in that world.

"Did you really believe that he'd let you walk away, just like that?"

A sad laugh falls from Kane's lips. "No, never. What I didn't anticipate was this..." He reaches over and takes my hand. "Nothing mattered before as long as Kyle was settled. I knew he wouldn't let me go like I promised, but so what, I was getting a shot at my dream. But I want more now."

"And what do you think will happen now that you've told him you're walking away and that he can take back all the favors he pulled for you?"

"I-I don't know. Best case, he lets me get on with my life, worst case... I don't have a future to worry about."

"It won't come to that," I blurt, although I'm more than aware that I have no control over any of this.

"Only Victor can decide the outcome of that," Mom says. "There have been very few men in the past to get away."

"I've got a few things on my side," Kane admits.

"Alana?"

"Yes, but not just her. There's something else too."

"Enough to make him turn his back on you?"

Kane shrugs. "Victor doesn't think like the rest of us. It's impossible to predict."

As if they knew we needed a little time alone to go through this, Kyle and Harley take their sweet time making the coffee but eventually their knock comes and they walk in with mugs for each of us.

"Anyway," Mom says, turning to her computer. "I was able to get my hands on your application, and I must say that despite all your... pastimes, it's a solid application and I fully understand why you were accepted. There's nothing here, or in your skill on the field that would not make them want you back. But the funding could be an issue. If this corruption is deeper than just Victor having a hand in the finance office somewhere then it could dig up some serious scandal.

"What I'm trying to say is... that even if we figure this out, get your scholarship back, it might not be a quick process."

"That's fine. I'll do whatever I need to do in the meantime to prove my worth."

Mom nods, taking a sip of her coffee. "I guess we just wait and see what tomorrow morning brings."

"I need to talk to Coach."

"You do. You need him on your side right now."

"Thank you, Jada," Kane says sincerely. "I don't know how I'll ever repay you for everything you've done for us." Kane shoots a glance at Kyle who's resting against the wall on the other side of the room.

"Look after this one, keep her safe and treat her right."

"Mom," I complain, my cheeks heating at her words.

"What? I always knew this would happen—"

"You what?" I ask, my brows almost hitting my hairline.

She shakes her head at me. "I always thought you should have been with Kane instead of Riley," she admits.

"And you didn't think to tell me this before."

She smirks. "Because you'd have listened," she deadpans. "These are the kinds of things you have to figure out yourself. And who's to say I was right about it. But despite the obvious issues, I'm glad you've found each other."

"Thanks, Mom. That means a lot. I mean, I thought you'd tell me that I'd lost my mind and disown me after everything."

"Never, baby. We all make mistakes, we all do things we regret. It's what makes us human."

I smile at her, feeling some of the weight I've been carrying around lift from my shoulders.

"Have you guys eaten?" she asks, pushing from her chair.

"Yeah, we have."

"Okay, well, I'm going to go and get something. You're all welcome to stay as long as you like, you know that."

We follow her out of her office and she heads straight for the kitchen while we loiter in the hallway.

"You wanna hang here?" Kane asks, looking down at me with a little hope twinkling in his eyes.

"I really, really don't," I admit. If I'm going back to Maddison and leaving him here soon, the last thing I want to do is hang out with our younger siblings for the night.

"Okay, good. Me either."

"We're heading out."

Kyle nods at his brother. "I'll come back tomorrow." He winks before smiling at me.

'Thank you,' I mouth to him.

"Call me if you find anything out, yeah?" he demands of Kane. "Everything will be okay. Jada will make it happen."

"Let's hope she can."

With a squeeze of my hand, he takes a step toward the door and we make our way out.

I wrap my arms around Letty's waist as she tips the dregs of her coffee down the sink and rinses her cup.

"Don't go," I breathe.

"Kane," she sighs. "I've got class. We can't both fall behind while this all gets sorted out."

I know.

"Do what you need to do today and then I'll see you after, yeah?"

"You got it."

When we got back last night, I called Coach. He needed to know what was happening before I didn't show up to practice this morning or he heard it from someone else. He's been on my side this whole time. I have no idea if that's really because he wanted me there or because he knew what was going on, and the claims that Luca was making about me at the beginning of the season were in fact correct. That I was only there because of Victor.

I like to think that's not the only reason I was there. Jada said herself that my application was solid, maybe I would go in off my own back. That maybe things will be okay.

I stand on the deck and watch as Letty waves and drives away from me.

I fucking hate that she's going back without me but before I show my face at MKU again and knock on the AD's door. I need to see Jada again, figure out a plan for how we're going to play this.

I slam the front door behind me with such force the entire house shakes.

Pulling my cell from my pocket, I hit call on Reid's number.

I give him a brief update and he tells me that everything is in place on his end. I just hope that having him on my side means I get to come out on top over his cunt of a father.

I shower, dress, and drop my cell and wallet into my pants, ready to head out when the sound of a car door slamming catches my attention. I don't think anything of it as I head to the door and pull it open.

The two figures standing on the other side of the door startled me enough not to see what was coming or to react before everything goes black.

Leon greeted me with a wide smile when I walked up to the Westerfield Building the next morning for our English lit class.

He wrapped me in a huge bear hug, asked me if I'd had a good weekend before the inevitable question came.

"What's going on with Kane?"

I knew I couldn't tell him the truth, so I was forced to mumble something about an issue with his scholarship. Leon looked at me like I'd grown a second head but thankfully, he didn't question me, obviously guessing that I was lying for a reason.

Luca looked at me when we entered the lecture hall and I took that as a small win.

He'll come around, I have no doubt in that but with Kane done for the foreseeable future, his life has just got even harder, so I'm not expecting him to do a one-eighty anytime soon.

It hurts, but it's fine. He needs to focus on what's

important right now, and I hope he knows that I'll be right here waiting for him when he's sorted himself out.

The second we found Ella in the coffee shop after class, she demanded to know everything about my weekend with my sister. I thought she was going to explode when I explained that things didn't really go to plan.

By the time we walk out of psychology later that afternoon, I'm more than ready to see Kane and to hopefully hear some good news, but as we emerge from the building, he isn't waiting like he promised me he would be.

"You can go," I say to Ella when I hover by a row of bushes, hoping that he's just got held up after seeing either his coach or the AD.

"You sure?" she asks, but I can see she wants to get back, she's already told me that she's got a deadline tomorrow and how behind she is.

"Of course. He won't be long, I'm sure."

I find myself a bench once she's taken off and pull my cell from my purse in the hope I've got a message.

Nothing.

Finding his contact, I hit call but it just rings out before going to voicemail.

Assuming he's in a meeting, I open up Instagram and start scrolling as I wait.

Students come and go before me, the sun begins to drop lower in the sky and Kane's cell continues to go unanswered.

With every minute that passes, the ball of dread in my stomach grows.

He wouldn't just flake out on meeting me today. I know he wouldn't.

"Kane, where the fuck are you?" I ask myself as I call his cell once more, already knowing that it's pointless.

"Fuck, fuck, fuck," I hiss to myself, trying to figure out what to do first.

There's a good chance he's on campus in a meeting with someone somewhere, but something tells me that I could search this place high and low and never find him.

My gut tells me that he's not in a meeting trying to secure his future, that it's worse than that. And if that's the case, then there's only one person I need to talk to right now.

Swiping my purse from the bench, I take off running until I'm in the parking lot. I slam the car door behind me, turn the engine, and slam it into drive.

I barely remember the journey to the Harris house. Every turn and stoplight passes me by. I have no idea if I drive through any and quite frankly, I don't care.

I leave my engine running and fly from the car the second I'm on the driveway, hammering my fist down on the front door like a maniac.

My chest heaves with my panic, my head spins and my hands tremble with my fear that something has happened to him.

I shouldn't have left this morning. I should have—

The door swings open and Devin's face immediately goes from smiling to murderous in a split second.

It makes me wonder if all the Harrises are complete psychopaths.

"What?" he barks, staring down at me as if I have no right to be standing on his doorstep.

"Have you heard from Kane? Have you seen him? Do you know where he is?" I ask in a rush, barely able to catch my breath.

"No. He'll be at practice."

"He's not. Hasn't he told you?"

He raises a brow for me to continue.

"He told Victor he's done and he's following through on taking college away. He's not at practice, he's lost his place on the team."

Devin's expression begins to change the more I say.

"When did you last talk to him?"

"I left him in Rosewood this morning to come to class."

"Fuck. Get out of the way."

He pushes past me, forcing me aside and immediately unlocks his car.

"What the fuck are you doing?" I bark at him as I right myself.

"Are you fucking coming or what?" I look from my car to Devin's and quickly run around to my driver's side and kill the engine.

"Yeah, I'm coming." I have no fucking clue where we're going but I'm all in right now.

He barely waits for me to climb into his passenger seat before he floors the accelerator and wheelspins down the street.

"Where are we going?"

"Reid's."

I nod. That's where I wanted to go but not knowing where he lives kinda halted that plan.

I sit with my leg bouncing up and down with my fingers drumming down on it while my stomach churns as I imagine all the things Victor could do to him for wanting out. He might not even be alive.

My breathing becomes so erratic that I think I'm going to have to ask Devin to stop the car so I can get some air.

Clearly realizing that I'm losing my grip on reality, he opens the window for me.

"Breathe in, breathe out," he repeats this until I begin to follow orders and my heart begins to slow.

"Okay, I think I'm good," I whisper after long minutes of panic.

"He'll be okay. He hasn't been through everything he has to give up now."

"He might not have a choice."

"Have faith, Letty. Kane and Reid have been planning for this. I have no idea what they've schemed up or what they've got over Victor but I have every confidence that they know what they're doing."

"Well, I'm glad one of us feels that way," I mutter as we pass the sign for Harrow Creek.

A shudder rips through me as we drive into a place I'd quite happily never set foot in again.

There are so many questions I want to ask Devin about all of this, but when I glance over at him and see the hard set of his jaw, I decide against it.

He's made it very clear in the past few weeks that he's not my biggest fan, so I figure the less we talk the better.

"Holy shit. Reid lives here," I gasp as he pulls to a stop before a massive set of secluded gates.

"Why, did you expect him to live in a cute little pink house with a picket fence?" he asks, amusement in his tone as the gates magically open for him.

"Well, no. But this place is haunted, isn't it?" I ask.

He pulls through and we make our way up the long driveway.

"That's what kids in Harrow Creek High like to spread. Truth is, the only one raining down terror in this place is my brother."

"Is that meant to make me feel better?"

"Absolutely not. It's probably best you realize now that my brother is a special breed of fucked up."

I swallow nervously.

I know Reid is... scary. Okay, terrifying, but I'm wondering if I might have underestimated him.

The imposing building emerges before us and a shiver of fear rolls through me at just the sight of the dark architecture.

"Welcome to the house of the devil," Devin announces as he pulls to a stop out front.

"Th-the house of the w-what?" I ask, thinking I just misheard him.

"Come on, Princess. Let's go and find out what the fuck our boy is up to."

I climb out of the car after Devin and follow him to the huge ominous black door.

He doesn't bother knocking, instead, he just pushes through the door. I assume he knows we're here and follows Devin inside.

"Yo, Bro. Where you at?"

"Kitchen."

The inside isn't half as scary as the outside. All the walls are a soft gray color and the furniture is all black but it's warm and somewhat homely, I guess. I look into a room that seems to be the living room as we pass, again everything is black and it's got a huge flat screen on the wall. It screams bachelor pad.

"Letty, this is a surprise," he says, giving me a double-take as I trail behind Devin.

"Do you know where he is?" I ask, desperation clear in my tone.

"N-no. Why?"

Fuck.

I tell Reid about Kane not showing up and he also tries his cell, only to find the same as me. It just rings out.

Anger hardens his face but he doesn't say anything or give anything away which only serves to piss Devin off.

"I know you know something, so can you fucking spit it out?"

"No, I can't. You just need to trust me."

"You know, that's getting harder and harder right now. I know you're the one behind our supply issue. Care to explain that one?"

"No. What's going on is bigger than your fucking supply."

"Well, did you want to tell Victor that because he's been riding our asses? If we don't do what he wants, then he won't initiate us."

"Of course he will. You're his fucking blood."

"You sure about that? He doesn't seem to give a fuck about Gray."

Reid's lips press into a thin line as his patience with his brother begins to run out.

"Enough, okay. I just need you to trust that I have all our futures—Kane's included—as my first priority right now. So will you just do as I say and shut the fuck up."

"Jesus, who got your panties in a twist? You need to get fucking laid or something, bro."

Reid actually growls like a wild animal at his brother's comment.

"Let's fucking go," he barks, physically shoving Devin in the direction of the front door.

"Where are we going?" I ask, hoping to calm the situation down a little.

"The clubhouse. If Victor's got him, that's where he'll be."

Fear freezes me to the spot at the thought of going back there. Images of Victor hurting my dad flicker through my mind, only it's not my dad sitting in that chair, it's Kane.

My vision blurs so I don't see Reid come to a stop in front of me and crouch down so we're at eye level.

"Letty, Letty. Scarlett," he snaps, dragging me from my nightmare. "Everything is going to be okay. I got both of you out of there, almost unharmed. I'll do the same for Kane. Victor just wants to issue his warning but he won't win. Not against me."

"W-what are you playing at?" I don't mean for the question to come out loud, but listening to him talk, I can't help but think he's got his own agenda where his father is concerned.

"That's for me to know, Princess."

A sob erupts at his use of Kane's nickname for me.

"If he's not okay, Reid. I-I don't k-know—"

"He'll be fine. We're one step ahead of that cunt. You have nothing to worry about."

"You're kinda scary, you know that?" I ask as he wraps his arm around my shoulders and guides me toward the door that Devin's already disappeared through.

"I've been told a time or two, yeah." He chuckles, leading me outside and toward his truck.

20

KANE

What the fuck?

I fight like hell to drag my eyelids open only to be blinded by a bright spotlight that's pointed straight down at me. It's the first clue that this time I'm not waking up in a hospital.

No, it's much worse than that.

I'm in hell.

"Ah, you finally going to join us," a familiar blood-chilling voice says as the pain in my body makes itself known.

My vision is blurred as I search for the owner of the voice in the brightness.

"What have you given me, you asshole?" I slur, my voice making it sound like I've spent the entire day drinking when I know I haven't.

"Just a little something to help make you a little more... agreeable."

"It's going to take more than what you've given me to make that happen."

"Oh, I don't know," Victor says, finally moving so he's in my eyeline. "I seemed to get you here fairly easily."

"What do you want?" I spit.

He chuckles, it's low and menacing and would terrify a weaker man. But that's not who I am.

As my vision begins to clear a little more, I find three men standing behind him. One of which is Alana's husband. I fight to keep the smirk off my face when I take in the dark shadows under his eyes and the obvious stress in his features.

Oh yeah, he cares that he can't find her.

Perfect.

"What do I want? You really are fucking stupider than you look, boy."

It takes every ounce of strength I have to push myself up from the cold, solid floor beneath me to sit so I'm resting against the wall.

My head spins, my eyes desperate to close and let the darkness consume me once more but I can't.

I knew this was coming. I knew he wouldn't just let me walk out without getting the final say. Sadly for him, I have a plan. I just need to stay focused enough to remember it.

"We're done, Victor. I told you, take away everything. I want nothing more to do with you or this bullshit life. I am done."

"You're a fucking idiot. You don't get to give this up because of a girl. A fucking Hunter girl at that.

Have those girls got diamond-encrusted cunts or something?"

"The only cunt around here is you, Victor. Let me go and I'll walk away and never look back."

"It's almost sweet that you think I'll allow that to happen," he mutters, smoothing down his obnoxious tie and turning to look at his henchmen who also smirk at my suggestion.

"I think you'll do exactly that, Victor."

"Oh yeah, and why is that? Why would I let someone who knows so much about me and my business just walk away scot-free?"

"Because I know things you don't."

"Oh?" he asks, barely looking interested in what I might have to offer.

I sit silently for a few moments and lift my hand to push my damp hair from my head. I have no idea if it's wet with sweat or blood and I don't look at my hand to discover the answer, I really don't want to know.

Averting my stare from Victor, I look to his right-hand man, Razor, and then to his son, Maverick, Alana's husband.

"You missing something that belongs to you, Mav?"

His jaw tics as he stares back at me, any attempt he's trying to make to look unaffected has failed.

"Yeah, you are, aren't you?"

"You're lying," he growls, earning him a scowl from Victor.

"Am I?" I shake my head. "I think you might be

missing some information when it comes to your pretty little *wife*."

"Oh yeah?"

"Victor, why don't you tell him?"

Maverick's eyes leave mine in favor of the boss.

"He's talking shit to get out of this."

"If you want to see her again, I highly suggest you ignore him, Mav."

Maverick parts his lips to respond but no words come out.

"You're fucking delusional if you think I'm going to let you go because of that whore."

Maverick's fists curl at his sides at Victor's barked words, making me wonder what the whole story is there. They're married, as far as I know. He seems to care about her, yet he won't sleep with her. The easiest assumption is that he's gay, but something tells me that's not it at all.

"Did you know that she's a whore, Mav? That Victor pimps her out to make men do as he so desires?"

His lips twitch as I'm sure his teeth grind hard enough to chip one.

"Oh, you didn't? So you didn't know that he's had me fucking her for over a year in the hope I'd fall in love with her?"

"You fucking asshole." Maverick flies at me, his fist connecting with my cheekbone making my head ricochet off the wall behind me.

"I'll take that as a no," I mutter, rubbing my face with my palm as Razor pulls his son back.

Silence ripples around the room as Maverick stares at me like he wants to kill me while Victor stands there with a smug as fuck smirk on his face.

"I don't give a shit about that slut, so threaten her all you like. It's not going to help your cause."

Maverick growls once more.

"You might not care, but he does," I say, tipping my chin in Mav's direction. "And I know that you have very, very limited alliances in this world, but Razor and Maverick are two of them."

His eyes flash with contempt and he knows I'm right.

"There's one other though, isn't there, Victor? The outside world might think that all your sons are equally as important as each other to you, but they're not, are they?"

He takes a warning step forward but I don't so much as flinch.

"I guess people might assume that Reid is your favorite. He is your underboss. The one who will continue this legacy because it's his birthright. But he's not the one you've been grooming to be your little bitch, is he? He's not the one who's been going around doing your dirtiest, most corrupt tasks, is he?"

Victor pales confirming what I already suspected. His nonchalance over his youngest son's disappearance is an act.

"You put so much effort into looking like you don't care, but we know the truth, don't we, Victor?"

"You don't know fuck-all about it."

"Don't I?"

He stares at me, the muscle in his temple pulsating.

"So I wouldn't know that you've sent men to infiltrate the Cirillo family because you think they have your youngest son?" I raise a brow as Victor's face begins to turn beet red.

"I wouldn't know that while you've been acting like you don't give a fuck if he's dead or alive that you've been fighting like hell to find his whereabouts?"

I shake my head and laugh at him.

"You've even sent men to England thinking that they smuggled him across the pond. There's only one idiot here right now, Victor. And I can assure you that it's not me."

"Where the fuck is my son, Legend?"

"Why the fuck do you think I'd tell you that?"

My heart thunders in my chest when he reaches around his back and pulls out his gun, clicking off the safety and aiming it right at my head.

"Go on shoot me, but I can assure you that you'll never find him if you do."

"Vic," Maverick pleads.

"I don't give a shit about you or your business, Victor. I want to be as far away from you and everything you stand for as possible. I'll keep your fucking secrets, how sick and twisted you are. It'll be like I was never here."

"And Alana and Gray?" he asks as if he's considering my offer.

"In time, I'll make sure they're delivered back to you safely."

"In time?" he asks like it's the most absurd thing he's ever heard.

"Yeah. Forgive me, Victor, but you're an untrustworthy cunt so I won't be handing them over the second you let me walk out of this room. You'll get Alana first, because I actually feel a little sorry for Maverick. He's clearly in love with a woman he shouldn't be for whatever fucked-up reason. Then Gray will follow if, and only if, you keep to your end of the deal and let me get on with my life."

He stares at me, his jaw tics with frustration as his outstretched arm begins to tremble.

"So?"

21

———

LETTY

The sound of a gunshot makes our race through the Hawks clubhouse slow for a beat.

"Kane," I whimper, fear for what that might have been races through me, paralyzing me. "No, no, no."

Reid reaches out and wraps his arm around my shoulder. Being comforted by him is weird. I should be scared of him, everyone else sure is. But as his warmth hits me, thankfully, it helps drag me back to the here and how and what we came for.

"Let's go," I say, swallowing down my fear and taking a step forward.

Reid leads me down a long dark hallway that I feel like I should remember, but I don't. My memories of my short time here are vague at best, aside from those minutes I was awake and sitting in the chair, the rest is just a blur.

The second we come to a closed door, Reid reaches out and swings it open.

"Stay here," he warns as he slips inside, but I'm long past doing what I'm told and the second he steps into the room, I bolt in after him.

"Oh my God," I cry when my eyes land on the illuminated figure that's laying on the floor, a small pool of blood beneath him. "What the fuck have you done?" I scream, racing toward Kane.

I don't feel anything as my knees collide with the concrete floor and I don't register Reid's low growl as he chastises me for defying his orders.

"Kane, Kane," I repeat, pressing my hand to his neck in the hope of feeling a pulse.

His face is black and blue, both eyes swollen and his lips cut with blood trickling down his chin. But those injuries aren't the ones that terrify me the most because that would be the hole in his shoulder.

"I-I'm okay," he manages.

"Kane! Oh my fucking God," I sob, leaning forward and wrapping my arms around him the best I can.

There are raised voices behind me but I don't hear a word of them as I pull back to find Kane's pained blue eyes on me.

"You're going to be okay," I tell him, cupping his rough cheek gently in an attempt not to hurt him.

"I know," he says. "You're here."

My heart splinters in my chest at his words.

"We're going to get you out of here. You're going to be okay," I repeat, more for myself than anyone else.

"Why did you bring that whore here?" Victor's

vicious tone sends a shiver down my spine and without thinking I stand and turn to him.

"What did you call me?" I bark, marching toward him without a second thought.

"Letty," Reid warns but I ignore him as I continue toward his father with every muscle in my body ready to fight.

"A whore. Just like your mother. Tsk." He shakes his head at me. "Coming in here and trying to save that cunt. He's just as fucking useless as you."

"Let him fucking go," I scream, flying toward him to help make my point. But arms wrap around my waist, stopping me from making contact with Victor and I'm hauled back into a hard, warm body.

"Enough, Princess," Kane growls in my ear.

"Shit, Kane." I rip myself out of his arms and spin around. He's on his feet but he's swaying slightly, the gunshot in his shoulder still oozing bright red blood.

"I'm leaving," he tells Victor. "I'll assume you accept my terms and will leave me the fuck alone. You've left your mark." He points to his shoulder. "If you keep up the rest, you'll get what I promised."

Wrapping my arm around Kane's waist in an attempt to help, we turn to walk out. We're at the door when Victor speaks, clearly needing to get in the last word.

"You go back on this and you're all fucking dead. All of you."

His warning ripples through me, turning my blood to ice. He doesn't say their names but I know he's referring to my family along with Kyle.

"Don't listen to him, Princess. You're all safe."

Kane looks over his shoulder at Victor one last time before we walk out of the door with Reid and Devin hot on our heels. The door has barely slammed behind us when Kane's legs give out.

"Oh shit," I gasp as he slips out of my hold but by the time I turn to him, both Reid and Devin have him.

"We've got him, keep going."

All eyes turn our way as we hurry through the communal area where the guys are hanging out. A couple look like they want to help, but the second they clock Reid, they quickly settle back down and continue with what they were doing.

"It's unlocked," Reid says when we get to his truck and I rush around them to pull the back door open.

Kane is now limp between the two of them, his head hanging low and his shoulder still spilling blood that's more than soaked his white shirt.

Somehow, they manage to maneuver him so he's laying across the back seat. The second they move, I rush to climb inside him but before I get there, a hand lands on my upper arm.

"I won't let anything happen to him," Reid says softly.

I glance up at his concerned eyes.

"It's a little late for that, don't you think?" I spit, nowhere near as scared of him as I once was.

"He'll be okay," he says before stepping around the door and waiting to get inside.

I climb in and lift Kane's legs onto my lap before

he slams the door closed and drops into the driver's seat while Devin takes the passenger side.

No words are said as we back out of the space and speed away from the clubhouse.

I keep my hands on Kane, my eyes focused on his face, hoping like hell that he might show some signs of life but he's out of it.

"I need to stop the blood," I say, staring at his shoulder.

"Shit." Reid looks around but comes up short.

"Here," Devin says, dragging his shirt over his head and throwing it at me.

"Thank you."

Balling it up, I press it to Kane's shoulder.

He doesn't so much as flinch as I apply pressure to the wound and it makes my stomach drop.

"Please, Kane. Please, be okay," I whisper, brushing my knuckles over his stubbled cheek.

Long, painful minutes pass as I sit staring at his chest, slowly moving and straining to hear his shallow breathing. When I finally look up, we're not heading in the direction I expected us to be going in.

"The hospital is that way." I point out the back window.

"We're not going to the hospital with a fucking gunshot wound, Letty."

"But he's bleeding—"

"Someone will meet us at my house. We're not going to let him die."

"Motherfucker isn't that lucky. He's going to have to wake up to our smiling faces," Devin deadpans.

"Reid doesn't smile," I point out, thinking of the handful of times I've seen him without his standard scowl on his face.

"Oh burn, Bro," Devin barks but predictably Reid doesn't react.

Only a few minutes later, we pull up outside Reid's house once more beside a car that wasn't here earlier.

The second the brothers climb from the car, a middle-aged man who's covered in tattoos emerges from the other vehicle.

Reid and the man briefly shake hands before the door beside me is ripped open.

Devin stares at me with his lips pressed into a thin line and an impatient expression on his face.

"Gonna get out of the fucking way?" he grunts, clearly still pissed at me despite the fact I'm the one who alerted him to this situation in the first place.

Quickly, I scramble from the car with Devin's ruined shirt in my hand. Reid passes me his keys and instructs me to go and open the door.

They manage to get him out of the car and I stand inside the house. I hold the door open and hope that I'm out of the way as the man who I can only assume is a doctor follows the three of them in.

They immediately go for the stairs, and after closing the door, I follow behind them.

By the time I turn to the room they've disappeared inside, Kane is already laid out in the middle of the bed and the doctor is cutting up the center of his shirt to get to his wound.

Devin backs up to a chair beside the window and drops down while Reid comes to stand beside me. The man opens the case I didn't notice he was carrying and injects Kane with something before properly cleaning up his wound so he can see the damage.

"Doc's the best, you don't need to worry," Reid mutters.

"Worry?" I ask as if the mere suggestion is absurd. "The man I lo—" I shake my head, swallowing down the words. "He's laying there with a fucking bullet in his shoulder and bleeding out."

"He's lucky, a few inches lower and—"

"Don't," I snap. Not at all in the right state of mind to be considering other worse options right now.

We stand in silence, my body beginning to ache from the tension as we watch the doctor work.

I have no idea what's going on but he mutters things like, "lucky," and "clean shot," so I can only assume things are really going to be okay.

"Right, he's all done," Doc says, turning to look directly at Reid. "I've cleaned and stitched him up. Given him some pain relief. He'll sleep for a while but when he wakes, give him these." He slaps a bottle of pills into Reid's hand. "Two every four hours."

"I know the drill, Doc. You know this isn't my first rodeo."

"I know, I know. Walk me out?"

"Sure thing." He gestures for the doctor to go

ahead before turning to look between Devin and me. "You two good?"

Devin nods and I just about manage the beginning of a smile. Happy that we're not about to kill each other, Reid leaves us to see the doctor out.

The second he's gone, I rush across the room and gently drop down onto the side of the bed beside Kane.

I take his warm hand in both of mine and stare at him with tears in my eyes.

Don't you ever fucking do that to me again, I silently chastise, the image of finding him slumped on the floor in that room light up like a fucking comedy act refuses to leave my mind.

Victor could have killed him. Could have killed him there and then, and if he hadn't planned to meet me, how long would it have been before anyone noticed.

A sob erupts from my throat at the thought of him going and no one who cares about him knowing.

"This is all your fault," a low menacing voice echoes around the silent room.

"M-my fault?" I stutter, turning to look at where Devin is still sitting shirtless in the chair.

"Yeah," he says, resting forward and placing his elbows on his knees. "You caused all of this."

"I didn't do any of this. I want nothing to do with your fucking family," I spit.

"Yet here you are. Good little Scarlett Hunter playing with the big bad wolves."

My teeth grind as I stare at him.

"What did you really think would happen when you made him choose between your pussy and us."

"W-what? I-I didn't—"

"Yes, you did."

"I never wanted him to walk away from you. You're a part of his life, all of you are."

"But we're Hawks, Letty. So by telling him to walk away from the Hawks, you're telling him to leave us."

"No, no, I never—"

He pushes from the chair, his anger tightening his features and pulling his brows together.

"You knew this would happen yet you're a selfish cunt who did it anyway."

"No. No," I cry. "I just want him to have a better life. I want him to live out his dream. All he ever wanted was football and college."

"Bullshit, Letty. He's a Creek kid. We all are. This life we're all living it's a fucking lie."

Releasing Kane's hand, I stand from the bed so I don't feel at a disadvantage in this exchange.

"That may be true for you, but it's not for me, for Kane. I've worked my ass off for this. I've fought through hell to be here, to succeed, to make a life for myself. I'm not just here because my daddy wants me to control the fucking drug ring."

"You want to talk about daddies, Scarlett? Then let's talk about yours." Devin takes a menacing step forward, looking at me through his lashes as if he's planning the most painful way to shut me up.

"That's enough," a deep voice booms, startling me.

"You two can argue all you like, but it's not going to make any of this any better. Kane is done, he's out. He's made a deal with the devil that the devil can only agree to. He's alive and will be fine in a few days. Letty's right, Dev. It's time for him to look to his future beyond the Hawks. Being with us was never his destiny and you fucking well know it."

Devin's lips part to respond but he never says a word.

"Go and make us a fucking coffee," Reid spits. "Letty's is white with one sugar, in case you didn't know that."

It's my turn to look like a freaking goldfish. How does he know how I take my coffee?

Devin disappears and Kane groans, shifting on the bed slightly and all my previous thoughts are forgotten.

"Ignore him, he's just pissed Kane found a decent girl before him," Reid says, although I don't believe him for a second. There's no way Devin is jealous of me. The guy is a player and he seems more than happy with it being that way.

"Right. Sure," I mutter, keeping my eyes on Kane once more. "What... um... what deal did Kane make, is Alana really that important? I got the impression she was just a slut who liked to play games."

He chuckles at that. "Yes and no. I think she enjoys the games, it's a distraction for her."

"A distraction from what?" I blurt before I think better of it.

Reid's jaw pops as he thinks. "Life." He runs his

hand through his hair. "Listen, when he's awake and you're up to it, you can talk to her yourself." For the first time ever, I think I hear a little hesitation in his voice.

"She's here?" I ask, trying to cover my shock.

"Yes. I'm... keeping her safe."

I narrow my eyes at his explanation.

"O-okay." I'm not sure how I really feel about the woman who tried to rip out my heart not so long ago. Let alone to know that she's here under this very roof where I know Kane has been hanging out.

"He doesn't want her, Letty. He never has. I don't know what he's told you, but anything that was between them, it was no more than a business deal."

I nod, accepting his words.

"Thank you," I say sincerely.

"Kane has wanted to get out for a long time. He's not doing this because of you, he was already doing it." I try to swallow down the lump in my throat. "As much as I hate to admit it because he's one of my best boys, he wasn't built for this life. He deserves to live out his dream, he deserves MKU and the Panthers, and you, Letty. I'm sure you don't need me to tell you just how much he's been through. He deserves happiness."

My eyes fill with tears at his words and all I can do is nod.

"I'll leave you alone. You're welcome to stay as long as you like."

He squeezes my shoulder and backs up toward the door. Just before he disappears, I find my voice.

"You're a good friend, Reid. He's lucky to have you."

"I'm not so sure about that, Princess. But I do my best. Call if you need anything."

I smile weakly at him before he closes the door and leaves me alone with Kane.

Kicking off my shoes, I gently slide down the bed. I'm careful not to put any weight on Kane as I wrap my hand around his upper arm, needing some kind of contact with him to feel his warmth.

I lay there with him for the longest time, just listening to his breathing and thanking anyone who will listen that Victor didn't aim that gun any lower.

"He's right, you know." His croaky voice startles me, and I quickly push up onto my elbow to look at him.

His eyes are closed but he's clearly awake.

"Kane?"

His eyes flutter open and the second I get to look into his slightly glazed blue eyes, I let out a massive sigh of relief.

"Hey, Princess."

"Oh my God." I can't stop the sob that rips from my throat or the tears that spill from my eyes at seeing and hearing him. "When we walked in... I thought... I thought you were..."

"Baby, I'm fine."

"You have a fucking hole in your shoulder."

"Meh." He shrugs, instantly regretting the move because he winces in pain.

"Do you need some pain relief? The doctor left some pills."

"I'm good. All I need is you." I swoon at his words. "Come here." He lifts his arm on his non-injured side and gestures for me to cuddle against him.

"I don't want to hurt you."

"You won't. Just lay with me for a bit."

Once again silence falls around us and the sound of his breathing gets heavier. After the stress of the afternoon, I find my own eyes drifting closed and I soon join him in sleep. Although it's fitful because I'm overly aware of moving too much and hurting him.

When I finally come to a while later and open my eyes, the room is in darkness. Only the light of the moon from the window on the opposite wall illuminates it. I look to find the bed beside me is empty.

"Kane?" I cry in panic.

I stand with my shoulder resting against the doorframe as I watch her sleep. The moonlight illuminates one side of her beautiful face and I can't help thinking that she looks like an angel. My angel.

Hell knows how long Victor and his goons would have kept me locked in that room for if she didn't raise the alarm that I never turned up.

I'm pretty sure I've done nothing in my life to deserve her. Everything's been fucked up and twisted for almost as long as I can remember. But fuck if I don't want to keep her and try to turn everything around.

I didn't hear everything Reid said to her earlier, I was drifting in and out. But he was right, my destiny was never the Hawks. It doesn't run through my blood like it does his. He's wanted it from the second he learned the truth about his father and his life, all I wanted was football.

I let out a sigh knowing that I might have screwed up that opportunity now. With my eyes still on Letty, I know that I'll find my way even if college is no longer an option for me. I've got her, I'm free from Victor as long as I make good on my promises, which Reid will deal with for me. The rest can just fall into place, hopefully.

A smile curls at my lips as I watch her stir. My body aches like fuck after the beating I took at the hands of Victor's henchmen and the burning through my shoulder where the cunt shot me. But she's worth all the pain and more.

She turns to where I was and stretches her arm out to find me. The second she realizes I'm not there, her eyes fly open and she sits up.

"Kane?"

"I'm right here, Princess."

Her eyes find me and her entire body sags with relief.

"You should be in bed," she warns, running her eyes up and down the length of me inspecting each of my cuts and bruises.

"I'm fine."

"I'm sorry, you're anything but fine. You were shot, Kane. Shot."

I can't help but laugh at her. "I know, baby."

Pushing from the wall, I slowly make my way back to the bed.

"You need pain relief, and don't even try to tell me that you don't. I can see it in your eyes that you're in agony."

"I'm a little sore."

"A little," she scoffs, climbing from the bed to help me with the final few steps. "Did you even look in the mirror in there?" She shoots a look at the bathroom.

"Yeah," I admit with a wince, remembering my bruised and swollen eyes, cut lip and brow and the dark bruising around my ribs, and of course the obvious hole in my shoulder.

"Get in bed," she demands, pulling the sheets back so I can slide under.

"Pants?" I ask smugly.

Her eyes hold mine for a beat before they run down to my waistband.

"You want me to be comfortable, don't you?"

"You're trouble, Kane Legend."

A smirk pulls at my lips as she moves around me and drops her hands to my belt before pulling it open.

Desire races through me the second her soft knuckles brush my sensitive skin and my cock swells. Momentarily pushing all the pain aside.

She pops the button on my pants and wraps her fingers around the fabric to pull them down my legs.

The second she has them over my cock, she gasps.

"Kane," she growls. I think she's meant to be warning me, but in my head, it sounds anything but.

"What? You're undressing me. I can't help it."

"Sure you can't," she mutters. "Sit down." I do as I'm told and drop onto the edge of the bed, sighing in relief that I no longer need to hold myself up.

She pulls my pants off my legs and then my socks before holding the covers back and nodding for me to get in.

"But—" I pout.

"Don't you but me, Legend," she sasses with her hands on her hips like she's the one in charge here. Wounded, I could still have her on her back in seconds and she knows it. "Are you hungry?"

"Starved," I rumble, my eyes taking her in from head to toe.

"For food, Kane. Everything else is off the menu right now."

"Spoilsport. Watching you wrap your lips around my cock right now would—"

She groans in frustration. I laugh for a second before I realize just how much it does actually hurt and I abruptly stop. Of course she doesn't miss it, if her raised brow and I told you so expression tells me anything.

"Take these," she says, holding out two pills and a glass of water. "Then I'm going for food. Don't do anything stupid."

She slips into the bathroom to freshen up before checking on me once again and leaves the room. My eyes follow her until she turns the corner, then I rest my head back and allow my eyes to close once more as the pain steadily throbs in every inch of my body.

I think back over my time with Victor and his goons. I knew it would be bad when he caught up with me, I was expecting the beating but I assumed that if he pulled the trigger then I wouldn't be around after to tell the tale. Maybe he is going soft in his old age, or and like I suspected, deep down he does care about more than himself.

It was no secret in the Harris family that he was grooming the youngest brother to be his protégé. Reid might be second in command and be the future of the Hawks, it was his birthright after all. But Gray, Victor saw something different in him and he was training— brainwashing—him to do all his dirty work. I mean, no one with half a brain cell would think kidnapping Harley earlier this year was a good fucking idea but he did it. I wonder if he's regretting it yet.

I picture the young Grayson Harris that Kyle was friends with and wonder where it all went wrong for him.

"Hey, how are you doing?" Reid asks, dragging my thoughts from his baby brother.

"Yeah, you know. On top of the world."

He laughs as he walks over to the chair beneath the window and drags it over.

"He took the bait then."

"I'm alive, aren't I?"

"Just about," he mutters, dropping his eyes to my stitched-up bullet wound. "Doc did a good job, eh?"

"He's had plenty of practice over the years," he deadpans.

"I guess so."

Silence stretches out between us.

"You confident with everything from here on out?"

"Of course, man. I've got this. I... uh... I told Letty

she could talk to Alana," he admits, rubbing the back of his neck.

"I told her she could talk to her too, let Alana explain her side."

"Want me to get her up or..."

"It's up to you, man. She's your prisoner."

He chuckles in a way that makes his eyes light up.

"You're enjoying having her here a little too much, aren't you?"

"What makes you say that?"

A loud crash echoes through the house followed by what I can only assume are a string of curses from Letty.

"I should probably..." He thumbs over his shoulder. "Yeah, I would. That sounded expensive."

Pushing from the chair, he walks to the door before looking back at me.

"You got a good one there, Kane. Don't let her go."

"Not planning on it, man."

After Letty brought me up sandwiches and confessed to smashing almost every one of Reid's plates on his tiled floor, I crashed with her wrapped around me like a monkey. It was perfect aside from the agony I was in and the fact she still refused to blow me.

The weight that had been pressing down on my shoulders for... well, years, had finally lifted. I was no longer Victor's puppet and I was free to get on with my life. As long as Reid follows through on his end—which I have no doubt he will, then it's over. Really over.

I lay watching the sun creep up through the window as Letty begins to stir beside me.

"Morning, Princess," I whisper when her eyelashes flutter open.

"Hey," she says, her eyes immediately lighting up when she looks at me and a wide smile spreading across her lips. "How are you feeling?"

"Like I've been hit by a bus," I confess.

"Well, you're looking hot. The blue and purple really suits you," she mutters, gesturing to my busted face with her finger.

"Yeah? I knew you'd like it," I joke.

"I fucking hate it, Kane. I kept waking up during the night with the image of him pointing a gun at you."

"It's over, baby," I assure her, holding her tighter and ignoring the searing pain that shoots through my body at the move.

"Is it though? Will it ever really be over? He's always going to be in the background."

"It's a part of my past I will never fully be able to put behind me," I confess. It's true. At any point he could go back on our deal but I'm confident he won't. Plus, there are other things at play here than me just trying to get out. Reid has not filled me in on any of the details but I know he's planning something. That mix-up with the shipments is just the tip of the iceberg, of that I'm sure. But I'm happy to let him do his thing while I restart my life properly this time.

"It's okay," she says, gently cupping my cheek and looking into my eyes. "I get it. And, it's a part of my past too. But it doesn't have to define our future. What do you want now, Kane?"

"You," I answer without missing a beat.

"You've already got that." She laughs. "What's next for the Legend?"

I throw my head back and laugh too and it feels so fucking good.

"I'm gonna get back into college, one way or another. Even if I do it online or community college. I want to get my degree, I want to get a decent job, I want to be the kind of man you can be proud of."

She smiles at me, her eyes glistening with tears.

"I'm so fucking proud of you." Leaning forward, she carefully brushes her lips against mine but I'm not having any of it. I thread my fingers through the hair at the nape of her neck and force her to kiss me properly.

My lip splits back open filling my mouth and I'm sure hers with the coppery taste of blood but our kiss doesn't falter. I smile into it knowing that she's just as wicked as I am because right now, I know she's wet as fuck for me, blood and all.

"Letty," I moan needily when she finally pulls back.

She bites down on her bottom lip and looks up at me through her lashes.

"I've got you, baby. Just... just don't move or try and take over, okay?"

"I can't promise anything, Princess."

She shakes her head at me as she climbs from the bed. But she doesn't do what I expect and I stick my bottom lip out in a pout when she tips two pills from the bottle on the nightstand behind me and hands them over with a glass of water.

"Take these," she demands before turning her back on me and walking to the bathroom. She's only wearing yesterday's shirt and her tiny panties that expose almost all of her ass. The sight does nothing for the situation I'm in thanks to that kiss.

She knows I'm watching and wiggles her ass before she slips into the room.

"Not fair, Letty," I complain as she kicks the door closed.

When she emerges a few minutes later, she's got her long hair twisted up on the top of her head and she's got a seductive smile on her face.

Dropping my eyes down her body, I find her pert nipples pressing against the thin fabric of her shirt. She clearly discarded her bra at some point while I was passed out, then I see her lace-covered mound and then her long, curvy legs.

My cock jerks against the confines of my boxers from just looking at her alone.

"Off." My voice is deep and rough as my demand fills the room.

Her teeth sink into her bottom lip before she lifts one hand to the hem of her shirt. "This?" she asks innocently, pulling the fabric away from her body a little.

"Yeah, baby. That. All of it."

"Sure you can handle it?" She stalks across the room and comes to a stop at the end of the bed, never coming close enough for me to touch her.

"You fucking know I can."

"You're pretty incapacitated at the moment."

"I'm so fucking hard for you right now, Princess. That is working perfectly fine."

"It's going to hurt you though. Maybe you should just watch me." Her hand slips up her shirt until she's cupping her breast.

"Fuck, Let." I throw the covers off me, my body burning hot with my need.

Following her move, I push my hand inside my boxers and wrap my fingers around my length.

A growl rumbles up my throat at the sensation but it's not what I really need. I need her. Her delicate touch and her hot and dirty mouth.

"Let me see," I demand when she obviously pinches her nipple and lets out a seductive little gasp of pleasure.

"What is it you want to see?" she asks, raising a brow, trying—and failing—to look innocent.

There's nothing innocent about Scarlett Hunter, I've ruined every innocent bone in her body and dirtied her up over and over. And I'm going to do it again, and a-fucking-gain.

"I want to see your beautiful body, Princess. I want to watch you pleasure yourself. I want to watch you push yourself over the edge and then I want to come down your throat."

"You want me to be your dirty little whore?" she asks, using my words.

"Fuck yeah, baby." I pump my cock faster. She hasn't really touched herself yet but already I can picture what her slender fingers are going to look like as she plays with her pretty little pussy. "Now take it off."

Slowly, painfully fucking slowly, she drops her hand from her body and wraps her fingers around the bottom.

Inch by torturous inch, she reveals her sinful body. I run my eyes up the curve of her waist, once again noticing how much she's filled out in just a few weeks. My fingers twitch to run them over her curves as she exposes the bottom of her breasts.

My mouth waters to lick over them, to tease her until she's begging me to take her nipple in my mouth and bite until it hurts.

Finally, she pulls it over her head, fully exposing herself to me.

"Fuck, you're beautiful," I blurt, unable to keep the thought to myself. She knows how much I love her body but still, my words don't stop her face from heating.

"Now what?" she asks, a shy edge to her tone that I fucking love.

"Panties, Princess. I want them."

She hooks her thumbs into the sides and shimmies them down her legs before bending over.

The move gives me a lingering shot of her ass and already slick pussy as she slowly swipes them up.

"Fucking killing me."

"You asked for it." She stands and flings her panties at me.

They land on my chest and I snatch them up, lifting them to my nose.

"Fuck, you're dripping right now, aren't you, Princess?" It's a rhetorical question. We both know that she is, and it seems she knows that I don't expect an answer because she never gives me one.

I suck in a breath to prepare for the pain that's to come as I push myself so I'm sitting a little higher. I push the waistband of my boxers down, exposing my throbbing length.

Letty's eyes immediately focus on my cock as I return to stroking it slowly.

"Sit in the chair." I tilt my chin in the direction of where Reid left it last night and she immediately walks over.

Lowering her ass to the edge, she sits all politely with her knees together.

"Nice try, Princess. Spread your legs, let me see your pretty cunt."

She swallows nervously but does as she's told, even going so far as to prop one foot on the edge of the bed.

"Good girl. Now run your fingers through and tell me just how wet you are, how badly you need my cock."

She ghosts one hand down her stomach until two

of her fingers press against her exposed clit as she gasps, her head falling back against the chair.

My heart thunders in my chest as I watch her, and I grip my cock tighter with my need to feel her tight pussy wrapped around it.

"Yes, Princess. Now push them both inside. Are you slick for me?"

"Y-yes," she cries as she plunges two fingers into her cunt.

"Fuck, you look so fucking hot fucking touching yourself, baby. I want to watch you come while you think about me fucking you raw. Can you do that?"

"Y-yes."

She pulls her fingers from her body and goes back to her clit, circling in a steady motion as her hips roll in time.

"You like knowing that I'm watching you? Does it turn you on, Princess?"

She lifts her head and her hooded eyes find mine.

"Yes."

She rips her stare from mine and lowers her attention to my cock.

"All for you, baby. I can't wait to get inside you. I'm going to fuck you until you don't know your own name."

"Kane," she moans, losing the fight with her body to hold her head up.

I watch as her free hand lifts to her breasts and she pinches and rolls her nipples as her movements between her legs get more erratic.

"That's it, baby," I encourage, my own hand getting faster with every second that passes. "I want to hear my name when you fall, you got that?"

"Yes, Kane. Yes," she whines as if she's practicing.

I smirk as I watch her beginning to lose control.

"Fuck your cunt, Let. I wanna see your fingers deep inside your pussy."

Releasing her breast, she drops it with the other and pushes two fingers inside.

"Oh God," she gasps as she stretches herself open.

"Yes, baby. Now ride your hand until you come for me."

"Oh God, Kane. Kane," she cries as her release builds. Heat burns across her chest as she heaves for breath. Her breasts swollen and desperate for my touch. I look lower, focusing on watching her play herself to orgasm.

Her entire body locks up when she finally falls.

"Kane," she cries as she begins to convulse on the chair, riding out every second of pleasure.

My breath catches as I watch her. So fucking beautiful and so fucking mine.

Her head lifts as she begins to come down from her high. When her eyes find mine, they're blown and glittering with desire.

"So fucking hot. Now get over here and suck me off, and don't stop until my cum is sliding down your throat."

Faster than I expected, she scrambles from the chair and crawls up the end of the bed.

Wrapping her hands around the waistband of my boxers, she pulls them down my legs and drops them to the floor, before kissing her way up my thighs.

"Princess," I half warn, half moan, already so on the fucking edge from watching her little show that I know I'm not going to last if she continues to tease me.

"So impatient, Legend. I'm in the driver's seat now, so sit back and enjoy the ride."

I groan because as much as I want to be inside of her mouth, a proper ride and sinking deep into her pussy would be so much better. But I already know she won't because she doesn't want to hurt me. And to be honest, I'm not sure I've actually got it in me anyway, not that I'm about to admit that to anyone.

She kisses all the way up before she licks and teases my balls as I continue to jerk myself slowly.

"Letty, fuck."

I watch her every movement as she begins to lick and suck up my length until I release myself so she can fully take over.

Holding the base, she licks and sucks all the way to the tip, my release already right there before she even parts her lips and sucks me deep.

"Baby, I really need—"

"Shush, I know what you need," she whispers before finally allowing me into her mouth.

"Oh shit, fuck. Fuck, Letty." Lifting my hand, I slide my fingers into her hair, but I don't take control. I just let her do her thing before I reach the point of no return only minutes later and I release everything I have down her throat just like I promised I would.

"Fuck, Princess," I pant when she pulls off me and wipes her mouth with the back of her hand.

Her eyes are still blown, and I know for a fact that she's so fucking ready for my cock.

"Get that look out of your eyes, Legend. It's not happening. Not until you've healed."

"But you're basically begging for it," I point out.

"I haven't said a word," she argues as she climbs from between my legs.

"I can read you like a book Scarlett Hunter and your entire body is screaming *fuck me, Kane. Fuck me until I can't feel my legs.*"

She laughs at me as she collects up her abandoned clothing. "It doesn't matter what you think my body is screaming. It's not happening."

"Okay, fine. But I wouldn't put any of those on because I'm gonna need your help showering."

"No, Kane. I don't think—" Her words vanish the second she looks up to find me sitting on the edge of the bed, ready to head for the bathroom.

"Help me or I'll go alone and I'm not sure I should be alone, you know, after I've been shot." I give her my best puppy dog eyes and she rolls hers in response.

"Low blow, Legend. Low fucking blow."

"Worked, didn't it?" I ask when she stands before me, still naked, and holds her hand out.

"Any funny business and you're in big trouble," she warns.

"When aren't I in trouble?"

"Jesus," she mutters as we make our way to the bathroom.

"I love this, you know."

"What, Reid's bathroom?" she asks innocently.

"No, Princess. Joking around with you like normal college kids." She releases me as she leans into the shower stall and turns the water on.

"Yeah, I like it too. Let's get you back in and we can be normal like this every day."

Wrapping my hand around the side of her neck, I pull her into me.

"Sounds like heaven, baby." I rub my nose against hers. "We're gonna find somewhere to live, just the two of us and I'm going to fuck you every day like I should have been doing for years."

"And here I was thinking you were going to make me sweet loving promises," she deadpans.

"Oh Princess, what's sweeter than multiple orgasms daily delivered by yours truly?"

"Okay, yeah. I guess you might have a point."

"Our future starts here, Scarlett. We can do and be whatever the fuck we want, together."

She lowers her head to my non-wounded shoulder and sucks in a shuddering breath.

"Letty?" I ask, concern flooding me that I just said something wrong.

She gives herself a second before she pulls her head away and looks up at me. Her eyes are full of unshed tears that she tries to blink away.

"I-I can't wait, Kane. I want this, I want you."

"Fuck, I love you, Scarlett Hunter."

My lips find hers before I have to see the conflicted look on her face every time I tell her those words. I know she feels it, I see it in her eyes every time she looks at me, I feel it in her every touch but for some reason, she's holding the words back. I want to be okay with it and give her the time she needs. Hell, I understand after all the shit I've thrown her way over the years but the selfish asshole that I am, I need to hear them. I need to know she really is mine in every single way.

We kiss for long minutes before she takes both of my hands and leads me into the stall where she very carefully washes every inch of me and is very careful not to get my wound wet. She's the perfect nurse, well, until she gets on her knees and pays my cock extra attention once more, then she's just my dirty little whore all over again and I wouldn't change it for the world.

LETTY

"He's got a fucking torture chamber in his basement, Kane. Tell me you don't think that's fucking insane," I damn near squeal as we drive away from Reid's house later that day.

I thought I was seeing things when I looked out of the window and saw my car sitting in Reid's driveway, but it seemed that while I was with Kane, keeping him... entertained, that we missed the other Harrises visit to drop my car off for me.

I see Kane shrug out of the corner of my eye as we pass through the massive set of gates and pull out onto the road. "Yeah, it's weird. But it's Reid. He's all kinds of fucked up," he says like I've just discovered he's got a tennis court in his home or something. Not a place where he literally tortures people, to death probably, but I figure I'm better off not having that confirmed.

"Who else does he have down there?"

Kane chuckles. "Honestly, I don't know. They could all be full or all empty—"

"Aside from Alana," I butt in.

"Yeah, aside from her. That's Reid's Hawk business. The less I know, the better." I glance over at him sensing that he isn't being entirely honest with me but I decide to let it go. I really don't want to know. It's bad enough that I now know it exists and that he's keeping Alana down there like a pet.

I might have disliked her from the second she wrapped her hands around my man outside the stadium the other weekend but still, I wouldn't wish that kind of life on anyone. I can only tell myself that she deserves it and hope that Reid isn't a total monster with her.

As if he can read my mind, Kane reaches over and squeezes my thigh as I drive. "I wouldn't worry about Alana, baby. Something tells me she's enjoying her time down there."

"What are you—no," I say, cutting myself off. "I don't want to know. I'm just going to forget he even has a basement."

"Probably for the best. She's not going to bother us again."

"Do you think she genuinely liked you?" I have no idea why I ask that question, it's not like I actually want to know the answer but my mouth runs away with me.

"I have no idea. I think she liked the idea of us but I think her life is more complicated than we can appreciate. I'm just glad not to be in the middle of it anymore."

"Same."

"I'm gonna miss the guys, obviously. They've been my friends since we were kids, but the life... I'm so done with anything to do with the Creek."

I glance over at him and smile, loving to listen to him open up properly.

It's easy to see the difference in him already since he woke up yesterday afternoon. I don't think I really appreciate just how stressed he was with everything he was dealing with. Looking at him now, bruises and swelling aside, he looks like an entirely different man.

"Same," I admit after a silent few seconds. "Well, aside from my dad, obviously."

"Reid's working on that."

"W-what?"

"Just give him some time and don't ask me any details because I don't know but he's trying to set your dad free too."

"Why?" I ask, my eyes darting between Kane and the road ahead.

"Because it's important to you, so it's important to me. I asked him to see what he could do."

"Kane," I sigh, twisting my fingers with his on my lap.

"Your parents deserve it, Let. They're both pretty incredible people."

"I'm glad you think so," I whisper with a laugh.

"Well, they made you so that makes them pretty awesome in my book."

I laugh. "You're an idiot."

"You love it."

"Yeah. Yeah, I do." I gasp as I realize what I just said but he doesn't react, or at least he tries not to but his hand tightens briefly on mine.

I know he needs to hear the words, I wanted to tell him this morning in the bathroom but the time just didn't feel right. I don't want to say the words after he could have died, and when he can't seal the promise between us properly. I figure the words can wait a few weeks while he heals and then we can celebrate it the right way.

"You don't have to take the week off, you know," he says as we drive into Rosewood. "I'll be fine if you want to go to class."

"Nope. I've already emailed my teachers and told them I'm going to do everything remotely for this week at least."

"Let, I don't want you falling behind because of me," he warns.

"I won't. Plus, you can do it with me so when you're let back in, you've got stuff ready."

"If, not when, Let," he reminds me.

"It's going to happen, Kane. Have faith."

Reid told me while he was helping me clean up the plates I smashed all over his kitchen that he'd spoken to some contacts in an attempt to cover up some of the corruption at MKU with Kane's scholarship. I'm not entirely sure how to feel about him trying to cover it with more corruption, but I thanked him and told him that my mom had it under control.

We just have to hope that's the truth and await the phone call that he can return and pick up where he left off. Although I think we both know that even if he is allowed back tomorrow, that his season is basically over. He might claim to be okay, but he just got beaten within an inch of his life and shot. The last place he needs to be right now is on the field no matter how badly he wants it.

"I'm trying, but I need to be realistic. I need a plan B."

"We'll figure it out, Kane."

The driveway is empty when we pull up at the house but we already know that Kyle is waiting for us. Kane told him that we'd be fine but I think he needed to see with his own eyes that his brother was okay.

The front door opens the second I pull the car to a stop and Kyle comes running out, confirming my suspicions. I get it, I'd be the same if I knew either Zayn or Harley had just been through what Kane had.

"How is he?" Kyle asks the second I step out of the car.

"He's okay, Kyle. Really. A week's rest and he'll be as good as new."

"I can't believe he got fucking shot," he says, scrubbing his hand down his face, a deep frown mars his brow as he looks off into space.

"This is all my fault," he mutters. "If I never got caught that night."

"No, Kyle. It's not. Kane was already tangled up with Victor long before that night."

"I know but everything he's done since, it was because of me."

"He loves you, Ky. He'd literally do anything for you."

"I know," he says, shoving his hand into his hair and tugging on the lengths. The move is so much like his big brother's it makes my chest ache despite the fact I can feel Kane's curious gaze burning into my back.

He's more than capable of getting out himself, so the fact he hasn't moved yet means he must think Kyle needs this moment with me and he's giving us the space he needs.

"It's over now. They've come to an agreement and Kane's free."

"That's good. That's so fucking good. But what now?"

"One step at a time, yeah?" I reach out and squeeze his shoulder in support. "You're both family now, and we look after our own. Everything will be fine. You just need to focus on graduating and where you want to go next year."

"Maddison," he says without missing a beat. I smile and nod, I can't say I'm surprised.

"Right, well let's focus on getting you both there then, shall we?"

He nods.

"Come on, let's get the invalid out. He really loves all the extra fuss he's getting."

"Really?" Kyle asks, screwing up his nose.

"No, he fucking hates it. It's amusing. Mr. Always In Control, has very much lost control."

"Sweet. Let's have some fun then."

I grab Kane's bags from the trunk while Kyle helps him from the car and leads him toward the house, much to his displeasure if the complaining I can hear is anything to go by.

My trunk is full, not only did the Harrises bring my car, but they stripped Kane's room at the house first. He didn't look surprised when Devin told them what they'd done. He knew he was going to have to move out. Living in that house meant he was connected to Victor and that was not an option. Walking away meant walking away from everything.

He put on a brave face and smiled at them all as if nothing was wrong, but I could see underneath it all that it hurt having his lifelong friends remove him from their lives so easily.

With everything weighing me down, I trudge up to the house and dump it all just inside the front door.

"Coffee?" Kyle asks me from his place in the kitchen.

"Please. White one sugar." He nods and sets about making them.

Leaving the bags where they are, I walk over to Kane who's sitting on the edge of the couch with his head in his hands.

"Hey, is everything okay? Do you need more pills?"

"No, I'm good." He looks at me and I can't help but gasp at the darkness in his eyes. "What's wrong?"

"I..." He runs his hands through his hair. "I-I just..." He looks behind me for a beat before pushing to stand. "I'm going to lie down. I just need..." He trails off once more before he disappears down the hall to his bedroom. The sound of the door closing echoes around the house and I blow out a confused breath.

Everything was good. Great, even. What the hell just happened?

"Okay, so I won't make his then," Kyle mutters from the coffee machine.

"I don't... shit. I thought he was okay," I admit, throwing myself back on the couch.

"He is, Let," Kyle says, placing my mug down on the coffee table and sitting in the chair opposite me.

"He wants to help everyone, fix everything. Be in control like you said out there, and he's not. He's got no job, no college, no nothing right now. He's freaking out."

I stare at Kyle as his words settle.

"Yeah, you're right. Fuck, I hate this. I wish I could fix it and just get him back into college."

"It'll happen."

"I hope so," I say, leaning forward to get my coffee. It's too hot to drink, so I just hug the mug and blow a stream of air across the top.

"I'm staying at your mom's place with Har so you guys can have some space."

"No, Ky. You don't need to move out because of me."

"I know I don't, but I think you two should have some alone time while he heals. I don't mind being there. Your mom's pretty awesome."

I smile at him, equally pleased that they get on so well and sad for him that he lost his own parents so young.

"Come over for dinner in a few days, yeah? I've got this week off classes so I can cook something."

"Sure thing. We'll let you know when. Things are kinda crazy for both of us with the team and cheer."

"Even more reason why you need a decent meal."

"Already looking forward to it."

We chat about Rosewood and life as a high school senior while Kane rests or sulks, I'm not sure which, before Kyle excuses himself to head to Mom's.

I pull him in for a hug before he excuses himself, feeling like after everything with Kane that he needs it.

"See you soon, yeah?" he says somewhat awkwardly after accepting my embrace for a few seconds.

"You got it."

I wave him off before turning back into the house to find Kane watching me from his bedroom doorway.

"Using your Hunter charm on Kyle now, eh?" he asks with a smirk.

"Well, we both know you have a weakness when it comes to us."

"That, Scarlett Hunter, is very, very true."

"Are you okay?" I ask him hesitantly.

"Yeah, I'll be fine." He walks toward me and takes my hand. Together we drop down onto the couch. "Just being back here, it reminds me of all the things I don't know how to deal with right now. Rent on this place, a job, college. I just hate being so unsure of everything."

"One problem at a time," I tell him. "How much money do you have, and how long can you realistically keep this place?"

"Probably a few months, but I'd have nothing left."

"Okay, so we need to look at living arrangements. Kyle just told me he wants to go to college next year so this place won't be needed soon. Maybe he could live with Mom and Harley for a few months before they start college. We could get our own place near MKU whether you're at college or not, I can get a job to help pay."

He stares at me with an unreadable expression on his face.

"As for college and work, we're just going to have to wait and see what happens. Have you heard anything yet?"

He shakes his head. "I'll call Mom for an update."

Reaching out, he wraps his arm around my waist and slides me closer to him. "I love you. Scarlett Hunter."

"Hmmm," I mumble into his kiss. I have no idea if he's giving me an out from having to say it or is actually terrified to hear it at this point.

"Who is that?" Kane groans the following night when we're curled up on the couch watching some sickly sweet movie he put on, apparently for my benefit. I think it was just an excuse to feel me up on the couch to be honest because neither of us are actually paying any attention to the TV.

"No clue. Harley said they were busy tonight."

Untangling myself from Kane, I right my clothing and walk to the front door.

"Oh my God," I gasp when I pull the door open and find our two visitors impatiently waiting on the other side.

"You're still alive," Ella squeals, stepping inside and wrapping her arms around me.

"El, I spoke to you yesterday."

"I know, I know. So how's the patient doing?" she asks, inviting herself inside. "Whoa, Legend. Gotta be honest, you've looked better."

"Thanks. Um... who let you in?" I shake my head at the two of them before turning back to our other, calmer guest.

"Lee," I say with a smile before jumping into his arms.

"Hey, Cupcake. How's it going?"

"It's... good. Yeah."

"You sure?"

"Yeah. It's just been a weird few days. What are you doing here anyway?"

"We missed you. Thought we'd come visit. Plus, we brought cupcakes," he says, lifting the bag I didn't see by his feet.

"Well, now that you've said that, come on in."

Elle is still talking Kane's ear off when I close the door behind Leon.

"Come help me make coffee?" I ask after he's gasped in shock at the state of Kane's face.

"He didn't just get jumped, did he?" Leon whispers to me once I've placed the bag of cakes on the side.

I blow out a slow breath and drag my eyes from the counter to meet his.

"The less you know, the better."

"Yeah, as I thought. What's going on with him and college? He's coming back, right? We need him."

"Honestly, I have no idea right now. We're working on getting his scholarship reinstated but who knows if that'll happen. But even if it does, he's not going to be playing anytime soon. He was shot, Lee."

Leon's eyes almost pop out of his head at my confession.

"In his shoulder, clean shot. But still. It's gonna take time before he's ready for the field."

"Fucking hell, Let."

"I know what you're thinking, but seriously, Lee. All of this is as much part of my life as his."

"Your old life," he points out.

"Only because Mom miraculously got us out. If she didn't..." A shudder rips through me. "We got a second chance, Lee. It's time Kane got one too."

"I'm not arguing with you, Let. I totally agree. I just wish I could help."

"I think we've done all we can right now, we just need to wait for decisions to be made. How's Luc?"

"Aside from being a miserable motherfucker, you mean?"

"What's new?" I joke but it falls flat because we both know that Luca is anything but miserable usually.

"He'll be fine. We've got a tough away game on Saturday, Dad's on his ass..."

"I'm with Kane," I add.

"Yeah, that too. It'll blow over. If you were it for him, then you'd have been together long before now. He just needs to hold on to something familiar right now as everything spirals."

"I get he's pissed at me, and the shit with your dad but—"

"Dad wants him to enter the draft early."

"Oh. He doesn't want to?"

"No, he wants to finish college and get his degree first. He might want the same career as our dad but he doesn't want to only set his sights on football and make the same mistakes Dad did."

"Understandable."

"He'll sort it out. Plus, if this season goes tits up without our star wide receiver then the draft won't really be an option."

"The season's barely begun, glad to see you're thinking positively," I mutter, shoving a mug under the coffee machine and hitting start.

"Something just feels off this season, and it's worse without him."

"Don't tell him that, he's already struggling enough right now," I tell Lee.

"S'all good. All we can do is our best, right?"

"Sure is. Here." I pass his coffee over before starting on the others.

We finally join Kane and Ella, much to Kane's delight because Ella's still talking to him like they're long-lost best friends.

"Thank you," he whispers to me when I pass his coffee over, although I don't think for a second it's the coffee he's so desperate for.

"So, Ella's caught you up on everything you've missed then."

"Sure have," Ella beams. "The dorm isn't the same without you, Let. When are you heading back?"

I look between Ella and Kane and swallow nervously.

"A-actually—"

"You're not, are you?"

I shake my head sadly, because I am sad. I love our dorm and the guys, but it's not where I belong. "I'm sorry, El. I'm going to stay here with Kane and commute for now while we look for a place of our own."

She smiles at me and although it doesn't meet her eyes, I know she gets it.

"Fair enough. We're going to miss you."

"I'll miss you guys too. You all were everything I didn't know I needed at the beginning of the semester."

"I'll be back in class next week so we can hang again and once we've got a place closer we'll be able to party."

"Hell, yes," she says, raising her mug like it's an alcoholic drink. "And now you two are official, you"—she pins Kane with a look—"won't have to drag her away from her friends to do wicked things to her."

"Ella," I warn as a smirk appears on Leon's face.

"What? We're all thinking it," she mutters, lifting her mug for a sip.

"So how come you two are here together?" I ask the question that's been nagging me since I opened the door.

"Oh, I bumped into him in the library after psych class, asked if he's spoken to you, one thing led to another, and here we are."

"Here you are," Kane mutters to himself, although not quietly enough if Leon's snort is anything to go by.

They end up staying a couple of hours. We order takeout for the four of us and once we've eaten they head back to Maddison.

"They make a cute couple, don't you think?" I ask Kane as I clean up the kitchen.

"Nah, they're not into each other."

"You think?"

"Yeah, I mean, Ella's got stars in her eyes. She's a jersey chaser—"

"Hey," I hiss, feeling the need to fight for my friend.

"I was going to say only a classier, less obvious one. She's not a Clara."

"Ugh, I hate her."

"Knew you were jealous, Princess."

"Yeah, well... she wants what's mine."

His warmth spreads across my back as he steps up to me at the sink and wraps his arms around my waist.

"I love it when you get possessive."

"You might have to get used to it when you come back and all the jersey chasers think they can have a piece of you."

"No one other than you is having a piece of me, Princess."

"Kane," I warn when he presses his length against my ass. "Not until you're better."

"I'm fine, Let," he lies. "It barely hurts anymore."

"Sure." I spin in his arms and look up into his eyes. "It's been two days since you got shot, Kane. It's not happening."

He lowers his head, pressing kisses up my neck. "You can do all the work again. I won't lift a finger."

"Not a finger?" I ask, raising a brow at him.

"I promise." He sucks the sensitive skin of my neck into his mouth and gently bites down. "Come on, baby. I know you want it as badly as me. I know you're wet for me right now."

A gasp passes my lips as he brushes one of my nipples with his thumb, sending a wave of heat racing through me and settling in my core.

"If it hurts at all, you tell me and we stop," I tell him firmly.

"Yeah, sure," he jokes.

"I'm deadly serious, Kane. You're meant to be resting."

"Oh I'll be resting, just while watching you bounce around on my cock."

"Fucking hell, you're insufferable."

"Yeah, and I'm all yours." He threads his fingers through mine and pulls me toward his bedroom. "We need to get to work on this place, we need to have fucked on every surface at least once before we move out."

"Kane," I chastise.

"What? I bet Kyle and Harley have been doing the exact same thing while we've been in Maddison."

"Don't... just don't. That's my little sister you're talking about."

"Yeah, and my little brother," he states proudly.

"Oh please."

The second we're in his room, he turns on me and pins me against the wall. But before I get to argue, he slams his lips down on mine and hitches my leg up around his waist with his good arm, ensuring his hard length grazes my core.

"Kane," I moan.

"Get naked. Now."

He takes a huge step back, leaving me desperate

for more of his touch as he unzips his hoodie and throws it across the room before dropping his sweats and laying back on the bed. His hard cock stands at attention as he holds my gaze.

"I'm ready for you, Princess. Do your worst."

Unable to resist, I shed my clothes in a blink of an eye and climb on the bed, immediately straddling his hips so his cock teases my sensitive center.

"Now that's what I'm talking about," he groans as I slowly slide down onto him.

I keep every one of my movements slow and considered, careful not to hurt him. He even almost keeps to his promise of relinquishing control and it's not until the very end when he grips my hips with enough force to leave bruises and thrust up into me with abandon as he finds his release.

The second we're done, I fold myself into his side and pull the covers over us both.

"I love you, Princess," he whispers in my ear.

I love you too, I say in my head, still waiting for the right time to let the words out.

As planned, I went back to classes on Monday. I'd secretly hoped that Mom would have sorted everything out, Kane would have his scholarship back and we could have gone back together. But that wasn't how it went.

Mom seems to think that things are moving in the right direction and that we just have to be patient for everything to be looked into. Kane came to Maddison with me yesterday to meet with a finance officer along with the AD and Coach. They all talked like it was going to be okay, that there were options for him but we've yet to get any kind of answer. With every day that passes, I can see it weighing down on him. At this point, he just wants an answer so at least he can start to plan with whichever direction it goes. Limbo is slowly killing him.

I was hoping to head home early after my sociology class this morning but I'm still so behind on some of my assignments that I told Kane I was going to spend the afternoon in the library in an attempt to catch up knowing that he's an expert at distracting me if I'm at home.

I find myself at a table with Brax and West as we work in silence. I feel them glance up at me every so often. I know everyone has questions about this situation with Kane and it's getting harder and harder to brush them off with half-truths but that has to be the way. We can't have anyone else involved with this shit with Victor.

The only good part of this whole thing is that, true to his word, he's stayed away from Kane. His cell has been silent and the only Harrises to get in touch have been the brothers.

"You sure you're not coming to the party tonight, we miss you," Brax says, pulling a puppy dog face.

"I miss you guys too, and I'll be back to partying again, I promise."

He blows out a breath.

"Don't do that, you're making me feel guilty."

"So you'll come?" he asks, his eyes lighting up.

"Give her a break, man," West says, slapping his shoulder. "She's already said she's got plans with Kane. Give it a rest. She said she'll be back and she will."

I smile at him, grateful for his input as butterflies begin to flutter in my belly as I wonder what Kane's got in store for us tonight.

I had a message from him waiting on my cell when I finished class, making me promise not to be late because he had plans.

As soon as I get to a point where I can stop, I pack up and say goodbye to the guys, impatient to get home to Kane who's been alone all day. Brax once again tries to convince me to come back tonight, but I once again turn him down.

With a hug to each of them, I head out of the library and almost skip to my car in excitement.

I blast Billie Eilish as I make the short journey back to Rosewood. I swear it takes longer than it has all week, but excitement and anticipation for what tonight might hold is getting the better of me.

By the time I pull up on the street outside of Kane's house, my hands tremble with my barely contained excitement.

I stare at the house for a moment, wondering why all the curtains are shut. He's here, his car is sitting in the driveway.

My heart thunders as I consider the possibility of Victor or his henchmen turning up, but then I spot the curtain twitch and Kane's face appears briefly at the window.

I messaged him on my way to my car so he knew when to expect me, and it seems he's as impatient as I am.

Quickly, I grab my purse and jump from the car, damn near running for the house.

I twist the doorknob the second I can reach it but find it locked.

What the fuck?

Curling my fist, I knock on the door, more confused than ever.

Footsteps head my way before the door is pulled open and Kane stands before me.

He looks better than he has since his ordeal with Victor. His hair is freshly washed and styled in a way I haven't seen since that day and he's dressed in something other than a hoodie and sweats; a smart button-down and cargo pants to be exact.

"Whoa, hot date tonight, Mr. Legend?"

"Yep, just waiting for my girl."

I glance over my shoulder as if I'm looking for someone. "Oh, should I go?" I ask with a smirk.

"No fucking chance." Reaching out, his hot fingers wrap around my forearm and I'm tugged against his chest. "I've been waiting all day for you, you're going nowhere, Princess."

I don't get a chance to look into the house to see what he's done, instead, he distracts me with a knee-weakening kiss that I feel all the way down to my toes.

"Missed you, baby," he whispers against my lips.

"Missed you too."

"Are you ready for your date?"

"I am."

"Good."

"What the hell are you doing?" I ask when he spins me around and presses his hand over my eyes.

"It's a surprise."

"Okay," I breathe, allowing him to guide me into the house.

He takes my purse from me and puts it down

somewhere before he presses the length of his body against my back.

"Ready?" he asks, and I nod against his hold.

He slowly removes his hands from my face and I blink a couple of times to clear my vision.

"Oh wow," I breathe, looking around at all the flickering candles and the fairy lights that are strung up everywhere. The table is set for two and there's a bottle of champagne chilling in the center. "Kane, this is incredible," I say, spinning toward him and smiling when I find a vulnerability in his eyes that no one outside of this house ever experiences.

"You like it?"

"What? How can you even ask that? It's amazing."

"I wanted to thank you for everything, but I didn't even know where to start."

"It's perfect. And you have nothing to thank me for."

"Letty," he sighs. "I have everything to thank you for."

I stare up at him with tears burning the backs of my eyes.

"Also, we're celebrating."

"Oh?" My heart thunders against my rib cage that he might actually be about to give me some good news where college is concerned.

He pulls his cell from his pocket and taps on the screen for a second before he turns it around.

My eyes fly over the screen, not really reading

what's in front of me but registering enough words to understand what I'm looking at.

"You're coming back!" I squeal. "You're coming back," I repeat, not able to believe what I'm reading. "Oh my God," I cry, throwing my arms around his shoulders, I hold him tight, the tears that were previously burning my eyes now freely streaming down my cheeks.

With his arms around me, he tucks his head into the crook of my neck, his own breath shuddering with emotion.

When he finally releases me and I get to look into his eyes, the sight of his own unshed tears rip me wide open.

"Kane," I breathe, taking his cheeks in my hands. "I love you. I love you so fucking much."

A groan rumbles from the back of his throat as he accepts my words.

"Fuck," he croaks, his voice deep and rough. "I've been dying to hear you say those words but now you have... fuck, Letty. I don't... I can't... shit." One of his tears finally drops and I catch it with my thumb. "I love you so much and I promise to spend the rest of my life making up for the past and proving to you just how much you mean to me."

"I know, Kane. You have nothing to prove."

"Fuck," he hisses, wrapping his hand around the side of my neck, the place he loves, and tilts my head to the perfect position so he can claim my lips.

His kiss is soft at first, gentle and full of emotion but in only a few short minutes, it turns heated.

"I need you, baby. I've waited long enough. I can't wait a second longer."

"Okay," I sigh against his lips and he immediately starts backing me toward the bedroom.

"This is it, Letty. This is where our lives begin."

Letty
Ten weeks later

Together Kane and I drove back to MKU the following Monday morning and we walked into our American lit class almost as if nothing had happened.

All eyes turned toward Kane, not only because of his sudden disappearance but also the fading bruises that still lingered on his face. He was almost back to normal but there was an obvious weakness on his left side that he was really going to need to work on in the coming weeks and months.

He had a meeting with the team doctor and then Coach that afternoon to discover that although he was officially back on the team, he was benched for at least four weeks while he continued to recover and build up strength.

Kane being Kane was determined to show them long before four weeks that he was ready. But Coach stood his ground and he wasn't allowed back on the field until the penultimate game of the season, and sadly, by then, the season was over for the Panthers. With Kane's absence and Luca's continuously declining mood, they ended up losing more games than they won.

With each game they played, it was clear to see the disappointment and tension in each and every player. But I guess that's how it goes, just because they made it all the way last year, it doesn't mean they'll be able to do it back to back.

Because of their lack of success, it did help to seal Luca's fate so that he's able to finish college before entering the draft, much to his father's irritation I'm sure. I haven't spoken to him about it, but I know from Leon that he is glad he's getting his own way with at least one aspect of his life.

Luca and I have talked, albeit briefly. But with his focus on his quickly depleting season, he hasn't really made any effort to fix things between us. But as the weeks have gone on, I've noticed him paying more attention to me in class. I can't help but wonder if the time is coming where we can rediscover our friendship and for him hopefully to accept that Kane is it for me.

"Okay, what do you think?" I ask, turning to look

at him where he's sitting on the couch with an amused expression on his face. "What?" I sulk.

He chuckles, pushing from the couch and stalking over to me.

We moved into our new apartment two weeks ago. We packed both our cars up with as much as we could fit in them and we moved in about thirty minutes after getting the keys in our hands. We had no furniture but we didn't care. It was officially our first home together and we weren't wasting any time in getting settled in.

Kyle and Harley had a couple of weeks together in the house in Rosewood before they handed the keys back and moved in with Mom. They've not complained once and I know it's because they understand, but at the same time, I can only imagine how frustrated they are losing their solace after weeks of alone time. But they've only got a few months and they'll be heading to college, hopefully here, if their plans work out.

"It's Christmas Eve," he says with a smile.

"I know, hence—" I gesture toward our small tree that I've just finished decorating.

"We're heading to your mom's first thing in the morning."

"I know, but I wanted our first Christmas together to be special," I say, ripping my eyes from Kane's amused ones to our twinkling tree.

Truth is, I didn't really need to spend money on a tree or decorations. We're only spending one night at Mom's and then we've got the rest of the holidays here thanks to my new job at a coffee shop not far from campus. I've been working as many shifts as I can, needing to help out financially and not having to rely on Kane's savings and scholarship.

"It will be, baby. We're together." His hand wraps around my neck and he brushes his lips over mine.

My entire body sags into him.

"Wait here," he instructs, taking a huge step back and removing his touch from me.

"But—" I pout.

"It'll be worth it, I promise." He rushes from the living room and I stand awkwardly beside the tree waiting to see what he's up to.

Things between us over the years might have been hell at times, but right now, I've never been happier. Kane is... Kane is everything. The man I've discovered who was hiding under all that anger and resentment is nothing short of incredible.

Finally, he's beginning to really accept the losses he's experienced in his life and he's truly managing to move on and really look to the future.

Victor is far behind us, although the Harris brothers are still a big part of our lives, just like my old roommates.

Right now, we're both living our best lives and I can't wait to see what comes next for us.

"Whoa," I say, my eyes wide when he walks into the living room with a big wrapped box. "What's that?"

"Your gift."

"Kane," I warn. We'd agreed not to exchange gifts

this year but to put the money toward things for the apartment that we're still missing.

Mom helped us out with some of the more vital pieces of furniture, like a bed, but there are still so many things that we need.

"I know, I know. I was going to wait but I couldn't."

"You're in so much trouble for this." Truth is, I got him something too, although it's only small and more just a sentimental thing than anything, but still. I want to be the one breaking my own rules, he wasn't meant to.

"Come and sit down," he says, placing the box on the coffee table.

"Okay." I rush over, more than ready to discover what he's got me.

I tear at the paper like a woman possessed and pull the lid off the first box.

"Huh?" I ask when I find another wrapped box.

Kane chuckles but urges me to continue.

I open that box, then find another, and another, and another.

"How small is this present?" I ask, opening yet another box.

"Pretty small. I wanted to impress you with the size." He wiggles his brows.

"I have no complaints about the size of anything, Legend."

"Good to know," he mutters before his breath catches as I open what I can only assume is the final box.

I pull the wrapping away to find a small black velvet jewelry box.

My heart thunders and my hands shake as ideas of what could be inside this box fill my mind.

"Kane?" I whisper when he slips from the edge of the couch and drops to one knee. "Oh my God," I gasp, my hand covering my mouth as he takes the box from me and flips it open.

The ring almost makes my eyes pop out of my head, it's different and beautiful and everything, but I can't keep my gaze on it because I have to look at Kane.

His eyes glisten as he stares at me.

"Letty, I know it's not been long. But when you know, you know, right? I'm pretty sure I fell in love with you when we were eight years old, I just had no clue what it meant or how to deal with it. You terrified me, you excited me, you captivated me.

"Our history is sketchy at best, but I've already told you that I want to spend every day of the rest of my life making it up to you. This is my promise, Letty. My real one."

"Will you, Scarlett Jada Hunter, stand by me for the rest of our lives, hold my hand when things get tough and promise to fuck me like a whore at every possible opportunity—"

A laugh erupts from my throat despite the fact I'm barely holding on to my tears.

"Will you, one day in the future when we've fully got our shit together, marry me?"

"Yes, Kane. A million times yes."

I drop to my knees before him, take his cheeks in my hands and kiss him as if it's the last chance we'll ever get.

By the time we break apart, we're both panting for breath and more than ready to seal the deal.

He stares into my eyes for the longest time making me feel stripped bare as he looks directly into my soul. But as scary as it is to know we've found this connection, it's the most exhilarating feeling in the world.

His fingers brush mine as he lifts my hand and plucks the ring from its cushion.

"It's taken me a long time to find this. I couldn't get you something normal, it just wouldn't be right for us."

I laugh at him as he slides the white gold ring up my finger but really, I couldn't agree more.

The princess cut black diamond is surrounded by normal diamonds which sparkle in the lights from the Christmas tree.

"Kane, it's perfect. I love it." Lifting my eyes to his. "But not as much as I love you." I throw my arms around his shoulders and hold him tight.

He allows me five whole minutes before he stands with me in his arms. He carries me to our bedroom, and throws me unceremoniously down in the center of the bed, promising to show me exactly what a life with him might be like.

I squeal with happiness as he jumps on top of me and claims my mouth.

Happiness rolls through me and for the first time in my life, I feel like I've really found my place.

Kane and I might have looked like a disaster waiting to happen. But the reality is, we were just meant to be.

He was right all those weeks ago. We had to experience the bad to know just how freaking good it could be. And I just know, I'm going to appreciate the hell out of it for years to come.

Because this is it.

I've officially been owned, claimed, and ruined by a Legend.

And I couldn't imagine it any other way.

EXTENDED EPILOGUE

Luca

It's Christmas Eve, I should be at home in Rosewood with Mom and Lee. It's where I said I'd be. Yet, I find myself still in Maddison in The Locker Room. Not the one at college, but the exclusive sports bar across town.

It's the only place in this town where men are really able to hide. There's a strict members-only policy that ensures that any paps are left out in the cold on the sidewalk. This is so that we can all drown our sorrows and indulge in our wildest fantasies without a camera in our faces.

Lee and I only turned twenty-one a few weeks ago, but we've both been coming here for years, thanks to its owner. Our father.

A bitter taste fills my mouth at the thought of him.

We've not spoken since the Panthers failed to make it to the playoffs this year.

He's pissed, I get it. I'm fucking livid after last year's success. This season it was like we'd forgotten how to hold a fucking football let alone how to throw one.

I scrub my hand down my face and rub at my stubble-covered chin. I can't remember the last time I shaved, I can't remember the last time I cared about much, to be honest. Everything is falling apart around me and every move I make only seems to make it worse.

I slide down on the leather couch I'm sitting on and gesture to the bartender for another. As he looks over I tip what remains of the amber liquid down my throat and slam the glass back down on the table.

Resting my head back, I allow the alcohol to warm my belly. I watch one particular waitress walk around collecting up empties in a tiny pair of booty shorts and a crop top that shows off the slim curve of her waist. Her legs seem to go on forever before they meet sky-high heels.

I readjust myself as my cock begins to react to her curves as I drag my eyes over her ass once more and up to her soft pink hair.

I track her movements, trying not to get ideas about a member of staff who works for my cunt of a father, not that he has any input on staffing of his beloved empire.

She moves from table to table, smiling and flirting with every man who looks her way. It's her job, I get that, but despite the fact I haven't so much as caught a glimpse of her face yet, I only want her eyes on me.

Finally, she heads back to the bar and I watch as the bartender slides my scotch over to her and nods toward my table.

Holding the tray over her shoulder she spins around and walks my way.

My heart jumps into my throat as I stare at her face, at the silver eyes I remember so well.

The second she registers who she's about to deliver a drink to, her steps falter and her tray slides from her hand sending my drink crashing to the floor.

"L-Luca?"

Sitting forward, I hold her eyes for a beat, a wicked smile pulling at the corner of my lips at the fear in her eyes.

Ripping my gaze away, I run my eyes over her body, taking in the front view of her. My cock swells more as ideas begin to swirl around my scotch-fueled brain.

"I-I need to go." She takes a hesitant step back as if she's unsure I'll even let her run.

"That's it, little girl. Run away," I snarl.

She swallows nervously as she continues to back away.

"Peyton," I call when she's almost out of hearing distance. Her entire body freezes. "You're not getting away this time."

She's gone before I can blink, leaving me with a sense that tonight might just have turned around.

I look at the bartender once more and hold up

two fingers. It seems I'm going to be hanging around a while because Peyton isn't going to be leaving here alone.

Merry Christmas, Luca. Your new toy has arrived.

Keep reading for a sneak peek of, *The Vengeance You Crave*, book #4 in the Maddison Kings University series!

Or alternatively you can grab your copy here.

Want more Reid? Merciless, the first book in the Harrow Creek Hawks series is available now!
ONE-CLICK YOUR COPY

Chapter 1
Luca

I'm drowning. Falling deeper into the darkness, and I have no idea how to claw myself back.

I remain in my car, in the darkest corner of the parking lot like I have for the past week and wait. I thought I wanted to stand before her and demand answers, but watching her and knowing she has no idea settles something inside me.

Maybe if I watch for long enough, I'll discover the truth.

I'll catch her out in a lie.

But I know that's unlikely, we haven't seen each other in almost five years. I have no idea who the girl I once knew is now. I have no idea why she's even back here.

I've run through all the possibilities in my head.

I've searched for her on social media. But I haven't found an account in her name, let alone any answers.

For those, I need her.

My fingers twitch with the thought of reaching out and touching her. My mouth waters for all the ways I want to show her just how much her lies hurt. How badly she broke me back then before Letty turned up like a guardian fucking angel and helped me put the pieces back together.

I thought when Letty arrived at MKU it was for me. I truly fucking did.

But now I know differently.

Because all this time, I've been waiting for *her*, and I had no idea.

The second someone pushes the back door open casting a bright glow across the parking lot, my eyes snap toward it, praying that it's time for her to leave.

When it's not her, but a guy taking some trash out, my teeth grind in frustration.

I need her. I need my fucking fix.

I've never been addicted to anything—okay, maybe the game—but this is different. This incessant need for her, the excitement about seeing her wide, fearful eyes when I finally catch up with her. Fuck. It makes me feel more alive than I have in weeks and I fucking love it.

I've lost everything else, but this, this right now, is mine and only mine.

I have the control when I reveal myself. I have the control with what I do and what I say for when that happens. No one can take this away from me.

Continue reading Luca & Peyton's story with The Vengeance You Crave

ACKNOWLEDGMENTS

Well... that's it. I'm not sure what to really say now other than, wow, this has been a seriously wild ride.

I have been planning Kane's story for months, he's been a part of my life for a long time before he actually began to appear in Rosewood in Hunter and Fury. I can't tell you how good it feels to finally let him free.

I have lived and breathed this trilogy and right now, it's been about a month since I finished typing and man, I miss them.

I might be knee deep in MKU #4 but Kane Legend is always going to hold a very special place in my heart. And it makes me so happy seeing you all accept his broken and dark ways, because under all of that, he's pretty incredible.

I always planned for Rosewood High to move onto MKU, I had plans for that way back when I first mentioned Maddison Kings University, but I never expected all the other worlds to emerge that I can't wait to experience more of. For one, I need a lot more of the psycho that is Reid Harris. I hope you're with me on that.

I have so many people to thank for all of this, and I know if I try that I'm going to forget someone. My alpha readers, my beta readers, Sam, my incredible PA, Candi for all the promo, Eric for the insane cover images and helping me bring this series to life and to Armando for his incredible shots. To all the bloggers, bookstagrammers and booktokers who helped me share and posted reviews.

But mostly, I want to thank you. I couldn't do this without you and it means so much to me that you've made it this far and that you're on this journey with me. So thank you. Thank you for taking a chance on me and my crazy characters. I LOVE YOU!!!!

So... now you know who's next. I'm already discovering so much I didn't know about our main man, Luca Dunn, QB1, and I'm so excited to bring you Luca and Peyton's story in the coming months.

Until next time,
    Tracy
    xo

ABOUT THE AUTHOR

Tracy Lorraine is a *USA Today* and *Wall Street Journal* bestselling new adult and contemporary romance author. Tracy has recently turned thirty and lives in a cute Cotswold village in England with her husband, baby girl and lovable but slightly crazy dog. Having always been a bookaholic with her head stuck in her Kindle, Tracy decided to try her hand at a story idea she dreamt up and hasn't looked back since.

Be the first to find out about new releases and offers. Sign up to my newsletter here.

If you want to know what I'm up to and see teasers and snippets of what I'm working on, then you need to be in my Facebook group. Join Tracy's Angels here.

Keep up to date with Tracy's books at
www.tracylorraine.com

<u>Rebel Ink Series</u>

<u>Hate You</u> #1

<u>Trick You</u> #2

<u>Defy You</u> #3

<u>Play You</u> #4

Inked (A Rebel Ink/Driven Crossover)

<u>Rosewood High Series</u>

<u>Thorn</u> #1

<u>Paine</u> #2

<u>Savage</u> #3

<u>Fierce</u> #4

Hunter #5

Faze (#6 Prequel)

<u>Fury</u> #6

<u>Legend</u> #7

<u>Maddison Kings University Series</u>

<u>TMYM: Prequel</u>

<u>TRYS</u> #1

<u>TDYW</u> #2

<u>TBYS</u> #3

<u>TVYC</u> #4

<u>TDYD</u> #5

<u>TDYR</u> #6

<u>Knight's Ridge Empire Series</u>

<u>Wicked Summer Knight</u>: Prequel (Stella & Seb)

<u>Wicked Knight</u> #1 (Stella & Seb)

<u>Wicked Princess #2</u> (Stella & Seb)

<u>Wicked Empire</u> #3 (Stella & Seb)

<u>Deviant Knight</u> #4 (Emmie & Theo)

<u>Deviant Princess</u> #5 (Emmie & Theo

<u>Deviant Reign</u> #6 (Emmie & Theo)

<u>One Reckless Knight</u> (Jodie & Toby)

<u>Reckless Knight</u> #7 (Jodie & Toby)

<u>Reckless Princess</u> #8 (Jodie & Toby)

<u>Reckless Dynasty</u> #9 (Jodie & Toby)

<u>Dark Halloween Knight</u> (Calli & Batman)

<u>Dark Knight</u> #10 (Calli & Batman)

<u>Dark Princess</u> #11 (Calli & Batman)

Dark Legacy #12 (Calli & Batman)

<u>Corrupt Valentine Knight</u> (Nico & Siren)

Corrupt Knight #13 (Nico & Siren)

Corrupt Princess #14 (Nico & Siren)

Corrupt Union #15 (Nico & Siren)

Sinful Wild Knight (Alex & Vixen)

Sinful Stolen Knight: Prequel (Alex & Vixen)

Sinful Knight #16 (Alex & Vixen)

Sinful Princess #17 (Alex & Vixen)

Sinful Kingdom #18 (Alex & Vixen)

Knight's Ridge Destiny: Epilogue

Harrow Creek Hawks

(Reid, Maverick, JD & Alana)

Merciless #1

Relentless #2

Lawless #3

Fearless #4

Ruined Series

Ruined Plans #1

Ruined by Lies #2

Ruined Promises #3

Never Forget Series

Never Forget Him #1

Never Forget Us #2

Everywhere & Nowhere #3

Chasing Series

Chasing Logan

The Cocktail Girls

His Manhattan

Her Kensington

www.ingramcontent.com/pod-product-compliance
Lightning Source LLC
Chambersburg PA
CBHW050751190726
48285CB00005B/1622